Outrageous hell-raisers let loose in Europe!

When London's most notorious rakes
embark on a Grand Tour they
set female hearts aflutter all across Europe!

The exploits of these British rogues might be
the stuff of legend, but on this adventure of
a lifetime will they finally meet the women
strong enough to tame their wicked ways?

Read Haviland North's story in
Rake Most Likely to Rebel
June 2015

And read Archer Crawford's story in
Rake Most Likely to Thrill
August 2015

And watch out for more **Rakes on Tour** stories
coming in 2016!

AUTHOR NOTE

Bonjour! Welcome to our first stop in ***Rakes on Tour***. Paris was the traditional first stop on the nineteenth-century Grand Tour for many, and Haviland's story is centred around a fencing *salon*. The *salle d'armes* in this story is modelled after a famous *salle* that really did exist at 14 rue Saint-Marc and was handed down from father to son. I have tried to be as true as possible to the various schools of thought mentioned in the story as Haviland continues his education as a fencer.

Gentlemen sought out fencing as an activity that furthered their education. Fencing was not only good exercise for the body, but it was also considered good exercise for the mind. To quote directly from *L'Ecole d'Escrime Français* by Roman Hliva, 'Handling a sword steeled one's nerves, provided courage and taught judgement under fire.' The *salles* were busy between four and seven in the afternoon, and many—like the one in rue Saint-Marc—had different practising areas, an area for paying members and one for day guests who also likely borrowed the *salon*'s equipment since they didn't have their own.

One other note: nineteenth-century French uses the word *'hôtel'* differently from its modern meaning. A *'hôtel particulier'*, like the Leodegrances', is not an inn but a large, private, free-standing home in town that does not share walls with other dwellings.

Enjoy Haviland's story and a glimpse into French fencing!

Stay in touch at bronwynswriting.blogspot.com or at bronwynnscott.com

RAKE MOST LIKELY
TO REBEL

Bronwyn Scott

MILLS
BOON

Published in Great Britain 2015
by Mills & Boon, an imprint of Harlequin (UK) Limited,
Eton House, 18-24 Paradise Road, Richmond, Surrey, TW9 1SR

© 2015 Nikki Poppen

ISBN: 978-0-263-24785-5

Harlequin (UK) Limited's policy is to use papers that are natural,
renewable and recyclable products and made from wood grown in
sustainable forests. The logging and manufacturing processes conform
to the legal environmental regulations of the country of origin.

Printed and bound in Spain
by CPI, Barcelona

Bronwyn Scott is a communications instructor at Pierce College in the United States, and is the proud mother of three wonderful children (one boy and two girls). When she's not teaching or writing she enjoys playing the piano, travelling—especially to Florence, Italy—and studying history and foreign languages. Readers can stay in touch on Bronwyn's website, bronwynnscott.com, or at her blog, bronwynswriting.blogspot.com. She loves to hear from readers.

Books by Bronwyn Scott

Mills & Boon® Historical Romance
and Mills & Boon® Historical *Undone!* eBooks

Rakes on Tour

Rake Most Likely to Rebel

Rakes of the Caribbean

Playing the Rake's Game
Breaking the Rake's Rules
Craving the Rake's Touch (Undone!)

Rakes Who Make Husbands Jealous

Secrets of a Gentleman Escort
London's Most Wanted Rake
An Officer But No Gentleman (Undone!)
A Most Indecent Gentleman (Undone!)

Ladies of Impropriety

A Lady Risks All
A Lady Dares
A Lady Seduces (Undone!)

M&B *Castonbury Park* Regency mini-series

Unbefitting a Lady

**Visit the author profile page
at millsandboon.co.uk for more titles**

For Monsieur Rouse,
high school French teacher *extraordinaire*:
Votre ardeur pour la langue insuffle mon fil. Merci.
(*Je regrette*, I have not conjugated 'to inspire' for some
time. I hope the form is correct on *insuffle*!)

And for Ro and Brony—we will see the City of Light
(La Ville Lumière) together soon.

Chapter One

Dover docks—March 1835

There were no pleasures left in London. One could only hope Paris would do better. Haviland North turned up the collar of his greatcoat against the damp of the early March morning and paced the Dover docks, anxious to be away with the tide.

All of his hopes were pinned on France now and its famed *salle d'armes*. If springtime in Paris should fail to stimulate his stagnant blood, the rest of Europe awaited to take its turn. He could spend summer among the mighty peaks of the Alps, testing his strength on their crags, autumn among the arts and graces of Florence, winter in Venice feasting on the sensuality of Carnevale and another spring, if he could manage it. This time in Naples, basking in the heat of southern Italy with its endless supply of the ancient. If those destinations did not succeed, there was always Greece and the alluring, mysterious Turkey.

The exotic litany of places rolled through his mind, a mantra of hopefulness and perhaps a mantra of fantasy. His father had promised him six months, not a year or two. It would all have to be managed very carefully. In truth, Haviland preferred it not come to that simply because of what the need for such lengths indicated about his current state—that at the age of twenty-eight and with everything to live for: the title, the vast fortune that went with it, the estates, the horses, the luxuries other men spent their lives acquiring—he was dead inside after all.

He'd had to fight hard for this Grand Tour, abbreviated as it might be. His well-meaning father had relented at last, perhaps understanding the need for his grown son to spread his wings beyond London and see something of the world before settling down. Haviland had won six months of freedom. But it had come at a great cost: afterwards, he would return home and marry, completing the plans that had been laid by two families three generations ago.

He could hear his father's voice, see him behind his massive desk in the estate office as he delivered his verdict.

'Six months is all we can spare. You're different than your friends. They don't have your expectations. Even Archer is a second son and when it comes down to it, his duties are different than yours. They can be gone for years. We can't possibly spare you that long. The Everlys are eager to see the marriage done, and why delay? You're twenty-eight and Christina is twenty-one. She's been out for three Seasons, which is very respectable at this point, but to make her wait any longer will arouse unnecessary suspicions where there are none.'

His marriage, like everything else in his life to date, had been arranged for him. Everything had been accomplished *for* him. He simply had to show up. He often thought it was the very idea that there was nothing to turn his hand to, nothing that required his effort that had spawned this dark yawning gap in him. He'd struggled for nothing, been denied nothing, not even good looks. He'd managed to snare the lion's share of the family's handsome genetics along with the fortune. Perhaps that was why fencing appealed to him so intensely—it was something he could work at, something he could personally excel at on his own merits.

Excel he had. Haviland touched his booted toe to the long, slim case lying at his feet to assure himself it was still there, the one piece of luggage he hadn't allowed to be stowed out of his sight: his rapiers, specially made for him from the fit of the grips to the weight of the thin blades. There wasn't a gentleman in London who could touch him in the art of the foil and still it wasn't enough. There was more to know and he hungered for the excellence that would come with new knowledge. He would go to Paris and study. With luck, he'd move on to the Italian masters in Florence. He knew six months wouldn't see him to Italy. It wasn't near enough time. He would need a miracle, but anything could happen if he could just be off.

Haviland took out his gold pocket watch, a gift from his grandfather upon completing Oxford several years ago, and flipped it open to check the time: quarter past five. His companions should have been here by now, which meant they'd show up any moment. None of them were extraordinarily concerned with punctuality but all of them were as eager as he for this journey, for reasons of their own. He closed the watch, his thumb running over his grandfather's carefully chosen, although not highly original inscription: *tempus fugit.* He'd wasted enough time already. This journey was a chance for the clock to start again, however briefly, for his life to start again.

Haviland's gaze strained in the lifting gloom, trying to make out the arrival of his companions. Who would come first? Perhaps Archer Crawford, his oldest friend. They'd suffered Eton together and then Oxford before moving on to the Season, exhausting the joys of London year after year after endless year until the pleasure had become *de rigueur.* Only loyalty to his mother had kept Archer in London this long. Now that anchor was gone and Archer was as anxious as he to be off.

Then again, the first to arrive might be Nolan Gray, depending on whether or not he'd had a good night at the rough tables of Dover. Nolan had ended more than one night with a tersely offered invitation to duel. His extraordinary skill at cards left many gentlemen lighter in the pockets. Over their years on the town, Nolan had developed the ability to defend his talent and his honour from the business end of a pistol at twenty paces.

Whoever arrived first, it wouldn't be Brennan Carr. He would most definitely be last and he most definitely hadn't spent his last night in England sleeping. If he knew Brennan, the night had been spent in the arms of a willing woman. Haviland chuckled to himself at the thought. Brennan could always make him laugh. Brennan had made London survivable long after it had lost its appeal.

Hooves and wheels clattered on the docks, a coach emerging from the lifting fog. Two men jumped out, coats swirling about them. One of them barked an order in a deep commanding baritone that carried in the morning air. Haviland smiled, recognising the voice. Nolan and Archer had come together and it looked as if Archer had brought a horse. Or the horse had followed Archer, which wouldn't surprise Haviland at all. Archer was always collecting stray horses the way some people collected cats or dogs. In the gloom, Haviland could see Archer tying the beast to the back of the carriage. He heard Nolan's voice carry across the pier.

'I win!' Nolan shouted as they approached. 'Haviland is already here *and* he has his case.' Nolan clasped him on the shoulder affectionately. 'Good morning, Old Man. Is everything loaded? I told Archer you'd be here overseeing.'

Haviland laughed. 'You know me too well. I saw the two coaches go on an hour ago and they loaded our trunks last night.' They'd decided the best way to make haste to Paris and then to destinations beyond would be to supply their own private coaches for travel. They'd have to buy or rent horses in Calais, but Calais was prepared for such purchases. Travellers who could afford it crossed the Channel with their own carriages. Those who couldn't afford to were reliant on public transport or whatever vehicles were for sale. Haviland had been more worried about finding two coaches for sale at prices that didn't border on extortion when they arrived.

'You trusted them with your trunks, which, may I emphasise, contain *all* your necessary belongings for the duration, but not with one small fencing case?' Archer pointed to the case at his feet.

'I told you that, too.' Nolan crowed. 'But, no, you insisted he'd have sent it ahead.' Nolan tapped his temple with his forefinger. 'I know these things. I'm a student of human nature.'

'Too bad you couldn't study that at Oxford.' Archer goaded him. 'You might have got better marks.'

But Nolan merely laughed. He and Archer had been sparring for years. They had each other's measure. 'What can I say? It's true. You two were the scholars, not me and Brennan.' He looked around. 'Is Brennan here yet?'

'No.' Haviland couldn't resist the ribbing. 'Did you expect him to be? Scholar of human nature that you are?'

Nolan gave Haviland a playful shove. 'A scholar of human nature, yes, a psychic, no.' He grinned. 'So who is she? We've only been in Dover a night. It's not the barmaid from the inn. She went off with another fellow.'

Haviland shrugged as the captain of their packet approached. 'Milord, you'll want to get on board. We'll be leaving in twenty minutes or so.'

'Thank you.' Haviland gave the man a short

nod. 'We're waiting for the last member of our travelling party.'

He didn't expect the captain to be sympathetic and the man wasn't. 'The tide does not wait, milord. You've been lucky. We can leave at once. Some folks sit in the inns for weeks, waiting for the right wind and weather.'

'Understood,' Haviland answered, casting a final look at the docks as if he could make Brennan materialise. The captain spoke the truth. He'd heard all nature of accounts from others who'd made the Channel crossing about the risk of having to wait, their travel plans at the mercy of the elements.

'I should have stayed with him.' Haviland said as the captain moved off. He blamed himself. One of the things that made his friendship with Brennan work was balance. Brennan made him laugh and, in return, he kept Brennan focused and out of trouble. But last night he'd been worried about the luggage and the arrangements and he'd left Brennan to fend for himself. Admittedly, he thought there'd be very little damage Brennan could do knowing there was an early departure. Apparently, he'd been wrong.

The trio headed towards the gangplank to

board. 'I'll wager five pounds Brennan misses the boat.' Nolan announced. 'Archer, are you in? If I'm wrong, you can win back your losses.'

Once on board, they leaned against the rail, all three of them scanning the docks for a last-minute sign of Brennan. Haviland checked his pocket watch, the minutes racing by. It wouldn't be the same without Brennan. Perhaps Bren could catch a later boat and meet them in Paris? Brennan knew the route they'd planned. Did he have enough money? Probably not. Brennan never had enough funds.

Beside him, Nolan started at the sound of chains rolling up. 'They're pulling the anchor. He's not going to make it.' Nolan blew out a breath and leaned on his arms. 'Dammit, I didn't want to win that bet.' The three of them exchanged glances, their disappointment silently evident. Their trip was off to an ominous start.

The boat began to nudge slowly away from its moorings as commotion broke out on the docks. A horse pulling a heavy dray full of crates reared in its traces, followed by a loud, vituperative spray of cursing. A barrel fell. More cursing. Something, *someone*, was on the move. Haviland squinted. There was something else running too. Was that a horse? He hadn't time to consider it, all of his concentration was fixed on the figure sprinting towards them, two more figures some paces behind giving serious chase. Bare headed, shirt-tails flying, and coatless, the figure came racing.

'It's him! It's Brennan!' Haviland shouted. He waved and called out, 'Come on!' He didn't like the looks of the men behind. As they closed, Haviland could see a pistol flash in one of the pursuers' hands. He definitely didn't like the looks of them now. Haviland cast a glance at the gradually widening gap between the boat and the dock. It would be impossible, even dangerous from where they stood, to hazard a leap. The gap was too wide, but at the rear, where the boat was still near the dock, it might be possible. It would be a hell of a jump, but Brennan would have his speed to carry him.

Haviland gestured wildly to the rear of the boat, shouting instructions through cupped hands as he raced towards the stern. 'The back, Brennan, head for the back!'

Nolan and Archer were behind him. Archer shouted something that sounded like, 'The horse, Brennan, get on the horse!' The horse

Haviland had spied had now passed the men in pursuit and had pulled up alongside Brennan, matching his stride to Brennan's as if to encourage him to get on. This was madness! But facing two men with guns didn't seem like much of an alternative. Brennan's pursuers were too close now, the boat moving too fast for Haviland's tastes. The horse would stand a better chance of making the leap. Haviland added his voice to Archer's. 'Bren, the horse, now!' he urged.

Haviland watched Brennan swing up on the fast-moving bay, and watched the pier end.

They leapt.

They landed.

The horse went down on his knees.

Brennan rocketed towards Haviland, taking him to the deck as a pistol report sounded from the docks, a bullet whistling overhead. 'Dammit!' In the excitement over the horse, he'd forgotten about the gun and nearly gotten himself shot. What a fine start to the trip that would have been. Instinctively, Haviland wanted to rise and see where it had come from. He grunted at Brennan's weight on top of him, but Brennan wouldn't let him up.

'Stay down!' Only when the boat had moved

a safe way from the docks and Brennan deemed it safe to rise did he let him up.

'Good lord, Bren, what have you got yourself into now?' Haviland rose and dusted off his trousers. Beyond Brennan's shoulder he could see the men on the docks shaking impotent fists their direction. Whatever it was, it had been worth shooting someone over.

Brennan stopped in the midst of tucking in his shirt tails and quirked an auburn eyebrow at him in mock chagrin. 'Is that any way to greet the friend who just saved your life?'

Haviland answered with a raised dark brow of his own. '*My* life, is it? I rather thought it was yours.' He stepped forward and pulled Brennan into an embrace, pounding him on the back affectionately. 'I thought you were going to miss the boat, you stupid fool.' Sometimes Brennan worried him. He took too many risks, treated his life too cavalierly as if he doubted his own worth.

Greetings exchanged, the horse being looked after in a makeshift stall by Archer who had some explaining of his own to do, the threesome took up their places at the rail. 'So,' Nolan drawled, tossing a sidelong glance Brennan's direction. 'The real question isn't where you've been, but was she worth it?'

Brennan threw back his head and laughed up to the sky as if he hadn't a care in the world, as if he hadn't been dangling over the side of a boat minutes ago with an angry man shooting at him. 'Always.'

Haviland smiled into the distance, a little spark starting to ignite deep inside of him. It was a good sign. He wasn't dead yet, wasn't entirely numb yet. England faded from sight. It would be a while before they'd see those shores again but in the meanwhile, it was going to be one hell of a trip.

Chapter Two

One month later—the viewing room of the Leodegrance salle d'armes

Mon Dieu! The Englishman was exquisite. Alyssandra Leodegrance's breath caught behind her peepholes as he executed an aggressive flèche against his opponent in the main training salon. Every movement spoke of lethal grace, his foil a natural extension of his arm as he effortlessly deflected Monsieur Anjou's sophisticated series of ripostes.

Alyssandra pressed her eyes more firmly to the peepholes of the *salle d'armes*'s private viewing chamber, hardly daring to believe what she saw: Monsieur Anjou, the *salle's* most senior instructor, was labouring now with all his skill to launch a counter-offensive and yet still the Englishman would not be thwarted.

'He has forced Monsieur Anjou into *redoublement*!' She could hear the excitement in her own hushed voice as she tore her eyes away long enough to toss a smile at her brother, Antoine, seated beside her in his wheeled chair, his own gaze as raptly engaged as hers.

Antoine gave a wry grin at her smug tone. 'You're enjoying it too, aren't you?'

Alyssandra shrugged her shoulders, feigning indifference, although they both knew better. There was the courtesy of professional respect between her and the senior instructor, but not much else. She put her eyes back to the holes, not wanting to miss a moment more. *Redoublement* was probably the last position Julian Anjou had expected to take up.

It had been ages since she'd seen Julian beaten and it did her heart good to see the arrogant master humbled. He hadn't been humbled since the time she'd beaten him. That had been two years ago and he would not admit to it. He preferred to call it a draw done at his expense to save *her* pride. Not that he wasn't an excellent fencer. Julian Anjou's arrogance was well deserved, but having earned it didn't make him any more tolerable.

The Englishman initiated an elegant *balestra* followed by a lunge, a traditional but fearless combination, his efforts confident and deliberate. He knew precisely what he was doing and what he hoped to accomplish. The sparring match had become a chess game. 'Checkmate,' she whispered under her breath as they circled one another again—Julian pressed to the extreme to keep the tight frame he was known for, the Englishman athletic and unwinded even after the long bout. A crowd of students and junior instructors had gathered at the edges of the floor.

He must dance like a dream, all that grace contained in those broad shoulders and long legs. The errant thought caught her off guard. After years of assessing men from a purely athletic standpoint as fencers, she seldom spared a thought for the more sensual applications of the male physique. Apparently, she was sparing a thought for it now. A shiver, wicked and delicious, shot down her spine as the Englishman moved in a tight circle around Anjou just out of reach of the man's foil. It was easy to imagine the confident press of his hand at a woman's back, of that hand guiding her skilfully through the crowded floor of a waltz. What woman wouldn't want to be led out on to the floor by such a partner, his body pressed ever so slightly to hers, their bodies attuned to the subtle pressures and nuances of the other?

She had to stop. Now she was being fanciful. It had been three years since she'd had a serious suitor or even been interested in one, nor was there any time for one at the moment with the tournament looming. She gave herself a mental scold. The *salle* and Antoine were her life now. Until that changed, there was no room for romantic games. A sharp movement from the floor refocused her attention. She'd been so engrossed in her little tangent of a fantasy she nearly missed it—the moment when the Englishman's blade slipped past Julian's guard and his buttoned tip pierced the master in the chest.

Julian swept him a bow, acknowledging the defeat, but his face was hard when he took off the mask and retreated to his corner to wipe the sweat from his brow. The Englishman did the same, pulling off the mask and tossing it aside, revealing a face a woman could study for hours and still not discover the whole of it; there was the strong, sharp length of his nose dominating the centre, the dark brows and long, defined cheekbones that likely did incredible things to his face when he smiled. Right now, he was not smiling and they lent him a slightly rugged air. And his mouth, with that thin aristocratic bow on top, and sensual, fuller lip on the bottom, was positively wicked. Suffice it to say, that mouth alone could keep a girl imagining all sorts of wicked things all night.

'He was perfect today,' Alyssandra remarked. She and Antoine moved back from the holes to talk, to plan. The Englishman would want to know if there was another master above Anjou with whom he could continue his studies.

Her brother's eyes held hers in all seriousness for a moment. 'Not intimidated, are we?'

She huffed at the idea, marking it as ridiculous with a shrug of her shoulders. 'Appreciating him is not the same as being intimidated by him.' Intimidated? Hardly. Excited? Definitely. Her body fired at the knowledge of it.

No, she wasn't intimidated. Men in general did not intimidate her. She'd faced men who'd believed they were the best, men like Julian.

She revelled in the thrill of matching blades, of wearing them down and striking when their arm was weak and their pride too strong. She sensed, however, that the Englishman would be different. A true challenge, but one she would overcome, she was confident of that. She'd been watching and learning. She was ready and now so was he.

The Englishman had been coming to the *salle d'armes* for three weeks. At first, she'd watched him because he'd been new and new was always intriguing. He had started with informal matches against the gentlemen who came purely to exercise. Having dispatched them, he'd moved on to those who came to study the art more seriously until there was no one left to face, no one left to coach him except Julian. It had been a testament to his skill and to his wealth that Julian had consented to take him on. Julian took on only a few select pupils with the skills and finances worthy of instruction from a great master. Now, Julian had been beaten. The Englishman had earned the privilege to face her; she, who was even more exclusive than Julian, not because of the money, but because of the secret. None of her clients ever knew they faced a woman. The mask gave her anonymity, her skill preserved it. No one would ever believe a woman could possess such a talent.

Alyssandra reached for her mask, her sword arm already feeling the grip of her hilt in her hand. 'Shall I go out now?'

Antoine shook his head. 'No, sit and watch with me. Your Englishman is not quite perfect, no matter what you believe.' He gave a crooked half smile and nodded towards the peepholes. 'They're about to start again.'

She and Antoine pressed their eyes to the holes once more. She watched and waited patiently for Antoine to make his point. They had done this countless times since his accident had rendered him incapable of fencing. She was his legs now and he was her mentor. One of the benefits of being a twin was being able to read her brother's mind after a fashion. He could read fencers, but she could read him. She knew what he was thinking quite often before he spoke. Like now. They weren't even looking at each other and yet she sensed he saw something in the Englishman's parry.

'There!' Antoine exclaimed in hush tones although there was no threat of being overheard. The room was soundproofed. 'Do you see it?'

She did see something, but what? 'No,' she

had to admit. She was astute at assessing her opponents, but her brother was a master at detecting the subtle movements of a fencer. It was what had made him so good.

'Right there, he drops his shoulder,' Antoine said. 'Watch closely, he'll do it again.'

This time she did catch it, but only someone of Antoine's skill would have noticed without instruction. Julian certainly hadn't or he would have taken the opportunity to drive his button into the Englishman's briefly unprotected shoulder.

'When he recovers from a parry, he drops the shoulder. It's when he's most vulnerable.' Antoine winked at her. 'We'll help him fix that, of course, but only *after* you've established yourself with him.'

'Bien sûr.' Alyssandra laughed with him. It was an effective strategy for gaining a student's respect to beat him a couple times before showing him why he'd lost. It proved the instructor knew what he or she was doing in theory as well as practice. But she sobered at the solemn look on her brother's face. 'What?'

'You *can* beat him, right?' he asked, worry creasing his brow. 'If you can't…' He didn't finish the sentence. They both knew the reputation of the salon was at stake, as it was any time Alyssandra faced an opponent, masquerading as Antoine Leodegrance, the famed Parisian swordsman.

She smiled to alleviate his concern. 'I will beat him. All will be well, as it always is. You have taught me perfectly,' she assured him. She understood his concern. He wanted her to be safe, but he was also frustrated with his own impotence to provide for them without relying on the masquerade. It had been three years since Antoine's accident, three years since they'd instigated this ruse in order to keep the successful *salle d'armes* running. No one would willingly study fencing under a woman's guidance.

Their *'petite déception'* had worked splendidly up until now. There was no reason to think it would not continue to work. Only one other knew of it and that was Julian, who had as much to lose as they if the secret was exposed. Of course, they had not thought to keep the ruse in place for so long. They'd hoped Antoine would recover the use of his limbs and return to his rightful place as the *salle*'s master at arms. It was only a matter of time, the physicians had said confidently at the beginning.

After three years, though, she had to wonder how much more time could be allowed to pass before they had to admit Antoine's recovery was an improbability? And if he didn't recover? What did that mean for the two of them? Antoine was all the family she had, but they could not sustain the masquerade for ever, for many reasons, not the least being her hopes for a family of her own. The longer she kept up the ruse, the longer she put off her chances to make a worthy match. It might be too late already. Etienne DeFarge had married another last spring, unwilling to wait any longer. Any hopes she'd entertained in that direction were gone now.

But those were thoughts for another time, for a far-off future if it ever came. They had no bearing on tomorrow or the next day. What *did* matter was the Englishman. Alyssandra turned back to the peephole, intent now on her quarry, all dark thoughts of the future thrust aside along with more seductive visions of a dancing Englishman complete with long legs, broad shoulders and a *very* kissable mouth. *Tomorrow*, she thought silently, *you, sir, shall meet your match*.

Chapter Three

'*En garde!*' Julian Anjou called out, stepping back from the two fencers in the private *salle*. Haviland assumed the position and faced his opponent, the masked and silent Antoine Leodegrance. Leodegrance had bowed to him respectfully, but other than that, all communication had taken place through Anjou acting as an intermediary. Masked and silent, Leodegrance had an almost surreal presence.

By pre-determined agreement, Leodegrance made the first '*attaque*'. Haviland understood this encounter was more an exercise than a bout. There would be no score kept. Leodegrance would want to see the variety and depth of his skills first-hand. And, frankly, Haviland wanted to see Leodegrance's. It wasn't everyone who had the privilege of viewing the selective Parisian's skill up close.

Parry and thrust, *balestra* and lunge, *battement* and *liement*. Haviland met the drills with ease, his eyes making a study of the great Leodegrance. The man had slim, graceful movements, elegance personified in even the smallest of motions. His parry from the *sixte* position was flawlessly delivered, his blade up, his wrist supinated. It was the subtlety of these motions that gave the man his edge, the litheness of his movements. Haviland dodged, barely avoiding the tip of Leodegrance's foil.

By Jove, the man was quick on his feet! With the slightest of efforts, the merest flick of his wrist, Leodegrance had nearly pricked him. There was a certain style to the flick of his wrist that was patently his own and Haviland made quick note of it. It seemed to give him an extra ounce of flexibility in wielding the foil—something easier to note without the Italian preference for a basket over the hilt. With the French blade, one's grip was exposed on the handle. Leodegrance was using that to envious advantage.

Gradually, the nature of their exercise began

to change. The space between them became charged with a competitive electricity. Something combative leapt and sparked between them, a lethal chemistry, more akin to sensual attraction. Leodegrance's manoeuvres became a seductive dance, stealthy and mesmerising; his strikes came more quickly until Haviland was fully engaged.

The exercise had transformed into an *assaut*. Haviland grinned beneath his mask, enjoying the thrill of competition. They circled, each one stalking the other, arms and foils held out in full extension to define their space and to protect it. Leodegrance's frame looked as fresh as when they'd begun, his arm appeared strong. Haviland wondered if it was a bluff. His own arm was starting to ache and yet he dared not waver. Surely, Leodegrance, as slenderly built as he was, was physically affected by the duration of this match.

Haviland wished he could see beneath the full-face mask. Was Leodegrance sweating? He could feel his own sweat trickling down his back, down his face. Leodegrance made a *flèche* at lightning speed, requiring him to put up a riposte and he did so, proud of the speed of his own reflexes. Haviland parried and moved to launch his own attack. That was when Leodegrance's foil found his shoulder. He felt the hard press of the wooden button before he saw it, so fast did the strike come. He stared at it in full surprise for a moment before remembering his etiquette.

He bowed as Anjou had bowed before him yesterday in acknowledgement of a fair match and in acknowledgement of the other man's superiority. It did not gall him to be beaten—*this time*—it did gall him, however, that he hadn't seen it coming. The final attack had been most unorthodox, coming as it did on the heels of Leodegrance's deflected offensive. Haviland had parried the attack. It had been his turn to initiate one of his own, only Leodegrance had not waited. Haviland saw in hindsight what Leodegrance had done—he'd turned the move into a feint, a move designed to distract his opponent both in body and mind, while the real blow was delivered—a most effective *fausse attaque*.

Leodegrance accepted his bow and offered a slight one in return. Haviland reached up to remove his mask, thinking Leodegrance would do the same. The man did not. Instead, he strode over to Anjou and conducted a conversation in low, hurried French, looked his direction one more time, raised his foil in salute and departed the room with a farewell as unorthodox as his final attack had been.

'*Bien, monsieur, bien.* You've done well. Master Leodegrance is very pleased.' Julian Anjou came to him, all smiles. It was the most pleasant Haviland had seen the instructor look. 'He has asked you to come back Thursday for another lesson. Also, there is a small competition in a matter of weeks. Master Leodegrance would be honoured to have you entered.'

'He could not tell me himself?' Haviland interjected sharply. This was by far the oddest lesson he'd ever had. 'Are we to never speak? Does he ever remove his mask?'

'Of course not!' Anjou sounded shocked, as if he'd uttered blasphemy. Anjou lowered his voice, tinged with a hint of French condescension. 'It is because of the accident, *monsieur.* You are an outsider, so perhaps you do not know. The scars are too hideous, too distracting for opponents. He wears the mask out of deference for *you, monsieur,* for all of his pupils.' He gave a thin smile. 'We are French, perhaps we are vain, but we put much stock in our beauty. Beauty is life to a Frenchman. We would not willingly inflict ugliness on anyone.' Anjou inclined his head in a dismissive gesture. *'Jusqu'à demain, monsieur.'*

Haviland watched him depart with a shake of his head. That was the trouble with Frenchmen. They never quite answered your questions even when they did.

'We're going to have trouble with that one.'

Alyssandra looked up in time to see Julian slip inside the private viewing room to join her and Antoine. 'He's no trouble. I can manage him. I proved it today.' She pulled her hair free of the pins that kept it tucked up and in place when she was Antoine Leodegrance and let it fall free about her shoulders. That felt better. She stretched her arms, relieving the tension that had built up in them during the match. She had handled the Englishman, but it had taken much of her strength and skill to do so.

'Not that kind of trouble.' Julian fixed her with a stare before moving his gaze and his conversation to Antoine. 'Our Monsieur North has been asking questions. "When can he meet you?" "Why don't you take off the mask?" "Why won't you speak to him?"'

'But you handled it all beautifully.' Antoine gestured towards the peepholes where he'd watched the entire lesson. 'I saw it. He understood.'

'But he does not accept it,' Julian answered sharply. 'He's been asking questions around the clubroom when the men gather after their exercise and in the main *salle*. He talks to everyone and everyone talks to him.'

'Let them talk, there's nothing anyone can tell him.' Antoine remained unconcerned.

Alyssandra walked up behind Antoine's chair to stand with her brother. It was a gesture she knew aggravated Julian, a non-verbal reminder that she and her brother were united on all things. 'We've seen his sort before. He's just another Englishman on the first leg of his Grand Tour. He's just passing through like so many of them.'

Julian gave her a shrug of concession. 'In that regard, you're right and perhaps we can use that to our advantage. Those Englishmen are all looking for the same thing on their tours; a little cultural experience and a lot of sex.' Julian paused thoughtfully for a moment. 'You should arrange for him to meet one of your more sophisticated friends. Perhaps Madame D'Aramitz?'

'Are you suggesting we spy on him?' Alyssandra rebelled at the idea of Helene D'Aramitz enjoying North's charms and reporting back all the details.

Julian's eyes were twin orbs of calculation. 'Yes, I am suggesting exactly that.' He flashed her a cold smile. 'I can keep an eye on him when he's here at the *salle*, but it will be up to you to use your connections and to keep an eye on him in society.' He gave Antoine a respectful nod. 'If you'll excuse me, I have a lesson to prepare for.'

'I don't think North is a threat,' Alyssandra said after Julian left.

'Maybe, maybe not.' Antoine blew out a breath. 'I hate being tied to this chair. It should be me out there fencing him. We shouldn't even have to worry about an inquisitive Englishman, but because of me, we do.'

What could she say? Her brother could no more change the facts of his existence than command his legs to walk. 'We'll manage. Julian makes too much of it.'

'I think Julian is right. He does bear watching so he's not given the chance to become trouble. But, I don't think Helene D'Aramitz is the answer. She's a terrible gossip and far too perceptive. Then we'll have her asking questions, too. She'll want to know why we're so interested in what North does.' Antoine's face became thoughtful. 'If anyone is going to watch him in society, it should be you. It will eliminate the risk of exposing ourselves unnecessarily to outside parties. Will you do it?'

Her stomach somersaulted at the prospect of engaging the handsome Englishman on two fronts: as the masked, mysterious Leodegrance, and in person as herself. Part of her—the very feminine part of her that responded to him as a handsome man— revelled in being able to meet him on her own merits. But the other part of her understood the enormous risk she ran. *'La petite déception'* had just become a *grande* one. She must don two identities in order to preserve one. The feminine part of her could not afford to be distracted from the professional goal of protecting the *salle* and Antoine. She would start tonight. She had a fairly good of idea of where North and his friends would be. Anyone of note was attending Madame Aguillard's Italian musicale.

Alyssandra squeezed her brother's hand. 'Yes, of course, I will do it,' she said as if there'd ever been a choice.

Chapter Four

The match lingered on his mind that evening, distracting Haviland from Madame Aguillard's elegantly appointed entertainment. The musicale was unable to hold his attention for long no matter how lovely the Italian soprano, or how talented the pianist who accompanied her or even how often the hostess herself trailed her beautifully manicured fingers down his arm in provocative suggestion. No matter the enticement, his mind drifted back to the faceless, silent Leodegrance. Even without words, without a visage, the man had a charisma that had drawn Haviland. The force of that presence was disturbing to say nothing of the circumstances in which it had been felt. Fencing with Leodegrance had been like fencing a phantom. He'd never faced an opponent shrouded quite literally in such mystery. He couldn't quite get over it, or past it.

'Stop brooding,' Nolan scolded *sotto voce* as they moved through the crowd at the intermission. 'It's bad form, and our hostess is bound to notice. You're still thinking about the match.'

'No, I'm not,' Haviland said defensively.

Nolan chuckled. 'Yes, you are. You're a terrible liar. It's a good thing you don't aspire to cards. It's probably some fetish of Leodegrance's. He's French, after all.' Nolan shrugged as if to indicate being French explained away any unexplainable eccentricities.

He clapped Haviland on the back. 'As for me, I'm off to the card tables in the other room. I, for one, won't risk disappointing my hostess. There's an inspector playing who is apparently unbeatable.' The French were mad for gambling, and Nolan had immediately become popular among the card set. After almost a month in Paris, Haviland still found it odd how the ability to gamble for large sums of money acted as a superior calling card in French society.

'I hear there's a certain pretty French widow playing tonight too.' Archer joined them, catching the last part of the conversation as he handed off the flutes of champagne he'd retrieved from the refreshment table.

Nolan smiled broadly. 'Madame Helene is a talented card player. I fancy she recognises those same skills in myself.'

'Well, probably not those particular skills, but certainly others if rumour is to be believed.' Archer laughed.

'What rumour would that be?' Nolan raised his eyebrow in mock chagrin.

'The "rumour" from our dear butler that you haven't been home before breakfast for the last week,' Archer supplied.

Really? Haviland hadn't noticed. He watched Archer and Nolan spar in friendly fashion and felt detached from their banter. He should be glad everyone was finding Paris so hospitable. Archer had found a horsey set of young men eager to share their knowledge of the Continental breeds. Nolan had been easily assimilated into the aristocratic gambling circles and Brennan, well—he had been easily assimilated into several French beds as far as Haviland knew. But what he ought to feel and what he did feel were different.

What he felt was lonely, left out. He'd spent

his waking hours at the *salle d'armes*. He was away as much as the others and he missed most of their days. They were together in the evenings in some form, two or three of them usually, although seldom all four. Even tonight, three of them were here at Madame Aguillard's, but Brennan was absent.

Perhaps it was better this way, establishing this sense of distance. Haviland sipped his champagne. At some point, the others would continue on the tour without him unless by some magic he wrested another six months from his father.

Nolan departed for the card tables, and Archer picked up the threads of their conversation from earlier that afternoon when he'd returned home from the *salle*. 'I've been giving your match some consideration,' he began thoughtfully as if that discussion had not been broken by hours of intermission. 'How do you know it was Leodegrance if he wouldn't remove his mask?'

That thought had crossed Haviland's mind, too, but he'd quickly discarded it. 'The man was too good to be anyone else. His talent spoke for him, which might be what he intended all along with his secrecy.' The effort seemed unnecessarily dramatic, but perhaps Leodegrance was a dramatic sort of man and there were the scars to consider as well.

'Then it's settled. You have your explanation and you can enjoy the evening.' Archer shot him a sideways glance etched with challenge and took a large swallow of his champagne.

'What is that supposed to mean?' Haviland said crossly.

'That you don't really believe your own explanation about talent speaking for itself. You think something is afoot. Admit it.'

'That's ridiculous. There *was* an accident a few years ago. We even heard about it in London. It's entirely plausible he's become a bit reclusive as a result. It's not as if Anjou's explanations about the scars don't make sense,' Haviland argued. Perhaps Nolan was right. He just needed to stop brooding. When Archer pressed him to see a conspiracy, he simply couldn't come up with a motive for such efforts. Perhaps that was what Archer intended all along; to make him see the foolishness of his notions. A silent look of comprehension passed between them.

Archer smiled in confirmation. Haviland had read him aright. Archer clapped him on the shoulder. 'Put it to bed, old friend, and have some fun. You need a distraction. Perhaps I could get our hostess to introduce you to one. There's several pretty ones here tonight.'

The crowd around them ebbed, affording Haviland a glimpse across the room. Archer shifted to the right to deposit his empty glass on a passing tray and there she was—a distraction to end all distractions. She must have come late. He would have noticed her earlier otherwise. She was the sort of woman who could command a man's attention without doing a thing. She was proving it right now, simply standing against a wall and stealing his breath along with any ability to formulate coherent thought.

'Archer, don't move. I think I've found my distraction.' She was a stunning brunette in an evening gown of crinkled taffeta the shade of gentian blue. The gown was plain by French standards, unadorned with ruffles or embroidered hems, yet the plainness lent itself to an understated elegance, as did the exquisite tailoring. For all its lack of affectations, this was not a poor woman's gown and no one would mistake the wearer for a peasant.

'I take it it's not a masked man?' Archer raised an interested eyebrow, but remained obediently frozen.

'Hardly.' Haviland inclined his head in the smallest of gestures for Archer to follow his gaze. 'Turn your head slowly and remember I saw her first.' He did see her, the woman beyond the dress. When he looked at her, he saw the confidence of her carriage, the delicate beauty of her very bone structure that declared her a woman of high birth. There was strength, too, in that delicacy. This was no retiring wallflower and yet she was alone.

Archer smirked. 'What are you thinking?'

Haviland gave him a wry grin that spoke volumes. 'I'm thinking I'm looking at Plan B.' One last *affaire*, one last opportunity to drink from passion's cup before settling into his marriage. He might not have chosen Christina Everly, but neither had she chosen him. He would not shame her with infidelities after they wed, regardless of the circumstances surrounding their union. Until then, however, a gentleman need feel no such restraint, especially if travelling abroad.

The woman in question looked their direction, catching his stare, the slight raise of his eyebrow. She answered his silent enquiry with the flick of her wrist, her fan opening in a sophisticated gesture that covered just the bottom of her face. Haviland's gaze dropped to her hands. She held the fan in her left, and Haviland smiled at the discreet sign to approach. Negotiations complete. Beside him, Archer let out a low whistle of appreciation. 'Now, that's a woman to cross a room for.'

'I doubt men stop there,' Haviland said under his breath. They'd cross mountains, even oceans for her. She was the sort of woman who could wreck a lesser man, one given to baser instincts and spontaneity. Thank goodness he wasn't such a man. 'Here, hold this for me.' Haviland handed his flute to Archer.

'Why? Do you think you'll be back for it?'

Haviland chuckled. 'With luck, no', and then he crossed the room.

Alyssandra felt a little tremor of anxious anticipation skate down her spine, so strong was her awareness of him. His eyes were on her, piercing and intense, demanding she meet his gaze as he approached, demanding she be aware of him. But it was too late to back out of this exquisite deception. This was what she'd wanted, what she'd orchestrated her evening around in the hopes of it happening.

She'd not known with certainty that he'd be here, but she'd known it was highly possible. The odds had favoured her. Madame Aguillard's soirée in the seventh *arondissement* was a coveted invitation and the Englishman and his friends had become coveted guests in certain circles. Men with money and connections could not be kept secret for long, and North was positively delicious on both accounts. He had looks and was heir to a title and a fortune, both English, which made him more impressive than his Continental counterparts. French nobles and Italian *contes* were thick on the ground and notoriously light in the pockets. In short, Haviland was the stuff of mothers' dreams. Even French *mamans*.

Who wouldn't jump, nay, who wouldn't *leap* at the chance to marry their daughters to such prestige and such security? There were those who would leap for much less than an offer of marriage. Alyssandra reminded herself she wasn't here for purely selfish reasons. It was what her brother *needed*. Her presence here tonight was professional. She had to remain objective just as if she were facing him from behind a fencing mask. There was no room behind the mask for carnal thoughts and there was no room for them now, although that didn't seem to be stopping them from trying to intrude.

She'd heard the women talking behind their fans all night. *'With a body like that, he cannot help but be extraordinary in bed,'* one woman had remarked. Another had commented, *'I just want to look at him, preferably naked.'* Alyssandra could understand the sentiment. He was gorgeously made, lean hipped and broad shouldered. She had studied that physique from behind peepholes for weeks now in anonymity. She had seen that body up close today during their exercise and it had been positively scintillating. It was in part responsible for the more feminine side of her wanting to risk the encounter tonight. She wanted to test the electricity between them. Would it happen again or was the spark between them limited to the fencing floor?

Around her, women whispered, watching his

approach with interest and perhaps hope, from behind their fans. His stride was purposeful, confident, his gaze locked on her, making his destination clear to those who hoped otherwise. Alyssandra raised her chin just a fraction, enjoying a moment of defiant victory. The Englishman was coming for *her.*

Alyssandra lowered her fan and met his gaze with equal strength. She let the rush of excitement over meeting him as herself fill her, let him take her hand and bend over it with eyes that never left hers. He would never look at her incarnation of Antoine Leodegrance the way he was looking at *her,* all banked fire and desire in those blue eyes. His lips brushed her gloved knuckles. Even that briefest of touches sent a jolt of awareness up her arm. The connection she'd sensed today at the *salle* was still there.

'*Mademoiselle, enchanté.* I must apologise for my boldness. I could not wait for a proper introduction. May I present myself? I am Viscount Amersham.'

She'd known all of his names, of course. It was on his application at the club although he preferred to go by his given name there. Therein lay her advantage. He was meeting a stranger.

But she was not. She knew him, whereas, there was nothing to connect her to Antoine save her name, and that would be revealed when and if she chose.

She let a little smile play across her lips, her eyes flirting coolly, her body trying to ignore the hot spark that passed between them upon contact. 'I know who you are.' She gestured to the groups gathered around them with her closed fan. 'Everyone knows. You've become quite the celebrity.' She rose and retrieved her hand, breaking the electric connection. 'Your reputation precedes you.'

'What reputation would that be?' He arched a dark brow.

She gave a laugh and spread her fan again, enjoying having the upper hand for the moment. 'Are you fishing for a compliment, *monsieur le vicomte*? I don't think vanity becomes you. I think you know very well what sort of reputation.'

'*Touché.*' He grinned, showing even white teeth in that kissable mouth of his. It was every bit as delectable up close as it was from the distance of the viewing room or from behind a mask. His blue eyes danced, his gaze taking in all she had to offer. She was acutely alert to the skim of his eyes roaming over the slender length of her neck, how they'd dropped discreetly to the low sweep of her *décolletage*. His attraction to her was not in doubt.

Electric awareness crackled between them, broken only by their hostess signalling the end of the intermission—a critical moment that would define the direction of the evening and perhaps even their association. Allowing him to go back to his seat would suggest at worst she did not return his level of interest or, at the very least, she had not been serious when she'd summoned him. She must act quickly. She had done the summoning; the next move was hers. She had to be one to establish the purpose of having called him to her.

Alyssandra placed a hand on his arm, braving the physical pull of him. Men had crossed rooms for her before. Tonight, she had even encouraged such a response, knowing how well she looked in the gentian blue and the careful upsweep of her hair, both of which showed the silhouette of her body and the profile of her face to advantage. Would it be enough? 'Some of the others will go to the card rooms instead of returning to their seats. Perhaps you might enjoy a tour of the gardens? I have been here before, if you're interested.' He was a sophisticated man. He would hear the *entendre* in her words and the invitation, just as he was aware she would see the silent interest he communicated with his eyes.

'I have heard much about the beauty of the French gardens. I would be delighted to see one in person if you could be spared?'

Alyssandra smiled. 'It would be my pleasure.'

He allowed her to step slightly ahead of him, his hand at the small of her back to guide her through the crowd finding their seats, his hand confident of its reception, as if it belonged there. She could hear his voice, low and familiar at her ear. 'It will be mine as well, I am certain of it.' She recognised, too, what this was; the touch, the words, the very closeness of him. His body was advertising its skills in his touch, in his bid for familiarity. These were the opening moves to a seduction and it would be up to her just how far they would go. Suffice it to say, it was much harder to be professionally objective just now.

Chapter Five

There was nothing wrong per se with the garden. It was inherently respectable with its paper lanterns and exotic-shaped shrubs. The incipient lure to wickedness was Alyssandra's construction entirely. She knew very well they'd not come out here to be respectable, or even to see the topiaries, although the famed shrubs did make a good ruse for the reality: They'd come outside to test the waters of their attraction in the way sophisticated men and women do who are not necessarily looking for attachment but something more fleeting: momentary pleasure, momentary escape.

While she understood the allure escape held for her, she was hard pressed to imagine the allure of escape for a man like Haviland North, whose life was already perfect. And yet what did she know of him? He was here after all, wasn't he? In Paris, hundreds of miles and a body of water way from home. The Tour itself was an escape of sorts and those on it escapees. It often stood to contrary reason that the more perfect something looked on the outside, the more rotten it was on the inside. What imperfections might the handsome viscount have, hidden away behind those blue eyes? It did make a girl wonder what he might be running from, and there was nothing sexier than a man shrouded in intrigue.

It was part of her mission to peel away those perfect outer layers and get to those imperfections beneath. Of course, she wouldn't peel all those layers tonight. That took time and trust. Tonight was about establishing the latter. 'Do you see the shrub shaped as a dog?' She pointed to the shape near a fountain. 'It was modelled after Madame Aguillard's favourite hunting hound. The fountain itself is made from marble imported from Italy.'

'Very impressive.' North said, walking beside her, his hand always at her back, offering a physical reminder of his presence.

'Very expensive, if you ask me,' Alyssandra shot back. It had always struck her as foolish to have imported the marble at extra cost when there were quarries nearby. It was darker now. There were fewer lanterns and even fewer guests in this remote corner of the garden. Her pulse began to leap. They'd reached their destination—somewhere private.

'It seems we have reached the perimeter of the garden.' North commented, his eyes full of mischief. 'What do you suppose we do now?'

Alyssandra wet her lips and turned towards him so they were no longer side by side, but face to face. 'I've talked far too long. You could tell me about yourself. What brings you to Paris?' She stepped closer, drawing a long line down the white linen of his chest with her fan. She'd genuinely like to know. She'd spent the past three weeks making up stories in her mind about what he was doing in France.

But she'd not come out to the garden to acquire a thorough history of Viscount Amersham. That would come in time, as those layers came off. Tonight was about making first impressions, ones that would eventually lead to…more. Even so, she rather doubted her brother had expected 'more' to involve stealing away to the dark cor-

ners of Madame Aguillard's garden with somewhat illicit intentions. Julian, on the other hand,
had envisioned exactly such manoeuvres when
he'd suggested Madame D'Aramitz.

'I *could* tell you my life story,' he drawled, his
eyes darkening to a deep sapphire. 'Or perhaps
we might do something more interesting.' Those
sapphire eyes dropped to her mouth, signalling
his definition of 'interesting' and her breath
caught. *Something more interesting, please.*

It was hard to say who kissed whom. *His*
head had angled towards her in initiation, but
she had stepped into him, welcoming the advance of his mouth on hers, the meeting of their
bodies; gentian-blue skirts pressed black-clad
thighs, corseted breasts met the muscled firmness of his chest beneath white linen.

Her mouth opened for him, letting his tongue
tangle with hers in a sensual duel. She met his
boldness with boldness of her own, tasting the
fruity sweetness of champagne where it lingered
on his tongue. Life pulsed through her as she
nipped his lip, and he growled low in his throat,
his arm pressing her to the hard contours of him.
She moved against his hips, challenging him,

knowing full well this bordered on madness. Desire was rising between them, hot and heady.

'You are bold for an Englishman.' She sucked at his earlobe until she elicited another growl of arousal.

'Is that a problem?' he whispered hoarsely against her throat, his lips nuzzling the column of her neck, his hands moving over her rib cage, warm and sure. A hand closed decadently over a breast, a thumb offering a circling caress over the fabric of her nipple. It was both a siren song and a swan's song. This had to end.

'It is if I have to go and I do.' She summoned the shreds of her resolve. If she didn't pull away, she'd end up half-naked in the garden, her dress around her waist and his hands on her breasts. The only layers that would end up being peeled would be hers and that would hardly bring him back for more.

Alyssandra stepped away, smoothing her skirts, taking a formal tone designed to cool anyone's growing ardour. 'It has been a most enjoyable evening, *monsieur le vicomte.*'

'Perhaps you might call me Haviland,' he offered abruptly as if the use of his title offended him. She thought she understood. After such an intimacy he wanted to be a man, not a title. It was not so different from the reason she was reluctant to give him her own name.

'*Bon nuit*, then, Haviland.' She dropped a little curtsy in a flirty farewell. Maybe she would escape this encounter unexposed after all.

She turned to go. His hand closed on her arm. 'Not so fast, my lady of mystery.' His voice held a tone of authority beneath the seduction. 'While we've had some pleasure tonight, one pleasure yet eludes me. Might I have *your* name?'

She did not mistake it for a request that could be denied or flirted away. How would Haviland North, Viscount Amersham, a man used to power and obedience, feel about her name now? Would he be angry? Would he feel betrayed or used? She dropped her eyes, assuming a demure, penitent posture. 'May I tell you a secret?'

'Absolutely. I love secrets.' His voice was a sensual whisper close to her ear, but she did not miss the firmness in it. His tolerance had limits.

'I must beg your forgiveness. I fear I have had you at a disadvantage.' She looked up beneath her lashes, gauging his reaction.

'Ah, so it's absolution you're seeking.' His eyes narrowed in assessment.

'Not absolution, sanctuary. If I tell you, you must promise not to be angry.' She let her eyes dance, building the mystery so that he would promise her anything to hear her secret.

He leaned close, a smile on his lips. She could smell the clean scent of linen and sandalwood soap on him, 'Sanctuary it is, then. Tell me your secret.' Good, curiosity had got the better of him. She hoped bad judgement hadn't got the better of her.

She locked eyes with him and let her secret fall into the night between them just before she fled. 'My name is Alyssandra Leodegrance.'

Curses tumbled through Haviland's mind. He'd spent four glasses of brandy and three hours sitting in the dark and he still could not get past it. He'd been kissing Alyssandra Leodegrance, his fencing instructor's...his instructor's *what*?

This was where things got fuzzy and it wasn't entirely the brandy to blame. What exactly *was* her relationship to Leodegrance? Was she his sister? His cousin? His wife? The latter wouldn't surprise Haviland, although it would repulse him. Frenchmen were forever throwing their wives at guests. It was considered rude not to ogle one's hostess as a means, he supposed, of congratulating the husband on such a splendid catch. If he had thought for one moment she was another man's wife, *any man's* wife, let alone Leodegrance's, he would not have kissed her no matter how lovely she'd been.

'You came home early.' Archer stood in the doorway of the sitting room, his form barely outlined by the lamp left burning in the entry.

'Maybe *you* came home late.' It was nearly three in the morning, after all. Haviland drained the last of his brandy.

'May I join you?' Archer gestured towards the decanter on the table, ignoring the cross response. He poured a glass and took the chair opposite him. 'I suppose this means the meeting with our lovely stranger didn't go well?'

Typically, Haviland enjoyed Archer's directness, but usually it was aimed at someone else. 'It went well enough, very well, actually.' Those particular memories were still warm. His mind was a riot of snippets, all of them full of her in bright, vivid colour: the mysterious spark that lit the depths of her chocolate-brown eyes; the long, black lashes that made her appear demure and seductive all at once. Those lashes had been quite engaging when she fluttered them, the perfect foils for her sophisticated conversation with its hidden messages, the blue of her gown, the lace and paint of that exquisite fan she'd employed so expertly, that sexy flick of her wrist… a flick practically identical to his instructor's.

Haviland had not fully appreciated that flick at the time. In hindsight, it was easy to say he should have recognised the resemblance right then. Antoine Leodegrance's wrist movement was signature.

'Then what's the complaint?' Archer nodded towards the empty glass. 'By the look of the decanter that wasn't your first brandy of the night.'

'Her name. She's Alyssandra Leodegrance, only I don't know what that means precisely.' Not just in terms of her relationship to Leodegrance, but in terms of what had she been doing with *him*? Had she known who he was ahead of time? Had she deliberately put herself in his path in the hopes of engineering what only appeared to be a chance meeting between two strangers? The more he'd drunk, the more it seemed likely and the more his mind had unwound each piece of the conversation, each gesture. When he held such speculations up against the oddness of his previous encounter with Leodegrance, meeting Alyssandra tonight began to look more than coincidental.

'If Leodegrance is a recluse, perhaps he sent her to vet you on some level?' Archer mused out loud, his train of thought mirroring Haviland's more private ones.

Haviland looked into his empty glass, debating whether or not to pour himself another and decided against it. Four was quite enough, and he had no desire to wake up with a thick head if it wasn't too late for that already. 'That makes little sense at this point. For Leodegrance's purposes, I've already passed. I've beaten his senior instructor. Vetting me now seems like an effort made too late.'

'Or it makes perfect sense. Now that you've reached Leodegrance, it may be that he wants to be sure you're worthy.' Archer raised his brows over the rim of his glass. 'We should have Nolan vet *him*. Nolan is far better at these sorts of games.'

But he and Archer weren't too bad at it either. One could not come of age in the *ton* without a healthy amount of social intuition. The second explanation, that Leodegrance felt the need to protect himself, perhaps reassure himself that his latest pupil was indeed an appropriate candidate for the honour, seemed logical. Haviland had already proven his skill, but Leodegrance would want more. He'd want to make certain Haviland's social credentials were what they were supposed to be and that his wealth was more substantial than mere rumour. Leodegrance would want to know he was a man who didn't just say he was rich, but was wealthy in truth. But that didn't explain most of what had happened with Alyssandra. Skilful conversation would have accomplished those goals. Frankly, there hadn't been that much conversation between them and what there had been had been pure flirtation. Fencing hadn't come up once.

'Ah, I see, she did more than vet,' Archer said softly when the silence stretched out between them. 'Did she fulfil your need for distraction, then?'

Good lord, yes. Just watching her had been a tantalising fantasy. Tasting her, touching her, had been a different elevated plane of sensuality altogether. That's where his pride came in. Had she'd been told to do those things or had they been part of the natural chemistry at work between them? Which all came back to the initial question: *Had she known him before he'd said his name?*

She had not told him her name until the end and she had done so penitently, knowing full well it would mean something to them both. And it had. She'd fled into the night, not waiting to hear his response, and he'd fled to the dark privacy of his rooms to mull that response over.

'I hope she isn't his wife,' Haviland said quietly. It would ruin everything. He'd have to leave the *salle*, have to forfeit instruction with Antoine just when he'd begun lessons with the master. He'd have to start over, one of his precious months of freedom now wasted. But most of all, he hoped she wasn't Leodegrance's wife because he wanted to see her again, wanted to kiss her again, wanted to feel what he'd felt this evening in the garden again. He wasn't sure he'd ever felt such initial, intense attraction before, hadn't ever felt such overwhelming fire course through him at a woman's touch. It was exquisite and quite obviously addictive.

'Because you are my friend, I hope so too,' Archer replied, rising from his chair. 'But be careful. A woman like that knows her way around a man. That makes her dangerous to a man like you who has so much to protect.'

A title, a family, a reputation, a fortune—Haviland knew all too well the things he had to protect. What he wouldn't give to forget all that for a while and simply be a man. He'd thought tonight, with her in the garden, perhaps such forgetfulness might be possible. But that was before he'd known her name. Now, his hopes hung in the balance of a kiss and its motives. Why had she done it? Why had she kissed him? For passion or for a plan?

Chapter Six

'You did *what*?' Antoine's disbelief radiated in all possible ways, in his tone, in the look on his face, even in the sloshing of his tea when he set it down too forcefully as her confession spilled out over breakfast.

'I kissed him,' Alyssandra repeated firmly, meeting her brother's eyes. She would not look away as if she was embarrassed by what she'd done. She was twenty-eight and well past the age of needing permission for her actions. If she could successfully masquerade as a fencing master, she was certainly capable of deciding who she was going to kiss. Her brother's attitude of indignation sat poorly with her this morning. She was not a child or even a naive girl out of her league with men like Haviland North. Alyssandra buttered a piece of bread with unnecessary fierceness. 'It was just a kiss, Antoine.' Had he forgotten she'd once been highly sought after before their fortunes had changed?

'Why? This is not what we'd talked about. You were supposed to talk to him, not kiss him.' Antoine fought to keep his voice from rising. 'It's not just a kiss! Who knows what he'll be thinking now.'

'It hardly matters what he thinks. He'll only be here long enough for you to make some money on him and that's all that matters to you and Julian,' Alyssandra shot back uncharitably. How dare he ask her to play this double masquerade and then question her execution of it.

'Yes, plenty of money; money from lessons, money from the tournament when I wager on him. Money for the *salle* when people see the kind of fencer we can turn out. That money keeps you in this fine house, keeps you in gowns like the one you wore last night,' Antoine retorted sharply.

She supposed she deserved that. It was an unfair shot on her part. Money always made Antoine prickly. He was acutely aware of the limits of his ability to provide for them. There was always enough, but just enough. She bit her tongue against the temptation to remind him just how much of that money she helped earn. He would not appreciate it and she already had one black mark against her this morning.

'Since he truly is only here a short while there's really no harm in it, is there?' Alyssandra soothed. She sensed there was something else bothering him. She felt terrible. Guilt niggled at her for causing her brother angst. She wanted to believe there was no harm in last night's kiss, that she could indulge herself just a little. At times she felt that she had become a recluse, too, along with Antoine.

Before his accident, she used to go out to all nature of entertainments. She used to dance, ride in the parks and the woods outside town, shop with her friends—many of whom had long since married and had children. Now, she seldom went out at all. When she did it was only in the evenings after the work at the *salle* was done.

At first, she'd stayed in because she felt guilty about dancing and riding when Antoine, who'd loved those activities, could no longer do them. They'd been things the two of them had done together and it seemed disloyal to her twin to enjoy them without him. In the early days after his accident, there had been nursing to occupy her. Then, there simply hadn't been time. Antoine had needed her at the *salle* and at home. Any attempts at maintaining her old social life had eventually faded, replaced by other needs.

'We have to be careful,' Antoine said. 'A conversation is one thing, but a kiss might have him sniffing around even more than he would have otherwise and that's hardly solving the problem.'

Alyssandra knew too well how fragile their masquerade was, how lucky they were it had lasted this long and how little it would take to see it all undone. Everything was done covertly. They kept only the most loyal of staff. No one could see Antoine leaving the house or entering the *salle*, carried by his manservant. No one could come to the house. Antoine conducted all his business in writing or at the *salle* where he had Julian and her to act as his legs.

She understood maintaining the ruse was a great sacrifice on Antoine's part, too. If he allowed everyone to know his injury was lingering, he could go about publicly in his chair, or with his manservant. He could attend musicales and plays, the opera, picnics even. But to do so would mean the end of the *salle* and the end of their income. Ironically, without income and means there would be no social invitations to such events. They would be nothing more than the impoverished children of a dead *vicomte*. It was not a bargain Antoine could afford to make. So in exchange for social security, Antoine had fashioned a secretive, reclusive life for himself—a life that consisted of his family home, the elegant Hôtel Leodegrance in the sixth *arrondissement*, his father's *salle* and his sister's well-being; three things only after a life that had been full of so much more.

'I'm sorry.' Alyssandra bowed her head. She had been selfish last night. She should not have kissed Haviland North. She should have resisted the temptation to seize a little pleasure for herself when Antoine could seize none. All the choices he had made had been for her, for them. She should do the same. They were all each other had left. Perhaps that was what was worrying him this morning—a fear of losing her.

The very thought of having caused him such pain when he already had so much to bear made her chest tight. She'd not thought in those terms last night—indeed, she'd hardly thought at all in Haviland's arms. She rose and went to Antoine, kneeling at his side and taking his hands in hers, tears in her eyes. 'I will not leave you. I promise. You mustn't worry about that, never again.'

Antoine placed a hand on her head. 'I know it's hard and I know it's unfair to ask you to stay,' he said softly. 'Don't think I don't know what it costs you. You could be out dancing every night. What would become of me without you? I am afraid I'm too scared to find out, but perhaps I won't always be. Maybe some day I'll find the courage to let you go.'

She shook her head in denial. 'You must never worry. You are my brother—' Hurried footsteps interrupted her. The butler stepped into the room. She rose and smoothed her skirts. 'What is it, Renaud?'

The butler drew himself up, trying with great effort not to look disturbed. 'There is a gentleman downstairs. He is asking to see you. He has given me his card.' The butler handed it to her, hiding a very French sneer of disdain. 'He's English.'

Her initial reaction was one of relief. No one was asking to see Antoine. People had stopped asking to see Antoine years ago at home. The story about facial scars had worked well in keeping people away. But the sight of the name on the card put a knot in her stomach that curled right around her buttered toast. She passed the card silently to her brother. Antoine had been right. It hadn't been *just* a kiss. The kiss had become an invitation to seek her out and he had. Haviland North was here, in a home that hadn't seen a visitor in three years.

'You'd better go down.' Antoine handed the card back to her.

'Take him for a walk through the back garden or over to the Luxembourg Gardens. That will look civil enough.' What he meant was 'normal' enough and it would get North out of the house, away from any telltale sign of Antoine's incapacity.

Antoine glanced at Renaud. 'Did he say anything about the nature of his business?'

'No, he did not.'

But Alyssandra knew. She had no illusions as to why he had come. He was here to make her accountable for last night.

'You played me false last night.' Haviland announced the intent of his visit the moment she stepped into the drawing room. This was not a social call and he would not treat it as such by dressing it up as one, nor would he allow her to escape the reckoning he'd come for. It would be too easy to forget his agenda in those deep-brown eyes, too easy instead to remember those lips on his, the press of her body against his.

He'd come as early as he dared in hopes that morning light would mitigate his memories of the midnight garden and show them to be just that—fantasies exaggerated by the lateness of the hour and his desire for distraction. He'd also come early simply because he wanted the situation resolved. Resolution would determine his next course of action.

He might have come earlier if finding the house had been easier. No one at the *salle* had been eager to give up the address, directing him only to the sixth *arondissement*. No one, not even Julian Anjou, had refused him outright, of course. They'd said instead in the indirect way of the French, 'The master does not receive anyone.' Haviland had been forced to rely on general directions from merchants and shopkeepers who recognised his description of Alyssandra and eventually made his way.

Alyssandra gestured to a small cluster of fur-

niture set before the wide mantel of the fireplace. 'Please, *monsieur le vicomte*, have a seat.'
He grimaced as she returned to formality as she
had at the last in the garden. 'Shall I call for tea
or perhaps you'd prefer something more substantial? Have you eaten?' The formality and
now this. It was a deft reprimand regarding the
hour of his call.

Haviland shook his head. The last thing he
wanted to do was sit and eat. He understood her
strategy. If he was determined to not make this
a social call, she was determined to do the opposite. A social call required a different set of
rules, polite ones. He was intent on something
a little more blunt, a little more direct.

She sat and arranged her skirts, the unhur-
ried movements calling attention to the elegant
slimness of her hands, the delicate bones of her
wrists. Haviland could not help but follow her
motions with his eyes. She was in no rush to answer his accusation and her sense of calmness
rather took the wind out of his bold claim. He'd
expected the passionate woman of last night to
leap to her own defence and deny him. He'd expected her to engage him in a heated argument
at his charges of duplicity. She did neither.

She arched a dark brow in cool enquiry as he sat. 'You are disappointed? Perhaps you thought to make some drama of this?'

'I do not appreciate being toyed with,' Haviland said tersely. 'You did not tell me who you were.'

She dropped her lashes and looked down at her hands as she had last night and, like last night, she was only playing at being penitent. 'I did not think it mattered so much at the time. We understood one another, I thought.'

Inside the drawing room perhaps they had understood one another. They had made eye contact, she'd given him tacit approval to approach, to flirt. At that point, a name had not been of issue. 'It mattered a great deal in the garden,' Haviland answered, his eyes resolutely fixed on her face, watching for some reaction, any reaction that might give her away, daring her to lift those deep-brown eyes to his. She was far too serene for his tastes. He wanted her agitated. She'd kept him up all night, damn it.

She did lift her gaze, a worldly half smile on her lips to match the hint of condescension in her eyes. 'Then I kissed you and apparently that changes everything for an Englishman. Are all of you so chivalrous? Tell me you've not come to propose marriage to atone for your *great* sin.'

'I am not in the habit of kissing women whom I do not know. That makes me particular, not chivalrous,' Haviland corrected. She was mocking him and he didn't care for it, although he recognised it was an offensive move of some sort, a protective strategy, something to put him on the defensive much like a reprise in fencing after an attack has failed. He recognised, too, that she would not be much help in supplying the answers he wanted without his asking directly. 'Are you his wife?'

She made him wait for it, studying him with her eyes, letting precious seconds pass before she uttered the words, 'No, I'm his sister.'

Haviland felt the tension inside him ease. One mystery solved, but another remained. He asked his second question, the one that mattered more in the larger sense. The first question had been for his private pride. 'You knew who I was last night the moment you heard my name. Why did you pretend otherwise?'

'You promised me sanctuary in exchange for my secret.' She stood and pierced him with narrow-eyed speculation. How had he lost the upper hand? She had played him and now, somehow, he was the one in violation.

'Is this how an Englishman keeps his word? By interrogating a lady?' Her retort was a powerful dismissal. Manners dictated that he should rise, too, but he knew where that would lead if he didn't change the direction of this conversation. It would lead to farewell and he had not yet got what he came for. Her manoeuvre had been skilfully done. She'd put his own leave-taking into motion, taking control of the interaction out of his domain.

Haviland rose. He was skilful, too. He wasn't going to be outflanked. He smiled charmingly. 'You are right, of course. My curiosity has got the better of my manners. I can do better if you would give me a chance. Would you do me the honour of accompanying me to the park? It's a lovely day, and I'd prefer not to walk alone. Or should I ask your brother?' He did not think she needed the approval. He'd added the request for formality's sake. He didn't want to risk angering the eccentric Leodegrance. It was also a goad. She wouldn't refuse a dare. She was old enough to make her own decisions as she'd exhibited last night. A woman who kissed like that didn't live under her brother's thumb.

'There's no need to ask him,' she said too quickly. 'I'll send for my hat and gloves.' He was not prepared for the odd look that crossed her face ever so briefly. Was that fear? Anxiety? She was hiding something, that much was clear. Perhaps it was nothing more than the fact that she hadn't told her brother she'd met him last night. And perhaps it was something more. Maybe Alyssandra Leodegrance was a woman with secrets.

Chapter Seven

In for a *sou*, in for a *livre*. Alyssandra drew a deep, steadying breath and slipped her arm through his with a confidence comprised mostly of bravado. She couldn't cry off now for at least two reasons. First, she'd promised her brother she'd keep Haviland close even if the two of them disagreed on the method. Second, Haviland had come back for more. Coming back had been the plan since the moment she'd put on the blue dress. She'd not flirted with him for the simple prize of a single night and a few stolen kisses. She'd played for bigger stakes and she'd got them in spades. The only surprise was how early he'd called. He'd wasted no time coming back for more.

That in itself was impressive. It was something of a feat for him to have made it this far.

'How *did* you find our home?' she asked as they made the short walk to the park. 'It's hardly common knowledge.' *For an outsider*, was the implied message. There were plenty of people who knew where they lived. The *hôtel* had been in the Leodegrance family since the sixteen hundreds. But everyone who knew them knew Antoine did not receive visitors. It was difficult to imagine which of their acquaintances would have given up that information to an Englishman. His only connection to them would be through the *salle d'armes* and while his skill was respected, he was still an outsider. Surely, no one there would have told him.

'By trial and error mostly. Shopkeepers.' His eyes rested on her. 'I did not think it would prove to be such a secret.'

'My brother likes his privacy,' she answered shortly, making sure he heard the warning in that and the caution not to come again. Visitors were not welcome.

'And you? Do you like your privacy as well?' Haviland was probing now and not so subtly.

'When I want company, I go out.' Her retort was pointed, in the hopes of dissuading him from pursuing this line of question. It would be a good time to let the subject drop. They'd arrived at the wide gates of the Luxembourg Gardens, and there was a small crowd of people to navigate: nannies with children, children with kites and boats for sailing in the fountains. She was conscious of Haviland's hand moving to the small of her back to negotiate the knots of people at the entrance.

Even the smallest, most mundane touch from him sent a jolt through her. Some men just knew how to touch a woman. Haviland North was one of them. Etienne's touch had been comfortable, but nothing like this. If a simple touch from him could ignite such a reaction, it made one wonder what other more intimate touches could do.

'Like last night?' he said once they'd found their way clear of the people at the entrance. *Touches like last night?* Those had certainly been more intimate. It took her a moment to remember where they'd left the conversation. Then she realised with no small amount of disappointment he was not talking about touches, but about company.

'Did you come looking for me or for any company in general?' His tone was edged with ice. He'd misunderstood her answer. He was thinking she was a loose woman, looking for intimate male company whenever and wherever it pleased her. She wanted him to be warm and charming as he had been last evening, as he had been before he knew who she was and everything had turned into a fencing match of the verbal variety. Her identity had made him wary as she'd known it would.

'*You* approached me, as I recall. *You* crossed the room.' It would be entertaining to banter with him if so much wasn't at stake. He was clever *and* bold, not afraid to say the audacious. It made conversation an adventure, wondering what would come next, what her response would be. 'I hardly think it's fair to blame me.'

He shrugged, contemplating, his eyes on her mouth. 'If I had known who you were from the start, it might have changed the, ah, "direction" of the evening. There's no denying being who you are complicates things. I kissed the sister of my fencing instructor. Surely, you can understand the precarious position that puts me in.'

Kissed was a relative understatement and they both knew it. They'd acted precipitously. She'd been a stranger to him. They'd owed each other nothing but passion in those moments. Then she'd become someone and everything changed.

'And I kissed my brother's star pupil. Certainly, *you* can understand the position that puts me in.'

He gave a wry smile. 'No, I'm afraid I don't. What position is that, exactly?'

She met his smile with a coy one of her own. They were expert wits toying with one another the way expert fencers tested the skills of their opponents. How much to reveal? How much to conceal? 'The position of deciding whether or not I can trust you. There's so much to consider if we were to become, shall we say, entangled.' It was hard to play cool with his body so close to hers, his eyes lingering every so often on her mouth, just enough to remind her of what their mouths could do. She had to resist. She could flirt all she liked, but ultimately, resistance was in her best interest. She needed to keep him close, but not too close. Too much intimacy and he would start asking more questions.

'What is there to consider?' he drawled, playing his end of the game with audacious charm. He was overtly in pursuit, driving her towards a particular conclusion to this conversation by stripping away her objections.

But she knew the game. Alyssandra ticked off the considerations on her fingers. 'First, I must consider your motives. Are you using me to gain an entrée with my brother? If so, it won't work. I don't appreciate being made an intermediary pawn and my brother doesn't receive anyone. Second, I must ask myself what kind of liaison are you looking for? Based on what I've seen of your like-minded countrymen, I can only assume you're looking for a short-term sexual companion, an exotic adventure to write home about. That, too, is an unappealing motivation. I have no desire to become an Englishman's souvenir, a story that is trotted out in his clubs back home when he's sloshed with brandy and reminiscing.'

Her words were sharp as she laid down her terms. She'd meant them to be. She wanted him to understand she would not be used no matter how strong their attraction. But Haviland merely laughed and gave her a wide smile. 'I agree entirely. Neither option sounds even remotely appealing. Those are not things I would ever want for myself.' That wide smile almost disarmed her.

Almost. Agreement was a most effective strategy and while she hadn't expected it, she was ready for it. 'I suppose you want me to ask what do you want?' She tried for a bored tone, or at least one that suggested she'd travelled this path before when, in reality, she couldn't tear her gaze from his blue eyes and her pulse speeded up in anticipation of his answer. What could a man with a perfect life possible want that he didn't already have?

His voice dropped, low and private, and the size of her world shrank with it until nothing existed but him, her and the tree at her back. 'What if I said I was looking for something else—an escape? What if I could offer that same escape to you? Don't tell me you wouldn't be interested. I can see the tension in you. Your life is not a free one. I can see it.' Those blue eyes dropped to her mouth again. 'Why not escape, even if it's just for a little while, to find pleasure with a man who knows how to provide it?'

He *was* bold. 'Are you propositioning me?' She could be bold, too. The game was heating up. Too bad she could do nothing more than let the pot boil.

Haviland shook his head. 'No, nothing as base as that. I'm merely asking you to consider the possibilities, that's all.' He smiled and leaned towards her ear, his voice a whisper. '*I have already considered the possibilities and found them positively delectable.*'

She was going to swoon right there and she might have if she hadn't been so sure that was what he was after. It took all of her sangfroid to muster the words, 'Has a woman ever said no to you, Haviland North?'

He grinned. 'No, not that I recall.'

She leaned into him, letting her mouth hover as near to him as she dared without touching. 'Then this is your lucky day. I'm about to be your first.'

He chuckled, low and throaty, a sexy invitation to repeal her decision. He didn't take rejection like any man she'd ever known. 'Then I shall delight in helping you change your mind.'

'You flirt like you fence, all *balestra* and lunge.'

'It's an aggressive combination.' His response was sexy and sharp in its immediacy. His eyes hooded so she couldn't see them, his forehead pressed to hers. 'So you *did* know me before last night. So you *have* seen me fence.' His tone was flintily accusatory.

She bit her lip. 'I *did* say your reputation preceded you. It stands to reason that you're a phenomenal fencer if my brother is willing to take you on.'

'So you did.'

She swallowed. He was going to kiss her. And he might have if Madame Aguillard hadn't swept down upon them with her little coterie of friends.

'There you are, *monsieur le vicomte*! And how nice to see you, too, *mademoiselle*.' She nodded at Alyssandra. 'You're out twice in as many days,' she added cattily, her eyes drifting between the two of them, but it was clear who the centre of her attention was. 'My friends have been dying to meet you, Amersham.' She gushed in rapid French to Haviland.

'Je suis enchanté.' Haviland smiled, overlooking the familiarity, but it was a polite smile only, nothing at all like the wicked smiles he'd been giving her. Alyssandra took a petty satis-

faction in knowing he preferred sparring with her over Madame Aguillard's company.

'I am giving a little dinner party tonight,' she said after introductions had been made. 'Perhaps you and your friends would like to come?' She stepped close to Haviland, affording him a view of her bosom if he so chose to look. Alyssandra noted Haviland did not. It was another small victory and one Madame Aguillard was well aware of. But she was not a woman who admitted defeat easily. She put a confiding hand on his arm. 'There will be cards for Monsieur Gray and ladies for Monsieur Carr. I have some especial friends who would like to meet him particularly and I'm sure you and I can find something special for you, too.'

Alyssandra wanted to skewer the woman for her audacity. She watched Haviland step back, freeing his arm from the woman's touch. 'I appreciate the invitation, but I must respectfully decline.' He offered no reason. The conversation mopped up after that with polite small talk and Madame Aguillard wandered off to join other groups.

'She'll be back,' Alyssandra said as the woman took her friends and left.

Haviland gave her a small, private smile. 'Well, what I'm interested in is right here.'

But for how long? They started walking, a slow, steady stroll, taking in the lush greenery of spring, the pleasant, warm air of the day. She was thankful for the silence as they strolled. Her mind was whirling and she needed a minute to think. How did she fulfil her promise to watch Haviland? How did she keep him from asking too many questions? How did she keep herself from rushing headlong into this forbidden attraction while not losing Haviland in the process? Or worse, losing herself? It would be too easy to capitulate to his charm, to set herself up for heartbreak when he left. How to balance all this?

The audacious Madame Aguillard might be routed for now, but the lesson was learned. Haviland was a person of interest to the women of Paris and a healthy male in his prime. Madame Aguillard might not be to his taste, but he wasn't a man used to being alone. It had crossed her mind as she'd watched Madame Aguillard jockey for position that if she didn't claim him, someone would.

Maybe the real question to ask was how much

was she herself willing to risk? Could she have it all? Could she reach for the pleasure Haviland promised, the escape he offered to explore with her, and still preserve her secrets? It was already the end of April.

'How long will you be in Paris?' She cocked her head to look up at him, letting her eyes give away a little of her contemplation.

His eyes danced in response. 'Long enough for you to take me up on my offer. Changed your mind already, have you?' He paused. 'All teasing aside, we plan to stay until June, unless Nolan offends any gamblers or Brennan angers any husbands. Then, it will be sooner.'

'Your friends sound delightful.' She had six weeks at most. Surely she could keep her secret and have her pleasure, too, if she dared.

He nodded. 'They are. The very best of friends a man could hope for, actually. Perhaps you'll get to meet them.'

'Then where will you go?' She shouldn't feel so empty at the prospect of him leaving. Her strategy depended on him leaving. She couldn't keep up this ruse for ever. He would go on to other places, other women, and she would still be here, her world much smaller than his and likely to remain so. *Don't think on it. He is here now, yours now if you encourage him. He's already made his offer, he is just waiting for you to accept.*

'My friends fancy a summer in the Alps, climbing the peaks.' He shrugged, and she thought she sensed some reluctance there.

'The Alps don't appeal to you?' They reached a fork in the walkway, and she gestured that they take the path to the right.

'The Alps do, just not as much as Paris,' he admitted. 'They are not known for their fencing *salles*. But it is on the way to Italy and Italy appeals a great deal.'

'Is it the *salles* alone that give Paris its appeal?' She might be guilty of fishing for a compliment here, but flirting was a way to keep the conversation light.

Haviland smiled. 'The *salles d'armes* are big part of it, but I love the coffee houses, the intellectual discussions. When I'm not at Leodegrance's, Archer and I sit for hours in the Latin Quarter, listening to the debates, joining in sometimes.'

'Surely you have that in London?' She shot him a sideways glance.

'I suppose we do. Soho is awash with artists and foreigners bringing their own flavour to the city, but it's not a place I am able to frequent often.' Wistfulness passed over his features and was quickly gone, but not missed. 'Perhaps it's not the city I love so much as the freedom I have in it. No one has expectations of me here.'

She gave a soft laugh of understanding. 'Le Vicomte Amersham has to keep up appearances?' There were places she no longer frequented, too, because life required otherwise. She thought about his comment regarding escape. Paris was about freedom for him. She'd been surprised a man of his background didn't already consider himself free, that he found it necessary to leave his home to taste freedom. She'd always thought money and power were the keys to freedom, and he seemed to have plenty of them. She and her brother had struggled to keep what little they had of either.

'Where does fencing fit with all of that?' She risked probing a little further.

'Fencing is a gentleman's art. A man should how to defend himself adequately.' It was a rote answer, the kind fencing instructors gave to build their student base.

'You've attained enough skill to have stopped ages ago.' She wouldn't let him get off with an easy answer.

He stopped walking and faced her, eyes serious. 'If you want to know, it's about freedom, the chance to prove myself on my terms and no one else's. Skill cannot be inherited, it has to be worked for, it has to be honed to perfection and that is something only a man can do for himself.'

'I know.' Her answer was a whisper. She did know. Better than he thought because that was how she felt every time she picked up a foil, every time she faced an opponent on the piste. How would she be able to keep her emotional detachment when he looked at her like that? Spoke to her in words that echoed in her heart? She swallowed in the silence. 'Come, the fountain I want you to see is just up here.' The layers were coming off. But his layers weren't the only ones being peeled back. She'd not bargained on the fact that exposing him would also mean exposing herself.

It was quiet beneath the shade of the leafy canopy overhead, the sound of trickling water growing louder as they approached the end of the path. 'This is the Medici Fountain, one of the prizes of our park.' Her voice was quiet out of reverence for the solitude.

'It's beautiful.' Haviland spared a glance at the stonework, but his gaze rested on her and she had no doubt his words hadn't been for the fountain alone. 'Is this what you wanted to show me?' His eyes dropped to her mouth, silently encouraging.

'And I wanted to show you this.' She stretched up on her toes, arms wrapping around his neck as she brought her mouth to his. This time there would be no mistake about who was kissing whom and who had started it.

Chapter Eight

It was both easier and more difficult to fence
Haviland on Thursday, two days later. Alyssandra had not bargained on this. She would have
thought the sensation of kissing him would have
waned by now. And, most certainly, fencing him
should have been easier. After all, this time she
knew what to look for in his attacks from the
experience of having opposed him before; knew
how he'd hold his body, how he'd move, how fast
he'd be. But the distraction of him, of knowing
that body and how it felt pressed to hers, was
mentally overwhelming. No wonder Eve was
not to have eaten from the tree of knowledge.

It took all her concentration to think about
flèches instead of kisses while knowing full
well he did not share the distraction. How could
he? He thought he was facing her brother. He

had no idea she was behind the mask. Yet, she sensed he carried his own distraction, too. The timing of his movements was off and he was dropping his shoulder more than usual.

Even so, it took her longer than she'd planned to defeat him. With a rather large sense of relief, her button pierced his shoulder in the same place. She put up her foil, nodding to Julian, and turned to make a quick departure as she had on Tuesday. Today, Haviland was ready for such an exit.

'Wait, aren't you going to explain to me how you do that?' he called before she reached the door. 'That's twice now, Leodegrance. There must be something you look for.' She did not turn. She kept moving. She could see in her mind the scene playing out behind her: Haviland stepping forward instinctively, wanting to follow her out, and Julian stepping between them. She could hear Julian as she slipped into the hallway.

'*Monsieur*, you were distracted today. Your movements were like an amateur's. *Mon Dieu!*' Julian picked up the instruction with a rapid cataloguing of Haviland's mistakes.

It was not unlike the discussion awaiting her

in the viewing room. She had barely taken off the mask and tugged her hair out of its tight bun before Antoine voiced his disapproval. 'You weren't concentrating!' He turned his chair from the peepholes with a fierce turn, his features grim. 'If this is what one kiss has done, it is too dangerous! He nearly had you today.'

Alyssandra shrugged, trying to give a show of nonchalance. It wasn't what one kiss had done, it was what one moonlit garden, one afternoon stroll, a rather charged flirtation up against an oak tree and another kiss at a fountain had done. 'If he had, we would have told him it was planned, part of the lesson to work on something or other.'

'That's not good enough,' Antoine snapped. 'You are supposed to be *me*. My reputation is on the line when you fence like that.'

It was true. Antoine would never have been distracted by thoughts of hot kisses or by anything for that matter. One of his many skills in fencing was his single-minded focus. Once, during a championship match, a fire had started outside but Antoine had been oblivious to all of it—people screaming, the fire brigade throwing water—until he'd defeated his opponent. It had become part of the legend surrounding him. She would never have that level of concentration. Privately, she wasn't sure it was a great loss. She'd rather see a fire coming.

She gave her brother a patient smile. 'Everything ended as we wanted. Shall I tell Julian to instruct him on his dropped shoulder tomorrow?' It would pacify Haviland and keep him from charging out of the room demanding answers from an opponent who wouldn't speak to him.

Antoine nodded, calming down. 'I'll tell Julian myself. We need to meet afterwards anyway.' He paused. 'I think I must apologise. It was wrong of me to ask you to stay close to the *vicomte*. I never meant for you to jeopardise your virtue. I thought you would be safe with him. I should have known better. I've seen enough of them come through the *salle* on their Grand Tours. They're all looking for the same thing. Your charming *vicomte* isn't any different, much to my regret.'

But he *was* different. He talked of freedom. He had offered escape, not a bawdy roll in the sheets. But how did she articulate those things in terms that wouldn't worry Antoine? 'I'll manage him. I'm not fool enough to lose my head over a kiss,' Alyssandra said tightly. 'I think I will change and go home now. I have a few errands to run on the way.'

Alyssandra changed quickly in her brother's office, her movements fast and jerky as she pulled off her trousers and slid into half-boots and a walking dress, mirroring the rapid, angry thoughts rushing through her mind. She wasn't mad at Antoine. She was mad at herself. He was right. Today's lesson had teetered on the brink of disaster. She'd nearly been too distracted and a second's distraction was all it would have taken. At the first opportunity, she'd failed to maintain the professional objectivity she'd promised herself.

He was right, too, about the uselessness of encouraging Haviland's interest in her. Nothing good could come of it outside of preserving their secrets. She had seen rich, titled heirs just like him come through the *salle*. The Grand Tour was supposed to be a time of intellectual enlightenment for young men, a chance to learn about the highbrowed philosophies that governed other cultures and countries. Alyssandra suspected that was simply the justification wealthy families gave for sending young Englishmen abroad to rut and gamble and drink so they couldn't cause trouble at home.

Alyssandra grabbed her pelisse from a hook on the back of the door and her shopping basket. It was hard to imagine Haviland fitting the standard mould, however. He looked to be a few years older than the usual fare they saw. Most of those men were in their early twenties and far too young to appreciate any of the cultural differences they might encounter. In contrast, Haviland had a polished demeanor to him, a sophistication that could only be acquired with experience. And the way he'd talked about freedom in the park hinted at depths behind those blue eyes. But that changed nothing. Even if he turned out to be different than the usual passerthrough, what could he offer her but a short *affaire* and a broken heart? He would leave. They *needed* him to leave.

Perhaps a short affaire *is best. What do you have to offer him or anyone for the long term? No one will want to take on an invalid brother-in-law*, the wicked argument whispered, tempting. She'd been so focused on Haviland, she hadn't spent much time thinking about her part in this equation. Alyssandra pushed open the door leading into the back alley behind the *salle* and stepped into the afternoon light. She couldn't leave Antoine in the immediate future. She might never be able to. Didn't Etienne prove as much?

'Alyssandra!' The sound of her name startled her out of her thoughts. The sight of the man who called it startled her even more. Haviland leaned against the brick wall across the narrow alley, his coat draped over one arm, his clothes slightly rumpled as if he'd changed in a hurry. He stepped towards her. 'I didn't mean to frighten you.' He took the basket from her arm. She could feel the heat of exertion through his clothes. He had indeed made a quick departure. How had he managed to escape Julian?

'I came down to bring my brother lunch. I just dropped it off.' Alyssandra improvised and gestured to the basket to give the fabrication credibility. 'Shouldn't you still be working with Monsieur Anjou?' According to the schedule, he was supposed to be with Julian for an hour to give her plenty of time to change and leave the building without *this* happening. Not that it mattered, she reminded herself. He didn't suspect anything. It wasn't unusual for a sister to want to bring her brother lunch.

'I had enough fencing for one day.' Haviland shook his head and gave a half smile. 'The lesson didn't go very well. Monsieur Anjou assures me I wasn't concentrating. I didn't stay long enough to hear everything else I did wrong.'

'Perhaps you weren't,' she teased, looping an arm through his and beginning to walk. It did occur to her that Julian and her brother were still inside. If they concluded their meeting, they would come out this door—this discreet door that hardly anyone knew about or paid attention to. She needed to get Haviland away from the exit before something happened she couldn't explain away.

'Your brother got me in the same place he got me on Tuesday, right in the centre of my shoulder. I must be doing something to leave myself open for it.' Haviland looked back over his shoulder towards the door. 'In fact, I was hoping to catch your brother afterwards and speak with him.'

She'd guessed as much. She gave him an exaggerated pout. 'I'm not sure that's what a girl wants to hear—that you've come looking for her brother, but not her.'

'I didn't know you would be here.' He smiled back and gave up on the door.

'Now that you *do* know, perhaps you'd like to accompany me on a few errands?' She told herself she was doing this for Antoine. If she didn't, he would exit the building sans mask, hefted in the arms of his manservant, and Haviland waiting to witness it. Haviland would learn the error was not in Antoine's face, but in his legs. Yes, all this was to protect the great ruse. But her pulse still raced at his nearness, at the thought of spending the afternoon in his company.

This would be new territory for her. She had not been in the company of such a gentleman. Most of her encounters had been at balls and soirées—in short, events that were heavily scripted, where everyone was expected to be on their best behaviour. She'd never been out in public, at a 'non-event' where there was no script except for the one the participants wrote between them. It was a new kind of freedom, and Alyssandra liked it. Even without the requirements of a ballroom, Haviland was solicitous. He carried her basket. He didn't show impatience when she debated, perhaps overlong, which bread to purchase at the *boulangerie*. He held the shop doors open for her. He walked on the far side of the pavement to shield her from any traffic.

It was all done effortlessly. Alyssandra hardly noticed, so easily were these little tasks performed. Maybe she wouldn't have noticed at all if she'd come to expect such treatment. As it was, it was new to her. Etienne had never had an opportunity to do these things for her. Their meetings had always been at events or carefully chaperoned in her home. Antoine might have done such things for her if he could have. But this was clearly not new to Haviland. These choices were ingrained in his being and it was intoxicating, a further reminder of his polish, his sophistication. This was no boy wet behind the ears. If he was this polished in public, how he must shine in private.

She shot him a saucy, sideways glance, wanting to flirt a little. 'You're very good at a lady's errands. Is this part of your "persuasion"?'

He laughed. 'A master never tells his secrets.'

'I can think of other ways a gentleman might prefer to spend his afternoons,' she teased.

'Really?' He gave her one of his raised-eyebrow looks. 'I can't.' He could melt ice with that look.

What was it the old wives said about flattery? It got you everywhere? There was definitely some merit in that when done right and, in her estimation, Haviland was doing it right indeed. It was hard to resist his charm even when she knew she so obviously should.

They crossed a street, skirting the edge of the gardens. They were just a few streets from the *hôtel*, and a few streets from the end of her glorious afternoon. Shopping had never been this much fun. Her stomach growled. Instinctively, she pressed a hand to her middle, trying to squelch the embarrassingly loud reminder that she hadn't eaten since breakfast and not much at that. Breakfast had been a hard roll and cheese.

'Are you expected back soon?' Haviland asked, his hand falling to the small of her back, guiding her towards the park entrance instead of home. 'I was thinking we might stop and try some of that bread you debated over for so long and some of that cheese. Maybe even some of that wine if you don't mind drinking straight from the bottle.' His motions suggested he was not expecting any resistance.

She liked that—confidence in a man was always attractive. Not Julian's over-confidence, which was really a combination of ego and arrogance, but the assumption that he knew they were enjoying their time together and would mutually like to continue it. She was also wary of that confidence. She'd not forgotten he'd given something up to be with her this afternoon. Maybe he thought this would be another avenue for getting what he wanted: a meeting with her brother. She'd warned him about such a ploy once before.

They found a patch of grass away from the path in enough shade to keep their eyes from being blinded by the sun. Haviland made to spread out his coat for her, but she declined with a laugh. 'I'm not so delicate as to need something to sit on. The grass is fine.' To prove it, she sat down and tucked her legs beneath her. She welcomed it actually, this chance to sit on the ground and just be.

Haviland reached into the basket and took out the wheel of cheese. 'You might as well take out the sausage, too,' Alyssandra said and then realised the flaw in their impromptu picnic. Bottles could be drunk out of in the absence of glasses, but they absolutely could not sit there and simply bite off hunks of sausage and bread with their mouths. 'Oh, no! We don't have a knife.'

Haviland grinned and dug into his pocket. 'Yes, we do.' He flipped open a small silver knife. 'It won't be elegant carving, but it will do.' In that moment, she didn't care. It was enough to watch this man smile, to know that he was smiling at her, enough to cling to the knowledge that he'd been interested in her before he'd known who she was.

Haviland sawed through a slice of bread and cheese and handed it to her. '*Bon appétit*, Alyssandra.' His blue eyes twinkled. Good lord, he was handsome but that didn't mean she wasn't cautious.

She tilted her head to study him. 'Why are you doing this?'

Haviland bent his knee in a casual pose. 'Does there have to be a reason?'

'There usually is.' She didn't particularly want to know it, but she would probably be better off in the long run knowing it now instead of later.

Haviland chewed his bread. 'You know. Persuasion. I made you an offer of pleasure and escape. The offer is still on the table.'

'I already rejected it,' she reminded him.

Haviland arched a dark brow. 'You didn't mean it.' He leaned closer, over the basket of food between them, his hand cupping her cheek. His voice was a low whisper against her jaw. 'You kissed me at the Medici Fountain. That's the most unlikely rejection I've ever had.'

She closed her eyes and let herself drink in the scent of him, the touch of his hand against her skin, his voice a caress at her ear. 'Then there's this electricity that jumps whenever I'm near you, like it's doing now. That's not any form of rejection I've ever known.'

She drew a deep breath and let herself pretend it could be real a moment longer before she uttered the words that would break the spell. 'Does that electricity have anything to do with wanting to meet my brother? Do you think seducing me will gain you an introduction to the famed Antoine Leodegrance?'

She expected him to rear back, expected him to take her words as a blow to his honour. It was what a gentleman would do, lie or not. No gentleman in good conscience would admit to such a thing. Haviland did neither. His mouth found hers, his lips brushed hers.

'Is that what other men have led you to believe? What fools.' He breathed against her and deepened the kiss until she wanted to forget that she needed to refuse him, that she needed to exercise caution. Too much too soon and perhaps he wouldn't come back having had all he'd come for, or perhaps it would push him to ask his insatiable questions. 'You don't want to turn me down, Alyssandra, you're just not sure how to accept.'

Maybe just this once, she could indulge. She knew her boundaries, after all. Perhaps she was making too much of a fuss over it. She leaned into him and gave over to the kiss, over to him, part of her mind remembering how far back they were from the public path. There was no one to see. His hand was in her hair at the back of her neck, massaging, guiding her into the depths of his mouth. He tasted of spicy sausage and fresh bread, of sun and grass, and of Paris in spring—hope and heat and possibility.

Alyssandra reached for his cravat, tugging him to her, letting him press her back to the cool grass. His hands bracketed her head, his body half lay against hers, her arms about his neck. Madness welled in her, want surged at the feel of him hard against her stomach. The madness was in him, too. Amidst this desire it was easy to believe this wasn't about Antoine, after all, but about her and about him. A hand slid up her rib cage, cupping a breast, and she gave a sweet moan and arched against him. There was only pleasure for a moment, before it exploded into chaos.

'*Bâtard!* Get off her, you English swine!' A booted kick seem to come out of nowhere, catching Haviland in the stomach. He groaned and rolled, staggering to his feet as she scrambled to sit up. Her first instinct was to grab a weapon, anything. Haviland's knife was on the ground beside her. She curled her hand around the tiny hilt. If only she had her épée.

Haviland was still bent double, but his fists were up, and he moved to stand between her and their attacker. There was no need for his chivalry or her puny weapon of a penknife. She recognised their attacker as he drove his fist into Haviland's jaw.

'Julian! Stop!' Alyssandra screamed, but neither man was interested in listening.

Chapter Nine

Haviland's head snapped back, taking the force of the blow. He vaguely registered Alyssandra's scream, but he was too enraged to heed it. He charged like a bull, burying his head into the midsection of the Frenchman. Julian went down, Haviland on top of him, delivering a few equalising punches.

'Haviland! Enough!' He was aware of hands tugging at him, trying to pull him off Julian Anjou. Alyssandra's hands. Some of the rage ebbed out of him at the realisation she was safe. There was no need for more violence unless Anjou chose to jump him again. He rose, straddling Anjou and dragging him to his feet. From the look on Anjou's face, Haviland wasn't so sure Anjou wasn't going to do just that.

'What do you mean by attacking a man without warning?' Haviland barked.

'That is hardly the greater crime here! You were all over her!' Julian roared. Haviland released him with a shake. It was a mistake to let Julian go. It gave the man a chance to focus on Alyssandra. 'And you!' He jabbed a finger her direction. 'You let him. That makes you a—'

Haviland stepped between Julian and his view of Alyssandra. 'I'd advise you to stop before you say something you regret.' His voice held unmistakable steel. He wouldn't mind punching Julian again—the slightest provocation would justify it.

Julian backed away, throwing one last threat at Alyssandra. 'Your brother will hear of this and he won't be pleased.'

With Julian gone, he could focus on Alyssandra. Haviland turned towards her. She was pale, but not entirely from fear or shock. There was anger in her eyes. 'Alyssandra, I am sorry—'

She cut him off sharply. 'Do *not* apologise. Neither one of us is sorry about what happened, only that we got caught. An apology makes at least one of us a hypocrite.'

True as that was, he knew better and to

carry on so in a public place was unconsciona-
ble. One moment he'd been stealing a kiss, the
next, things had progressed far beyond what
he'd intended, but not beyond what he minded.
Although perhaps he *should* mind if the consequence was getting hit in the face. His cheek
was starting to throb now that the adrenaline
had receded, and his lip was split.

'Julian had no right,' Alyssandra insisted, still
fuming as she gathered up their picnic.

'Doesn't he?' Haviland crossed his arms and
leaned against the tree trunk, watching her,
thinking. He knew so little about her and yet
he'd risked so much in those unguarded moments. 'It seems to me that he felt he did. Is
there an understanding between the two of
you?' He'd not considered that. Up until now,
he'd been focused on her as merely the sister
of his fencing instructor. He'd not thought of
her as belonging to another. An Englishwoman
would never have invited his attentions the way
Alyssandra had if she was claimed by another.
Maybe that was his mistake. This was France,
after all, the country where husbands begged
guests to flirt atrociously with their wives.

She stood and faced him, hands on hips,

looking gorgeously defiant. Her hair had come down and now it hung in a long chestnut skein over one shoulder. 'There is an understanding between Julian and me, but not the sort you think.' She slid the basket on to her arm and handed him his discarded coat. 'Thank you for the afternoon.' Her tone was terse, perfunctory. 'Now, if you'll excuse me? I have to go home and clean up this mess.'

'I'll come with you. Perhaps I can explain.' Haviland shrugged into his coat. His split lip and bruised cheek could wait. He owed her this much. A gentleman didn't let a lady face scandal alone even if the scandal wasn't likely to leave the house.

She gave a harsh laugh. 'What do you think you'll explain, exactly? It's not as if Julian misunderstood what he saw. No, I don't think an explanation would improve the situation.' She stepped away from him, her voice quieter now, but no less sharp. 'It would be best if I did this alone. I am sorry if that thwarts your plans yet again to meet my brother. *Au revoir.*'

It didn't occur to Haviland until after she'd disappeared from sight that he might not see her again. Ever.

* * *

'She doesn't trust me,' he groused to his friends in the common room of their apartments, a cold rag held to his cheek.

'And you don't trust her. She hid her identity from you on purpose,' Archer reminded him, handing over another cold rag to replace the one he held. 'It seems you have something in common.'

'She thinks I am using her to meet her brother. Even today when I offered to walk her home and explain, she refused on the grounds that I was manipulating the situation into a meeting.' Lucifer's stones, he'd made a mess of things. He'd never been so ham-handed with a woman before. Usually, he was discreet, masterful, charming. His *affaires* were smooth associations. Women could and did trust his lead.

Brennan snorted from his corner of the room where he lounged casually in a chair, his shirt open, his waistcoat undone. It was nearing evening and he looked as if he'd just risen. 'What did you think you were going to explain? The angle of your tongue in her throat?'

Haviland threw him a quelling look and winced. It hurt his face to move. 'Don't be crass. It's not funny.'

'I disagree.' Brennan laughed. 'It's hilarious. It's the sort of the thing that happens to *me*, not you. I am going to enjoy the shoe being on the other foot. Thoroughly.' He pushed himself out of the chair. 'If you'll excuse me, I have to get dressed. I'm anticipating a busy night at Madame Ravenelle's.'

'Stay in the Marais, Bren,' Haviland cautioned out of habit. He couldn't go with Brennan tonight, and Brennan was in the routine of slumming in the more dangerous parts of the city. At least in their more aristocratic neighbourhood, Brennan would be safer. Although 'safe' was always a relative term when it came to him.

Brennan clapped him on the shoulder as he passed. 'I can take care of myself, old man. Don't worry. Take care of you. You'll have quite a bruise in the morning. I'm an expert at these things.' Then he grinned. 'Was she worth it?'

Haviland chuckled even though it hurt. 'Yes.' God, yes, she'd been worth Julian's fist in his face. Julian would look worse, though. It was a male sort of consolation.

Nolan raised his head from his book. 'She was worth it? Truly? I find it interesting you would say that about a woman you don't trust. It is as if you are saying "I trust whatever you are keeping hidden from me will not be damaging to me".'

'*This* is exactly why I like horses.' Archer sighed. 'Horses don't require cynicism. Your thoughts on human nature are so uplifting.'

Nolan shrugged. 'I'm sorry if the truth offends you. Humans require more cynicism than others in the animal kingdom.'

'More than wolves? I would have thought...' Archer began.

Haviland stood, grabbing a spare rag to take with him. He didn't particularly want to hear what Archer thought. He wasn't up to listening to Nolan and Archer debate wolves, horses and humans. He wanted to retreat, nurse his cheek and think in the privacy of his room where his friends couldn't voice their well-meant opinions.

Alyssandra Leodegrance had him spinning. She was beautiful and intriguing. It was the latter that concerned him most. What drew him to her? Where did the intrigue come from? Some women could naturally affect an air of mystery. Was she one of them or was there truly a mystery about her?

Haviland lay on his bed, eyes closed, his thoughts turning inward. He suspected the mystery had to do with what she wanted with him. She wanted him and yet she didn't. It was as if she was afraid to get too close. Her actions where he was concerned were things of contradictions. She'd signalled him to approach at the musicale, she'd gone into the garden with him knowing who he was. She'd kissed him knowing that, too, and yet she was reluctant to accept his offer for pleasure in full.

Today had followed much the same pattern. She'd spent the afternoon with him and then pushed him away when they had to confront the consequences of their brief indulgence.

He knew what Brennan would say. *She's using you for sex, reeling you in nice and slow until you're mad for her and nothing more. That's every man's dream. Embrace it.* It wasn't quite *his* dream, particularly. His dream was freedom. His dream was choosing his own destiny. A thought came to him. Haviland's eyes opened slowly, as if opening them too quickly would cause the idea to evaporate. Suddenly, he knew why she intrigued him. She'd not been selected for him by someone else. He'd chosen her. She was his choice alone.

Julian Anjou chose to remain near the long windows in the main foyer of the Leodegrance *hôtel* while he waited for Alyssandra to return. He schooled his anger, focusing instead on the green expanse of the back garden. Perhaps a nobler man would contain his emotions better, but he was not that man. He was a man who had pulled himself up the social ladder rung by painstaking rung with the talent of his sword. He might look like a gentleman on the outside after years of cultivation, but inside he was a scrapper from the streets and a desperate one at that.

So close and yet so far as the expression went. He had free access to the elegant, generations-old *hôtel* of the noble Leodegrances, he worked side by side with the *vicomte* himself. His own mother had been a washerwoman. She would have been beside herself with her son's success. But it was not enough for him. He understood how fragile his elevated status was, how pre-carious. He was not permanently bound to An-toine Leodegrance in any way and yet all his own status rested on Antoine's. Should the *salle* fail, should Antoine be exposed, Antoine would survive it in some fashion, reduced though it might be. But he would not. No one would care where he landed. Fencing instructors without references were cheaply come by.

Behind him he could hear the front door open and Alyssandra's voice as she passed her pelisse to a waiting footman. He turned from the window and watched her face pale when she saw him, but she did not try to evade him or his reason for being there.

'He will be gone in six weeks, what harm can come of it? I'll never see him again,' she said baldly, her dark eyes meeting his in challenge. She joined him at the window, unafraid. She was far too bold. If he was Antoine, he would have taken a strap to her and demanded obedience. This latest adventure of hers could ruin them all and for what? For a roll in the grass with an Englishman? For momentary pleasure? There were far safer ways to achieve those ends.

Julian exhaled, letting his mind clear. Anger would not endear him to her and that's what he needed—endearment, and if not that, at least tolerance. 'When I suggested we use feminine wiles to keep him from asking questions, I was not suggesting we use yours.'

Images from the park began to stir in his mind where he'd trapped them. He'd rather not think of her as he'd seen her this afternoon, her hair loose, her face flushed, her eyes closed, savouring her pleasure, the Englishman pressed against her. And that sound she'd made, that mewl of unmistakable delight. He wanted to be the one who offered her those pleasures. He could, too. If it was pleasure she was after, he had more than one talent to his repertoire. It might be time to remind her, get her to reconsider what he'd once offered her.

'I'm surprised you're here.' Alyssandra ignored his remark. Her tone was cool, but not entirely. There was concern beneath it. 'I didn't think you'd really tell Antoine.'

'And hurt him like that?' he queried. Alyssandra was a loyal creature. It would be worthwhile to stir that particular pot with a little guilt. 'Do you know what that would do to him?' Julian replied. 'He will not hear it from me that his sister was playing the harlot in the park.'

'Of course not.' Her words were filled with acid. 'It hardly suits your purposes.' She made to move past him, but Julian wasn't done. His hand shot out and gripped her arm. She was not going to walk away from him as if he were a servant, as if he didn't wager his fate every day on the twins Leodegrance. He deserved her respect.

'What are you running from? Are you afraid of what I'm going to say? Are you afraid I'm right? Only a coward would walk away and leave things unsettled.' Julian knew just where to poke her. She was a temperamental one, any dare would spark her tenacity. She wouldn't walk out of a room where her courage was in doubt.

She wrenched her arm free. It was the only defiance she could afford and he knew it. 'There is nothing you can say that would frighten me.'

'I hope so.' Julian softened his tone. He didn't want her angry, he wanted her confused, wanted her to doubt her attraction to the Englishman. 'It's not my intention to hurt you, Alyssandra. We are family, the three of us, we're all each other has. We all guard the same secret for the same reasons. The truth is, the Englishman is just using you. I'm not telling you anything you don't already suspect. He wants to get to your brother and you're his best chance.' He reached for her chin, trapping it between his thumb and forefinger, forcing her to meet his eyes. 'In your heart, you know this is true. He tried to follow you out of the salon today, thinking to speak to your brother. He was waiting in the alley for your brother today, not you. You were a surprise.'

'How did you know he was out there?' Alyssandra jerked her chin away, the answer coming to her before he could supply one. 'You followed me.' Her eyes flashed with accusation.

'I followed *him*,' Julian corrected. 'He left his lesson early, walked out on me, in fact. I suspected what he was up to and I was worried.' They were standing toe to toe now. The world had narrowed to just the two of them. He was conscious of the rise and fall of her breasts, of the scent of her. He had not been this close to her in ages. It was arousing even to fight with her. But he had to be careful. He didn't want to engender danger or she would never come to him.

'And you kept following us. You spied on us the entire afternoon! It's the only way you could have known where we were at.'

She was making him look obsessed. That was

not the image he was going for. 'I was protecting you,' Julian answered swiftly. He dropped his gaze to the floor as if to appear humble, perhaps momentarily vulnerable before he dissembled. 'Your brother is not the only one who cares for you.' It had the desired effect. She closed her eyes and gave a tired sigh.

'Julian, we've been through this—' she began.

He held up a hand to stall her words. 'Don't say it, Alyssandra. I cannot stand by and let you throw yourself away on an Englishman who will offer you nothing. You are too fine, you deserve better than that and *I* know it. I doubt your Englishman does.' He left her then by the windows to ponder his warning, his offer, and strode off down the hall.

It was time to make his next move. He needed to speak with Antoine and start laying his groundwork. He just needed Antoine to take up his suit with Alyssandra once more— perhaps this time it would succeed. When he'd approached her before, it had been three years ago, during the early stages of Antoine's accident. In hindsight he could see it had been too soon. She hadn't been nearly desperate enough.

She was full of hope that Antoine would recover. Frankly, so was he. But those hopeful days were long past. He wondered if Alyssandra had admitted her brother would never walk again. There would be no miracle. She needed to start planning the rest of her life. He needed to convince her he was part of that plan. Together, they could keep the charade up, the salon running until a son of their own could take over.

Who better to leave the *salle* to than Alyssandra's husband, his very own brother-in-law? If that happened, Julian needn't wait for a son to establish his claims. He could claim it outright. Truly, how long would Antoine last? Cripples didn't live long healthy lives and he'd already put in three years.

He knocked on the door to Antoine's study and stepped inside. 'I need to speak with you. It's about Alyssandra.'

Marriage to Alyssandra would solidify his dreams. He was so close and one damn Englishman wasn't going to get in his way.

Chapter Ten

'Alyssandra needs a husband.' Julian had meant the words to shock and they had. Antoine looked up from the papers spread before him, worry and confusion on his face. 'What? Why? Is she all right?' His instant concern almost made Julian laugh. Antoine was such an easy puppet to manipulate. Mention his beloved twin and he melted. It even took him a moment to notice. '*Mon Dieu*, Julian, what happened to your face?'

Julian took the chair on the near side of the desk, shrugging off the reference to his purpling eye. 'Just a small accident after you left the *salle* today. It is nothing. It looks worse than it is.' He reached for the decanter on the desk's edge. Sometimes Antoine took a little brandy for the pain. He helped himself to a glass. They'd become equals, partners, over the past three years. Older than Antoine by seven years, Julian had painstakingly cultivated the complex role of mentor, friend, uncle-cum-older brother when the case demanded it. Antoine had bought into it wholeheartedly first during his grief over his father's death and then in the throes of despair after his accident. Today, he was claiming that role to the hilt: taking a chair without permission, helping himself to the brandy—an equal interacting with another peer.

'It's time she marries,' Julian repeated. 'A husband, a family, is what she needs. She's twenty-eight. Most of her friends have long since wed.'

'I know.' Antoine's eyes were thoughtful. 'I've been thinking about it for a while now. Perhaps it's time to give up the ruse and accept the fact that I will never walk again. We could sell and Alyssandra could go on with her life.'

Julian interrupted abruptly. This was not where he'd imagined the conversation heading. If Antoine were to sell, it would be devastating to him. 'Why not have the best of both worlds?' he prompted in silken tones. The *salle d'armes* was Antoine's other weakness. It meant the world to him. He must be worried indeed about Alyssandra if he was willing to consider giving it up. 'Keep the *salle*, you can "retire" if you like, but let Alyssandra and I run it as husband and wife. I am offering myself as a husband for her.' He said it quietly, humbly, watching Antoine's eyes lose some of their softness and become shrewdly assessing.

'You?' Antoine said.

'Yes. Who better? I have been with your father and with you. All total, I've spent twelve years in the service of your family. I have known Alyssandra since she was sixteen. I have been with you through death and through despair. What better than to have your sister marry your friend and keep your father's fencing legacy, *your* fencing legacy, alive? Some day, there may even be a nephew to look after that legacy.'

Antoine smiled at that, as Julian had known he would. Family was important to Antoine. 'What does Alyssandra think?'

Julian shrugged. He chose his words carefully. This answer had to be handled delicately. 'She's a wild creature. I don't know that her opinion is the one that matters most here.

She may not know what is best for her over the long term.'

Something affirmative moved in Antoine's brown eyes, and he gave the most imperceptible of nods. Julian pushed his advantage. 'I fear her head may be turned by the Englishman. He is a fine figure of a man,' Julian offered. 'But I think it is nothing more than a sign of how lonely she is, how ready she is to move on with her life. It is too bad Etienne DeFarge has wed.' The reference to Alyssandra's old fiancé would make Antoine feel guilty.

'I like the Englishman, although I'm not sure of his motives. So many of them are just passing through,' Antoine said tentatively but it was enough to ring alarms.

'I'm sure North is a fine man. He's a real man's man. The other men at the *salle* seem to enjoy him,' Julian put in blandly, wondering what Antoine was thinking. He took a swallow from his snifter, hoping Antoine would elaborate.

'He has desirable qualities; a title in England, wealth, good manners,' Antoine mused out loud. Julian wanted to argue the last. Those manners had his hands on Alyssandra and his tongue in her mouth. 'Alyssandra is not without recommendations of her own. He would be a good match for her, and the *salle* could use him.'

Julian felt his insides freeze. He'd been right not to tell Antoine about the park. It would be all the provocation Antoine would need to start negotiating a marriage. He'd not counted on this. Antoine agreed with him on marriage, but not on the groom, and now Antoine was thinking of giving the Englishmana place at the *salle* too. Julian's ego didn't like that one bit. He was the senior instructor and he didn't like to share, which was precisely what he'd be doing.

Julian gave a sigh. 'That's a nice fantasy, Antoine, but I don't suppose it will work, do you? He's a viscount, heir to an earldom. He's not going to want to *work* as a fencing instructor.'

Antoine was far too quick to clarify. 'Of course not! He would be an owner. If he married Alyssandra, I could leave the *salle* to them and you certainly. I could retire and you could carry on. He could show up and offer instruction whenever he felt like it, make it a hobby for himself. He's talented enough.'

Julian took a healthy swallow of brandy. This was getting worse by the minute. It would be complete torture to have to answer to Haviland North at the *salle* every day, knowing North was going home to Alyssandra every night. He'd have to live every day with the man who'd taken everything from him. That was a lot of 'everys' and it was not to be borne.

'I think you're forgetting one thing.' Julian gave a sad half smile as if commiserating with Antoine. 'He'll want to go home some day. He'll have to go home when he inherits. There wouldn't be much good in that for us.' This was the second time Antoine had mentioned retiring. It was a bit disconcerting.

Antoine nodded his head. 'Well, still, it's a nice fantasy to think of Alyssandra with him, happy, safe, secure. I think she fancies him, and he'd be a fool not to fancy her.'

There was nothing left to say. Antoine seemed determined to ignore his own offer and now was clearly not the time to push it. Julian could only hope a few of his doubts would take root in Antoine's thoughts. Meanwhile, he needed a secondary plan. Alyssandra could not marry a man who wasn't there, nor could Antoine hire a man who couldn't fence well. It might be time to call in a few favours from the streets. With the tournament nearing, there would be ample opportunity to eliminate Haviland North.

Haviland was not going to let one Frenchman stand in the way of his training. Or maybe two Frenchmen depending on how Leodegrance had taken the news about the park. Haviland couldn't imagine him taking it well. He squared his shoulders as he entered the Leodegrance *salle d'armes* on Rue Saint Marc.

He was unsure of his reception. Perhaps it was good news he had yet to receive a challenge. He had no desire to fight a duel with the master. For one, the outcome would be uncertain at best. He had yet to beat the master in their lessons. And two, fighting a duel abroad over a foreign woman was exactly the type of scandal his family had prodigiously avoided for generations. His father would be appalled if news of such a thing reached English shores. It would validate all the reasons his father wanted to keep him close to home. 'Going abroad to sow wild oats suggests there's something wrong, something that can't be aired in public at home,' he'd argued on more than one occasion when Haviland had brought up his desire for freedom.

Inside, the *salle* was busy, filled with the clash and slide of steel on steel. It was mid-afternoon and all three fencing salons were busy with clients, pupils and day guests. The sight brought a smile to his face and he allowed himself a moment to drink it all in. Whatever else the reclusive Leodegrance might be, he'd certainly made a little world for himself here. From the moment Haviland had first entered the *salle*, he'd felt the energy of the place. To his right was the long day salon with its medieval shields and antique swords decorating the walls to set a tone of respect. This was the place where clients could pay by the day to use the services of the *salle*. Haviland had noticed the price was slightly more than the other *salles* in the city, but perhaps that increased the prestige. The fee included the use of the *salle*'s changing rooms and its weapons for those who didn't have their own.

In the centre was the large main salon for members only. It looked more like a ballroom with its two enormous chandeliers at either end. Weapons and fighting equipment through the ages adorned these walls too, interspersed with silver cups set in niches bearing testimony to the greatness of Antoine Leodegrance and his father before him. The elegance, the trophies, the historic weaponry only a noble family would possess were all subtle, or perhaps not-so-subtle reminders that the fees for this club were well worth it.

Not for the first time, Haviland felt a stab of envy for the eccentric Leodegrance. This *salle* was his. It might have been his father's before him, but he'd maintained it through his hard work and his talents. It was a different kind of accomplishment than simply inheriting estates others ran for you. To do what you loved every day and see those efforts grow into a place like this, now that would be a legacy.

The third salon was smaller than the other two and more private. This was where Julian held his lessons, where Leodegrance met with the elite pupils. He would go there later and seek out Julian for his latest lesson, but for now he'd join the other members in the main salon.

The others present were glad to see him. Of course, they were unaware of the contretemps in the park. Haviland soon found himself engaged in a few bouts, helping another member master his *in quartata*. During his time here, he'd discovered he had an aptitude for teaching. Helping others with their fencing was something he enjoyed doing. 'Don't turn too far,' Haviland instructed. 'Turn to the inside, bend at the waist and get your left foot behind you so you can deliver a counter-attack. Perhaps if you moved your feet like this.' Haviland demonstrated.

'Too much footwork! Do you want to fence like an Italian, Pierre?' Julian's harsh tones broke in, scolding the younger man although Haviland knew the scold was directed at him as well. Haviland turned to face the surly senior instructor. He stifled a smile. He'd been right. Julian did look worse. True, he was sporting a bruised jaw of his own but that could almost be overlooked. There was no overlooking Julian's purple eye which stood out against his paler skin. 'You fence like the Italian school.' Julian spat the words in disgust at him. 'In the French school, it's all in the wrist.' *If you were a real Frenchman and not some upstart* Anglais, *you'd know that.* Haviland could almost hear the hidden derogatory message being spoken out loud.

'Are you ready for your lesson?' Julian queried coolly. The question was designed to remind everyone just who was the instructor and who was the pupil. 'Although it looks as if someone already gave you one.'

'And yourself?' Haviland enquired politely. 'Did someone give you a lesson, too?' There were a few nervous snickers from those who'd gathered around to watch. Julian's talent might have won him respect from the members, but his cutting wit hadn't won him many friends. Left with no response, Julian narrowed his eyes to a glare.

In the private salon, Julian set to the lesson with brisk efficiency. 'Today, we will study the methods of the Spanish school.' He began pacing the floor with an occasional flourish of his rapier. 'We have a few Spaniards coming to the tournament and no doubt they will be eager to show that their methods are superior. If at all possible, you must have some ability to anticipate their moves. If you have done your reading, you will know that Carranza's *La Destreza* system has been the leading influence on Spanish swordplay for nearly three hundred years.' This was said as a challenge, as if to expose an intellectual weakness.

Haviland decided to go on the offensive. He picked up his foil and joined Julian's circling so that now they circled each other. 'The primary difference between the Spanish and Italian schools is that the Spanish focus on defence whereas the Italian school focuses on attacks,' Haviland answered. He'd done his homework. One of the many aspects he liked about the salon was the clubroom, an elegant gentleman's gathering place where fencers could meet for a drink or take advantage of the excellent library lining the walls. The library contained nearly every known treatise on fencing from all the major schools in Europe and even a few texts on the katana from Japan.

'Very good.' Julian gave him a begrudging nod. He stepped back and went to the weapons cupboard, unlocking it with a key and pulling out two rapiers. He handed one to Haviland. 'Then you will also know these are Spanish rapiers. You are not required to compete with one, but you should know what kind of weapon your opponent is using, how it manoeuvres, how it feels in his hand.'

Haviland took the blade, noting the difference in design. The Spanish rapier had a cup hilt that covered the hand. He tested it, giving a few experimental thrusts. It was lighter and shorter. It would definitely have an advantage in a longer bout where arm stamina might become an issue, but it would also be at a disadvantage against the reach of a longer French blade.

They worked throughout the lesson on the Spanish defences until Haviland was sweat-soaked. Whatever he thought of Julian Anjou, the man knew his fencing. 'Will I see Leodegrance on Thursday?' Haviland asked casually as they put their blades away.

'I do not know. He has not told me if he has time.' Julian did not look at him. It was impossible to know if he was lying. 'He is very busy organising the tournament. There is much to be done.' He gave a shrug. 'There is plenty you and I can work on in the meanwhile.' Julian gave him a hard look. *'Jusque à demain.'*

'No,' Haviland said with quiet fierceness. 'We are going to talk about her. We are not going to pretend Leodegrance is too busy to meet with me because of the tournament and we are not going to pretend you didn't ambush me in the park yesterday because I was kissing her.'

Julian's face was a study of subdued anger. 'You misunderstand the situation. We are not talking about her because doing so would validate the absurd idea that you have any claim on her.'

'And you do?' Haviland took an unconscious step towards Anjou, his body tensing, fists clenching.

'I have been with the family for years. I will be with them long after you've left,' Julian said tersely. 'If you would exit the room, *monsieur le vicomte*? I have another lesson.'

The situation was deuced odd. Haviland took a chair in the clubroom close to the bookshelves, nodding for the waiter to bring him a drink. It wasn't that he *wanted* to fight Leodegrance in a duel, but it did appear strange that there'd been no outrage on the man's part. If he had a sister, he'd have been furious. The family would have required marriage. Yet Leodegrance was acting as if nothing happened. Had Julian told him?

Ah. Haviland took a swallow of the red wine. It was starting to make sense. Julian hadn't reported the incident for exactly that reason. Seeing Alyssandra married to an Englishman wasn't what Julian wanted. He wanted Alyssandra for himself. That's why there hadn't been any repercussions. Antoine Leodegrance didn't know.

'*Monsieur*, a message.' The waiter extended a salver towards him bearing a single folded sheet of heavy white paper.

Haviland took it and thanked him, waiting until the man left before he read it. A little smile played along his mouth, he could feel his lips twitching with it. He was to meet Alyssandra at Madame LaTour's salon that evening. It was further confirmation Julian hadn't told Leodegrance. She'd never be allowed out of the house otherwise. A silver lining indeed, although not without an edge of madness to it. Alyssandra Leodegrance had proven to be dangerous to his health. Surely, there were far easier seductions to be had.

She must be mad to seek him out so boldly. Alyssandra wove a path through the guests crowded into Madam LaTour's Egyptian-themed drawing room, discreetly searching the room for any sign of him. Dancing had started and the sidelines were a crush of people as room was made for the dancers. It was early yet, far too soon to conclude he hadn't come. Although, such a conclusion was within the scope of possibility. Why should he come? The last time she'd invited him to come with her, he'd ended up with a bruised jaw and publicly brawling. She doubted the handsome, mannerly Viscount Amersham had ever resorted to public brawling. He'd known how to bloody his knuckles, though. So many gentlemen were useless outside the *salle d'armes*. But he'd known how to use all that muscle in practical application. He could defend a woman. Not that she needed defending. Still, it was nice to know he could. And, more importantly, that he *would*. A woman would be safe with him in all ways. Perhaps that was why she'd risked the invitation. She would be safe with him, body and honour both.

Alyssandra slipped outside onto the veranda at the first opportunity. The fresh air was welcome after the heat of the drawing room. It was a chance, too, to escape the gossips. Julian might not tell Antoine about the park, but that didn't ensure the gossip tonight wouldn't reach Antoine's ears if someone saw her with the Englishman. It stood to reason that if she was with him, Antoine must condone him as an escort. Anyone who knew them well knew Antoine to be a socially reclusive but protective brother when it came to her welfare.

Alyssandra unfurled her fan, this time a white one painted with pink roses to match the rose of her gown. She would rest here for a moment and go back inside to dance with friends and to wait. And to see. If he would come.

'I knew I'd find you out here.' His voice was low and sensual at her ear, his hands at her shoulders ever so briefly. She could smell the vanilla and spice of his soap. All men should smell this good. She closed her eyes for just a moment to take it all in in her mind before he stepped back.

'How did you know I'd be outside?' She turned with a smile, her eyes skimming his face for signs of yesterday's altercation. It was hard to see any damage in the dark. She had seen Julian, though, and it made her cringe. She didn't like thinking of Haviland being hurt because of her.

'I would know you anywhere.' It was a lie, of course. She fooled him enough times in the practice room. In there, he had no idea who was behind the mesh mask. He grinned and she could make out the remnants of his split lip, but just barely.

She reached out her fingertip to it. 'Ouch!' Haviland scolded, jerking his head back.

'Does it hurt?'

'Only when people touch it.' He laughed and then turned serious. 'Am I to understand your brother remains unaware?'

'Yes. It doesn't serve Julian's purposes to bring yesterday to Antoine's attention.'

Haviland nodded. 'I figured as much. Still, I don't like secrecy or the idea that we have to sneak around. It seems deceptive. Perhaps I could call on him and formally ask permission to take you driving in the park or to escort you to these sorts of gatherings.'

Her stomach clenched. *This* was hardly deceptive. She could only imagine how he would feel about *the* deception. *If* he ever found out. Another thought came to her. 'I think the sooner you can accept the fact that my brother will not meet with you, the sooner we can move forward.'

'We're back to that again?' Haviland's eyes darkened, his body stiffening. 'You insult my honour to imply I am using you for an entrée.' His mouth came down close to her ear, the harshness of his voice roughly erotic. 'You know damn well I wanted you before I knew your name.'

'How do I know that hasn't changed?'

'*You* sent me the invitation.' He growled, his teeth nipping the lobe of her ear, sending a delicious trill down her spine. 'Now it's my turn. There's a carriage parked at the kerb, pulled by two matched greys. If you believe me, get in. The driver knows where to go. He will wait only fifteen minutes.'

Her throat went dry at the implication. One choice and everything would change.

Chapter Eleven

Get in the carriage. Don't get in the carriage. It was somewhat amazing how one simple decision could set in motion a series of significant events. But she'd been making 'simple' decisions about Haviland North since she met him: going to Madame Aguillard's musicale, unfurling her fan, taking a walk in the gardens. All were simple decisions and all had led to this moment of choice. Would she make one more simple decision that would move her forward on this path?

Her feet registered the decision before her mind. She was already moving towards the entrance before she fully realised the import of the decision. What she meant to do was reckless. She'd had a lover before, but not an *affaire*. She and Etienne had been together two years.

They'd meant to marry. They would have, too, if not for Antoine's accident. An *affaire* was terminal. There would be an end—such a liaison *began* with that assumption in mind. It was the end that contained the risk. How would it end? With her heart still intact? With Haviland angry and knowledgeable of the deception that had been perpetrated on him? With Haviland happily naive to the drama around him and moving on to his summer in Switzerland?

Alyssandra came up short at the top of the steps leading down to the kerb, partygoers moving about her as people entered and exited the mansion. The carriage was there, an expensive, shiny black-lacquered vehicle complete with glass windows and lanterns. Two greys pranced in their traces, eager to be off. Seeing tangible proof made the decision real. Twenty more feet and there'd be no turning back.

The decision might be reckless, but that didn't mean it hadn't been thought out. Being with Haviland would mean far more to her than it would to him. He would go on to be with other women, she would be one of many to him if she wasn't already. A man like him must have women begging for his attentions. But she would live on this for ever. The coachman pulled out a watch to check the time, and she felt a surge of urgency. He was getting impatient. Had fifteen minutes passed already? What if she missed the carriage?

Then she would miss it—her one chance to date at experiencing true, unbridled, physical passion. She didn't hold out much hope there'd be other opportunities. Tonight had been Haviland's gauntlet thrown down. There would be no more arguing over trust and motives. If she did not take the carriage, he would not ask again. All would be settled between them whether she liked that settlement or not. Haviland North was not a man to be toyed with. Nor was he a man who tolerated having his word challenged.

Alyssandra hurried down the steps. It was time to be reckless. What had caution ever done for her anyway? The coachman nodded at her approach. A footman waiting at the kerb lowered the steps and helped her in. It all seemed so disturbingly normal when she felt as if the phrase 'I'm off to a clandestine rendezvous' was scrawled across her forehead.

The interior of the carriage bore out its external luxury with plush grey-velvet seats and matching draperies held back with maroon ties. But the carriage was disappointingly empty. Haviland was not inside. She supposed discretion demanded he be picked up at a separate destination a distance away from the venue, but she was disappointed all the same. Now that she'd decided to take his invitation, she wanted that invitation to begin right now.

She didn't have to wait long. The carriage pulled over three streets later to pick up Haviland, who managed to look urbane and quite comfortable with these arrangements as if he had assignations all the time. For all she knew, he probably did. He certainly *could*, anyway.

Haviland took the rear-facing seat across from her and gave the signal to move on, a rap of his walking stick on the carriage ceiling. He reached under the seat and drew out a thick lap robe of luxurious fur. 'Are you cold?' He settled the blanket across her knees. The warmth felt good and helped to quiet her nerves. Spring evenings and pending anticipation had their own special brand of chilliness.

'I thought we would drive for a while and enjoy the evening. Then, I have some place I would like to show you.' Haviland reached under the seat and pulled out a basket this time. 'I have champagne and if we drink it now, it should still be cold.'

His dexterity was nothing short of amazing. He managed to pop the cork *and* pour two glasses without spilling while the carriage moved over the rough cobblestones of the Paris streets. 'Years of practice.' He handed her a glass with a wink, and she had the feeling that 'years of practice' referred to far more than pouring champagne.

'Pour champagne for women in carriages often, do you?' she teased, sipping carefully from her glass.

Haviland laughed and had the good grace to look slightly abashed. 'I am hoist by my own petard, as the expression goes. Can I just answer "maybe" and leave it at that?'

'Absolutely. A gentleman with a bit of mystery to him is far more intriguing than an open book.' She smiled and risked clinking her glass against his—a difficult manoeuvre to accomplish in a moving carriage without spilling. She liked him this way; more relaxed, less intimidating than he was at the *salle*. It was the way he behaved around the men in the members' salon. She'd seen him in there on occasion working with others. He was a natural leader even in casual circumstances. It was how he'd been the day he'd come on her errands, as if a mask had been stripped away. When he was with Julian and even with 'her brother' he was different. In those lessons, he exuded a formality, an intensity that was as magnetic as his casual charm. She wondered which persona he'd bring to the bedroom.

'As is mystery in a woman, up to a point.' His eyes held hers, blue and intense over the rim of his glass. *Mon Dieu*, those eyes of his could sell a line. 'I think the mystery lures a man in, but after a while, he wants to know more and that desire for knowledge outweighs the desire for mystery.' That was the urbane rake in him delivering a practised line for certain—a remark designed to compliment and pursue, to bring a woman into his circle of sophistication.

Even knowing it, she couldn't stop a thrill of excitement from racing down her back. Still, she would not be an easy conquest. She might have agreed to this assignation and they both might be fully aware of the evening's intended conclusion, but she didn't have to be a quivering blancmange just because he was handsome and silver-tongued beyond reason.

Haviland looked out the window. 'Pont Neuf. Right on schedule. I thought we could take a walk. It's still just early enough in the evening to be safe out.'

Alyssandra laughed. It was only ten o'clock, early by Parisian standards. 'The streets aren't truly dangerous until after midnight. Surely, London streets are no different.'

Haviland jumped down to set the steps. He reached out a hand to help her down. 'They're wider though. For such a modern city, Paris has the narrowest of streets. I think a medieval merchant could walk through town and find the city unchanged in many regards.'

'I think that's true of most European cities.' Alyssandra stepped down onto the pavement. 'You will find Florence much the same.' She thought she detected the fleetest of grimaces. In the gaslight, it was difficult to be sure. It might have been a trick of shadow and light. 'You are going on to Italy, are you not?'

He smiled, and she felt sure the grimace had been nothing more than shadows. 'It is one of my greatest wishes.' He tucked her hand through his arm and signalled the driver to meet them on the other side of the bridge. They began to stroll, joining other couples taking the evening air. She had not been out like this for years and it was intoxicating; to be out with this man, in this place. The Seine was dark below them, smooth and still, the gaslights lining the stone vestibules of the bridge, casting a kind light on everything around them.

'I meant it, a few minutes ago, about trading mystery for knowledge.' His voice was low, weaving privacy about them even in public. 'Tell me about yourself, Alyssandra. Have you always lived in Paris?'

'The Leodegrances have a country home in Fontainebleau. We were raised there, but we've lived primarily in Paris since I was eighteen.' No need to mention that living in town allowed them to close up the country house and economise. The beautiful home in Fontainebleau was too big to keep open for just two people. It was enough of a financial commitment to live in the family *hôtel*.

'The *salle d'armes* occupies a great deal of your brother's time, but what about you? What do you do all day?'

'It might surprise you, but my days aren't much different than yours.' She offered him a coy smile and stepped into one of the vestibules, out of the flow of pedestrian traffic. She didn't want to lie to him, but she wasn't above distracting him when questions became more akin to an interrogation.

'*You* might be surprised what I spend my days doing.' His words were husky. His eyes darkened, his gaze falling on her mouth. 'I think about doing this.' His mouth took hers in a firm press of a kiss, and then another one. 'And this,' he whispered against her mouth. His hands fell to her waist, drawing her against him, his touch low and intimate on her hips where his thumbs imprinted themselves through the thin chiffon of her gown.

In the distance, she could the hear strains of a roving musician's violin. Haviland heard it, too. 'Perfect,' he murmured against her throat. He began to move in a slow circle of a dance, his hands still at her hips, his lips still at her neck, her ear, her lips. She moved, too, her arms lifting about his neck, her body swaying with his. This was like no ballroom waltz or indeed like any dance she'd ever experienced. This was intimate and close. This was bodies pressed together, the hard planes of him against the soft curves of her. This was two people falling into each other. She could drink in the whole of him; she could taste the lingering fruity tang of champagne in his mouth, smell the spice and vanilla of his soap, feel the power of him where their bodies met. Her fingers dug into the depths of his dark hair, her body hungry for every inch of him.

This was precisely what she'd wanted when she'd issued her invitation: to forget who she was for a while and a man who could help her do it. Tonight was for her, not to talk about Antoine, or the *salle*, not to think ahead to the next day's lessons. It was just to enjoy, to feel alive again.

The music ebbed as the violinist passed into the street beyond the bridge. Their dance ended. She rested her head against the wool of his jacket, reluctant to step back just yet. Here on the bridge, surrounded by strangers who were too wrapped up in their own lives, their own romances, she was anonymous. She could do as she pleased in a way Antoine Leodegrance's sister never could.

'I know a place we can go.' Haviland's voice was low at her ear, whispering temptation.

'Yes.' Her own response was not more than a whisper of its own. She hoped it wasn't far. They crossed the remainder of the bridge in silence, hands interlaced, his grip firm and warm, her body awake, every nerve on edge, alert and raw to even the slightest sensations. She *needed* satisfaction.

In the carriage, they drank the rest of the champagne. The ride was short. The carriage came to a rolling halt and his eyes met hers over the empty glasses, the intensity of his gaze proof he was as primed for this as she, his eyes two intense blue flames, his body taut with wanting. It was flattering in a primal sense to be desired by such a man.

Haviland handed her out and she looked up at the building in question. It was an elegant building in a prestigious neighbourhood. 'Your place?' she asked quietly. Only a man for whom prices were no object could afford quarters like these.

Inside matched her expectations—expensive carpets, airy rooms in a city that was cramped for space. Behind her, Haviland lit a lamp. 'This

is the common area, my room is this way.' She
liked the feel of his hand at her back, confident
and strong, as they made their way down the
hall. He pushed a door open revealing a room
dominated by a tall four-poster bed with carved
pillars and dressed in pale-green damask lin-
ens. French doors on the side led out to a small
garden.

Haviland left her for a moment to shut the
door and set the lamp down on the bureau. It
was a beautiful room for seduction, for making
love. She wandered to the bed, a hand reaching
out to caress the coverings. A decorative pillow covered in satin and trimmed with dangling
crystal beads lay in the centre of it. Useless, but
beautiful. They hadn't had such luxuries at the
Leodegrance *hôtel* for years now. The heat in
her began to build again, subdued momentarily
by the intermission of the carriage ride. The bed
conjured a thousand fantasies on its own, of rolling entwined among the rich fabrics.

Haviland turned towards her, playing the
host. 'Would you like something to drink?
There is more champagne. We've fallen in love
with it, all four of us, and laid in cases. Perhaps

something to eat? Our cook always leaves something in the larder.'

She shook her head, locking eyes with him.

He gestured to the two chairs set near the French doors. 'We could talk.'

Alyssandra let a smile slip across her face as she crossed the room to him. She let her hips sway. She pressed a finger to his lips before he could say another word. She kissed him once on the mouth, hard, and then stepped back, pulling her hair free of its butterfly clip in one deft movement. She let it fall, her tongue running across her lips. 'I don't want to talk, Haviland.'

Chapter Twelve

'I don't want to talk, Haviland.' Good Lord. Was there a more seductive line in the whole world? His entire body was on full alert. He watched her hair fall and his groin hardened. He shouldn't be surprised. *She'd* sent the invitation after all.

'Alyssandra.' His voice was a rasp, made hoarse by desire.

A knowing smile spread across her face. She knew precisely how she was affecting him, the vixen. She wet her lips in a slow, passing lick, her eyes locked on his. 'Shall I undress you first?'

She didn't wait for an answer, but moved towards him. Her hands rested at the waistband of his trousers, her fingers warm against his skin where they curled inside the band, tugging at the tails of his shirt until they were free. Her hands moved beneath the fabric, sure and confident, sliding up his torso, over his nipples. Her touch was a hint of the intimacy to follow, of being skin to skin. But the most searing aspect of her play was her eyes—dark flames that held his with a bold message: *I know what I'm doing to you, I want to watch you come apart under my hands, under my mouth.* He would, too, Haviland had no doubts of that. It was just a matter of when.

He cupped her face between his hands, taking her mouth in a full kiss. She answered aggressively, her teeth sinking into the tender flesh of his lower lip, her hands working his shirt open, pushing it from his shoulders. Then her hands were on him, on his chest, her thumbs stroking the nipples they'd so recently glided over in an effort to divest him of his shirt.

He kissed her hard, his hands taking possession of her waist, his thumbs reaching to stroke the underside of her breasts, sending a bold message of his own. He would be no passive lover. She could not play him without consequence. For every stroke, every caress she used to heighten his arousal and prolong his desire, he would apply himself in equal measure. His arousal would become her arousal, his waiting would become her waiting.

She gave a little moan as his tongue found hers, their mouths hungry, devouring one another as desire spiked. He could feel her breaths come shorter, her excitement rising. Her hands were rough at his waistband, fumbling with his trousers, her movements no longer focused, premeditated strategies of arousal. He knew a moment's pleasure at having distracted her, of knowing her desire for him was no longer a calculated thing, but something organic that was taking on a life of its own.

The moment was short lived. Her hand closed about his length, firm as she began to stroke him. She had the advantage just now. Haviland could not remember a time when he'd been handled so boldly, so enticingly. She pushed him with a gentle shove into the chair waiting by the French doors, kneeling before him, pulling his trousers down his legs. She ran her hands along the sensitive skin of his inner thighs, spreading him for more pleasure. Her eyes glittered mischievously before their gazes broke and she dropped her head between his legs. She took him in her mouth with a dilettante's skill; slowly at first, her tongue laving his head, her mouth sucking before it travelled his length inch by sensual inch.

He gripped the arms of the chair, fighting the urge to slide, the urge to explode. Her fingers squeezed the sac behind his phallus, and he nearly lost the fight. But losing would mean ending this and he was loath, oh, so loath to see this glorious torture end. And yet his body was priming to return the favour, such as it was. He wanted this—her mouth on him, her hand on him—but he wanted her beneath him, too, wanted her writhing as he did, wanted her eyes to go dark, wanted moans to escape her mouth in acknowledgement of what *he* could do to her, for *her*.

His eyes were shut tight, his senses overwhelmed when his body began to pulse, his balls drawing up tight. He felt her warm mouth leave him so she could catch his release in her hand. Once, twice, three times, four, five, he convulsed against her palm. His breath came ragged and short and when he looked at her it very nearly didn't come at all. He'd expected the smug superiority of a victorious woman, but the look she wore was one of amazement, the classic lines of her face soft with awe as if they'd witnessed something significant together, *done* something significant together.

Haviland leaned forward, taking her face in his hands, and kissed her softly in recognition of it. 'I am naked and you are not,' he whispered against her cheek. 'We must rectify that immediately.'

Laces loosened, silk slid. Alyssandra could not have said when her dress had fallen, or when her undergarments joined it in a heap on the floor. All of her senses were riveted on the feel of his fingertips against her skin, the pressure of his mouth on hers. It was a wicked sort of heaven to press against him, skin to skin, to feel him rise hard and strong against her stomach without any barriers between them.

He swept her up into his arms in a slow fluid motion and made the short journey to the high, gloriously bedecked bed, depositing her amid the luxurious pillows as if she were a precious gem. 'All the better to see you.' The gravel of Haviland's voice sent a tremor of anticipation through her.

'And you, too.' Alyssandra tucked a hand behind her head and held his eyes before letting her gaze drop slowly down the length of him. The lamp favoured him with light and shadows, showing off the carved perfection of his torso, the sculpted muscle of his abdomen, the masculine contours of his lean hips with their defined, square bones. 'A man can be such a beautifully made creature.' Haviland North was definitely that. Years of physical exercise had created the masterpiece standing in front of her.

'But you, Alyssandra, you are a goddess.' He came to the bed then and stretched his length down beside her. She fought a moment's self-consciousness. This was so much more intimate than standing naked together. Then they could only *see* the other's face. But now, he could see all of her, could reach all of her and he did. Haviland's fingers started a slow journey down her body, drawing heat where he touched her, drawing desire.

Haviland North was a tactile lover. With him, it was all about touch, how he could make her *feel*, and she revelled in it; the feathering caresses that ran from breastbone to navel, his fingertips light and sensual on her skin; the deeper, firmer touches when he cupped her breasts, his thumbs passing over her nipples, coaxing them to erectness much as she had for him earlier. Had it felt like this? This exquisite friction?

Alyssandra arched, hips lifting to him, her body asking for more and for less. There must have been an end to this heat, this slow burn that existed somewhere between torture and pleasure. Her legs opened in invitation, and he settled between them, rising up over her, the muscles in his arms taut with the effort and the discipline of pacing his desire to hers. Their eyes met one more time, one last time. He was looking for consent, waiting for it, she realised, when many men would have been hasty in their lust and seen to their own wants first. Alyssandra gave the signal. She wrapped her arms about his neck and took him full on the mouth, leaving no doubt as to what she wanted.

He thrust, and her body welcomed him, stretching, accommodating as they took up the rhythm, finding one another in the motion of joining and parting only to join again, each time more intensely until the rhythm consumed her, defined her. Nothing existed outside of this. There was only Haviland, there was only pleasure and it pushed her, *he* pushed her with each stroke towards some unknown cliff.

This pleasure, brilliant as it was, was unsustainable. It would end. She knew it empirically. They could not keep it up for ever. Haviland's shoulders were sweat-slicked with effort, her own legs strained from wrapping about him, but unwilling to release him. And yet it built, achieving the unattainable. She heard herself cry out, a series of sobs strung together between ragged breaths, desperate and satisfied at once. She felt the muscles of his arms tighten where she gripped them, felt his body tense, his muscles gathering themselves, her own body matching his. He gave a hard, final thrust and pushed them both into completion, into fulfilment.

This was new territory. It was her first coherent thought when she could think again. Long after Haviland had rolled to one side and taken her against him, his arm slung comfortably across her hips, she'd simply *felt*. She'd felt the rhythm of their breathing start to slow, their bodies start to cool, a hundred other sensations, not the least being the irony of feeling such completion while feeling as if her body had shattered into a thousand crystal shards, each a shining point of light.

Her body had awakened and it was greedy.

Having discovered this place where nothing mattered, nothing existed but pleasure, her body wanted to stay. But to stay, it would have to happen again. Could it? Clearly it didn't always happen. It had never happened...before. She gave a little moan and pushed the thought away. There was not room in this bed for memories or for comparison. Or for hopes. Tonight existed in a vacuum, one time only.

'How are you?' Haviland's voice was at her ear, warm and comfortable as if they were more than acquaintances who'd found temporary pleasure together.

'Fine. I was just thinking,' Alyssandra murmured, turning over to face him.

'Don't do it. Thinking is dangerous.' He smiled at her, the sight of it warming her. Probably because he did it so seldom, not a genuine smile, anyway.

'You're very handsome like this.' Alyssandra pushed a strand of dark hair back from his face.

'Like this? Do you mean naked?' Haviland chuckled.

She shook her head and smiled. 'No, just being, I don't know, relaxed, as if the mask you show the world is off and you're very simply yourself.'

His eyes drifted away from her, and she felt a moment's anxiety over having gone too far, which seemed absurd in the extreme considering what they'd already done tonight. A simple observation shouldn't tip the balance. Yet when his eyes strayed back to hers, she knew it had.

'Do you know me so well after an afternoon and an evening spent together?' His tone carried a hint of sharpness beneath the quietness.

She met the challenge and placed a hand against his chest. 'I know how you look when you kiss me and there has been plenty of that.'

'How is that?' The fire was starting to stir in his eyes again. He was going to forgive her intrusion into his privacy.

'Like a man who could be happy,' Alyssandra whispered and decided to push her advantage. She pressed against him and kissed him, effectively distracting them both from any chance of dangerous thinking. She didn't want to contemplate what lay beyond this night, nor did she want to contemplate why Haviland was so very private. 'Private' was often a polite euphemism for secrets. People who were private had something to hide. People like the Leodegrances.

Chapter Thirteen

This was going to be complicated. It was the one thought Haviland's mind kept returning to as the sky began to lighten outside the carriage windows. Alyssandra drowsed against his shoulder even though the drive to the Leodegrance *hôtel* would be a short one. Neither of them had been overeager to leave his warm bed and they had in fact already lingered longer in that haven than was prudent.

Paris had been waking up around them, or going to bed, depending on one's perspective, when they'd finally dressed and slipped out the gate at the back of the garden. He didn't think Archer and Nolan had come home yet, but he hadn't wanted to risk going through the common room. If the milkmaids and early vendors were out, his friends wouldn't be far behind.

There were a few carriages like his out, too, taking the wealthy home from a night of revels. It was not at all odd to be out this time of day—and night—but there'd been no question of waiting any longer to see her home. They'd escaped her brother's detection over the kiss in the park, but that would look like a minor infraction if he caught them after tonight. Nor had Haviland wanted to encounter his friends. Nolan would most likely still be drunk and Archer would ask too many questions.

It wasn't that he was afraid of them or of Antoine Leodegrance. He simply didn't want to share. He wanted to keep Alyssandra to himself. She shifted in her sleep and murmured something softly incoherent. He looked down where her head rested against his shoulder. She was beautiful even in her sleep, with all that hair falling over her shoulder in a silky curtain of caramel, the sweep of dark lashes against her cheek.

He was already planning when he could see her again and how. After tonight, he knew that once would not be enough. That was the complicated part. There were the logistics, but there were also the ethics. How long could he go on seeing Leodegrance's sister without telling him? She was of an age to make her own decisions, but Haviland felt something of the cuckolder to face Leodegrance across the fencing *piste* while pursuing the man's sister behind his back, regardless of her age. Although it might be best if Leodegrance remained oblivious. The man would want to know his intentions and those were hardly classified as honourable.

Despite the concerns, Haviland knew it wouldn't stop him. Tonight had been heady stuff indeed. It had been hard to tell who was seducing whom. They'd been partners in pleasure. The result had been explosive and satisfying. The result had also been dangerous—it had created an intimacy, that if pursued, would eventually make demands of its own. There were already signs of it. *When I kiss you, you look like a man who could be happy.*

She saw too much and he could not give her that part of himself. She wanted to know him, but therein lay the rub. If she knew him, she wouldn't want him. How could he tell her he was expected to return home and marry Lady Christina Everly? Not only was he expected to marry, but it was a match he'd known about since he was eight years old. He could not plead ignorance.

But neither could Alyssandra, on different grounds. She was no blushing English virgin expecting marriage. She'd come to him for pleasure, not a proposal. She'd come to him tonight knowing full well what could happen and she'd certainly initiated a fair share of it. One night did not qualify as an *affaire*. However, the longer this went on, expectations *would* form, a consequence of intimacy that went beyond physical pleasure. It occurred to him that just as he'd never indulged in a purely self-motivated pursuit of a woman, neither had he indulged in a free-standing *affaire*. It was different than dealing with mistresses where the terms and expectations were less emotional and far more defined. The carriage pulled to a halt and Haviland gave Alyssandra a gentle shake. 'We're here.'

She lifted her head and gave him a drowsy smile that had him wishing the driver could take another turn around the city, but the sky was already considerably brighter than when they'd left his rooms. He jumped down and helped her out, insisting on watching her all the way to the door when she refused to let him walk her any farther. He doubted Antoine Leodegrance was awake this time of day, but the servants would be up and servants would talk.

'Goodnight, or should I say good morning?' She gave him one last smile and turned to go before it became too difficult. He wanted nothing more than to haul her back to his rooms and lock the day out. Haviland caught her arm before she could slip away. There was at least one detail they could settle that would make the rest of the day tolerable. 'I have to be at the *salle* this afternoon, but this evening, where can I find you?'

She gave him a coy smile. 'I'll send you a note.'

Haviland arched a brow. 'It's to be a puzzle, then?'

Alyssandra stepped away, dancing backwards with a little trill of laughter. 'I have it on good authority you like a woman of mystery. *À ce soir*, Haviland.'

Haviland folded his arms across his chest and leaned against the carriage, watching her until she disappeared. Even the Leodegrance home was private in the extreme. A high stone wall set it apart from the street, making the house accessible only through the arch that led into the inner courtyard. Certain she was safely inside, Haviland climbed back into the carriage for the lonely drive home.

Only he wasn't alone. She had not left him entirely. The carriage smelled faintly of her soap—lavender and lemongrass—as did his coat where she'd rested against him. The seat was still warm from her body, *he* was still warm. It was something of a novelty to realise he wanted her again, or was it that he wanted her *still*? After a night of rather thorough love-making, he would have thought he was ready for a respite, not just for a chance to recover, but to reclaim his space. He'd always been happy after a night with a woman's charms to be back in his space, to have his privacy. He enjoyed women, but he didn't need them clinging to him every second of the day. He liked an independent woman. But this morning he'd not been ready to let Alyssandra go.

Back at the rooms, Brennan had returned, looking entirely unkempt. Most of his clothes were draped over a chair instead of on his person, a sure sign he'd had to make a quick exit from somewhere. Apparently, he wasn't in any great danger, though, because he'd stopped for breakfast. French rolls, cheese and a block of rich creamy butter were laid out on the dining table.

'Just getting in?' Brennan said around a mouthful of bread. He motioned to an empty chair. 'I'll have Guillaume bring coffee.'

Haviland gave a tired smile, the night catching up with him at last. 'Thank you, but I think I'll go to bed.'

Brennan winked. 'I've already been there tonight, twice in fact.'

'You can tell me about it later.' Haviland tried to laugh, but it came out as a yawn. He didn't know how Brennan did it; up all night, every night, and always cheerful as if his personal life didn't teeter on the edge of disaster.

Haviland knew what he'd find before he opened the door to his room. The carriage had been fair warning, but he was still unprepared for the lingering effects of her scent in the confines of a closed space. Lavender and lemongrass mingled with the musk of sex. She was everywhere in his room, *they* were everywhere. Haviland smiled to himself and tugged off his boots. All the better to dream of her. The only problem with getting up so early was that it took night that much longer to come. He had nothing to do except wait for her note and go to the *salle* for another lesson at three. But that was ten hours away. Until then, sleep could help. He lay back on the pillows amid the rumpled sheets, eyes closed, and let the dreams come.

Archer woke him shortly after one. 'You've slept the day away, lazybones. Don't you have to be at the *salle* for lessons at three? And...' He stopped there and grimaced. The grimace had all of Haviland's attention. 'You have a letter from home.' He held up the letter as proof.

Haviland groaned. 'Leave it for me. I'll read it after I get dressed.' He'd slept too long. He should have been up at noon. He rolled out of bed and did a quick wash. Anything more would have to wait until tonight—some time after fencing, but before he went out. The letter kept creeping into his periphery. He'd best get it over with. Shirt half-buttoned and feet still bare, Haviland picked up the letter and ripped it open. It was from his mother. The handwriting was a collection of neatly regulated loops. He sighed and slouched into a chair.

My Dearest Son,

*I hope you are well and that you are
finding Paris lovely. I appreciated the one
letter you sent upon arrival...*

He could hear the rebuke in that for not sending others. She would want a full accounting
of the parties and the fashions. He felt guilty.
He should have written. It would have been the
dutiful thing to do, but he'd wanted to keep Paris
to himself.

*I have been busy with the Marchioness
of Dunmore. We have begun plans for the
wedding. It will be a Christmas affair at
the abbey, the Dunmore family seat. We've
decided to make the most of the holiday
season and greenery.*

*The abbey will look stunning all done
up with boughs and berries and garlands.
Christina and her mother have met with
the dressmaker and selected the fabric for
her gown. I have seen it; it's an ice blue
that shows off her eyes and her hair to perfection. You will have the most beautiful
bride in the* ton.

He stopped reading.

Archer came in with a small tea tray. 'I thought you might want to eat before you left.' His eyes flicked sideways to the letter. 'Bad news?'

'It's from my mother. It's always bad news.'

Archer sat down and poured him a tea cup. 'Don't say that, Haviland. She loves you in her way and at least you have a mother.'

Haviland took the tea cup, regretting his words. 'I'm sorry. You're right, of course.' He nodded to the letter. 'You can read it if you want. She sends her love to you, it's down at the bottom.' He reached for the small decanter of brandy Archer had thoughtfully included with the tea tray and poured some in, giving time for Archer to scan the contents of the letter.

'It goes on for pages, but you get the gist.' Haviland sighed and eased back in his chair, one bare foot crossed over his knee.

'I can see that.' Archer gave him a shrewd look. 'It's really going to happen, then. You're going to marry Christina Everly.' He tried for a smile. Haviland knew he was trying to make him feel better. 'Congrats, old man. You'll be the first of us to marry and no doubt you'll have the loveliest wife of us all. Shall I tell Brennan and Nolan? We could go out and celebrate to-night, all four of us, when you get back from fencing.'

Haviland shook his head. 'No.' Getting three sheets to the wind with Nolan and Brennan was usually quite entertaining, but it wouldn't solve anything and it certainly wouldn't make his situation go away. Besides, he had plans to be with Alyssandra, plans to escape.

Haviland got up and paced the room. 'I shouldn't complain. I feel like a petulant child when I think about all I'm resisting. Men would kill to have what I have.'

Archer didn't argue. 'What will you do?'

'I don't know.' Haviland pushed a hand through his hair and blew out a breath. 'I don't know what I stand for any more.'

'You have a little more time,' Archer said soothingly.

'A little.' Haviland looked out the French doors leading into the garden. There would be no petitioning his father for extra time now, his mother had neatly ruined that option with her wedding plans.

'I suppose this means you won't make Italy,' Archer said quietly after a while.

Haviland nodded his head, not daring to look back at Archer for fear emotion would get the better of him. 'I would have liked to have seen you race. It would really have been something to see you win the Palio, flying around the Campo.' It wasn't just the Palio he'd be missing. There would be no summering in the Alps, no second spring spent in Naples, no afternoons spent in the Italian *salles d'armes* of Florence. All the adventures he'd imagined would never be.

'Perhaps you can go as far as Switzerland with Brennan and Nolan,' Archer put in.

'Perhaps,' Haviland replied noncommittally. What would the point be? He'd just have to turn back. Why not stay in Paris a little longer with Alyssandra? These were all horrible thoughts and there was no time for them, so in customary fashion whenever the subject of his future came up, Haviland pushed it away. 'I have to go, Archer, but I'll see you later.'

Archer rose, concern etched in his face. 'Will you be all right?'

Haviland tried to smile his reassurance. 'I'll be all right. After all, there is still a little time.'

She'd thought she'd have more time. Alyssandra stared at the list of clients on the desk in front of her. It was to be business as usual, although the idea of anything being 'normal' or 'usual' felt decidedly surreal after last night. It seemed even more impossible after seeing the list of the day's clients. 'Antoine Leodegrance' was giving three lessons today; the first two were regulars, young wealthy students from the university. They would be no problem, but the third name on the list held all of her attention. Haviland North.

'Is there a problem?' Julian leaned forward from his seat across the desk. They were alone in the *salle*'s office and she felt the absence of her brother's presence acutely. Antoine had not come in today. It was the first time she had seen Julian since their conversation after the park incident and he'd had a couple of days to recover. His black eye had faded to a yellow-grey halo, making it difficult for her to look at him and not remember who put it there.

'No,' Alyssandra lied swiftly. Of course she'd

known she'd have to face Haviland again in the guise of her brother. She'd just hoped it wouldn't be so soon, not when she could still feel the delicious remnants of their lovemaking on her body. She'd hoped to have time to settle into it, into him. Leading a dual life certainly had its complications. 'Today, we have to tell North about his dropped shoulder. He'll need to control the habit for the tournament. This will give him two weeks to work on it.'

Keep it business as usual, she told herself one more time. This was good. If she could keep the conversation focused on the work at hand, perhaps she'd forget how uncomfortable Julian made her feel or how fabulous Haviland made her feel. 'Let's be clear on what I will need from you in the lesson today. I will need you to show him. I can't touch him.' Especially not now. Perhaps earlier with her full-face mask on, she could have touched him to demonstrate a point during the lesson, but not after last night. Surely, he would recognise her touch or she would do something to give herself away if she got too close. Better to maintain the aloof distance she'd already established in her relationship to him as Antoine Leodegrance.

'No, I suppose you can't.' Julian's response was snide. 'Hopefully you do understand in hindsight just how ill advised your little rebellion was. It has even jeopardised your ability to give a lesson.'

Alyssandra fixed him with a hard stare. 'Scolding does not become you, Julian.' For a man who insisted he had feelings for her, he certainly didn't understand her. He ought to know berating her would not prove to be an effective suit. She stood up to avoid giving him a chance to respond. She didn't want to fight with him. She had too much threatening to distract her without adding worry over Julian. 'It's time to change. Our first pupil will be here soon. I will see you in the private practice room.'

Changing did help to soothe her thoughts. The ritual of wrapping her breasts flat, of pulling on the trousers, worn loose enough to hide any telltale curves or lack of them under the guise that they provided freedom of movement, of putting on one of her brother's white shirts. She twisted her hair up into a tight bun and settled the mask over her head. Thirty years ago, her masquerade wouldn't have been possible with just a leather mask that covered the eyes, but the new invention of the full-mesh face mask gave her the social anonymity she needed. The genetics of being a twin gave her the rest.

Alyssandra opened the wall case and took out her foil, giving it a few experimental slashes. The grip felt solid in her hand. She could feel peace settle over her. All was right with the world when she held a blade. It always had been. She went through the eight parries, stretching her muscles to warm up. She moved about the room, calling sequences in her head: *Balestra flèche! Balestra lunge! Coup lancé!*

Her body took over automatically, letting her mind focus on the upcoming lessons. The first pupil needed to work on the pronation of his wrist while he executed parry three, *tierce.* The second pupil's lesson would focus on *coups d'arret*, stop cuts, as a way of improving his mediocre defence.

Alyssandra brought her exercise to a halt and blew out a breath. She felt good. Her body was primed, her mind was ready. Everything would be fine. Everything would be business as usual.

And it was. Through the first two pupils. Then Haviland stepped into the room. The air crackled, the tension ratcheted. The tenor of the room changed entirely or was it merely a trick of her imagination? His reserve was back, his polite aloofness in place. Gone was the man she'd been in bed with just hours before. What was he so determined no one see?

Haviland eyed Julian with a gaze that managed to convey respect and disdain all at once. Julian responded in kind. But Julian was far more wary. As he should be. Haviland could beat him. She wondered what would happen if the two met in competition at the tournament? If they both made the final rounds, they would most certainly face each other.

She smiled behind her mask. Two years ago at the tournament, *she'd* beaten Julian. Everyone had thought it was Leodegrance who had beaten him, but the three of them knew the truth and Julian had never forgiven her for it. Perhaps this year, she'd be facing Haviland instead.

That thought wiped the smile from her face. Facing Haviland would be dangerous in the extreme. Julian knew his duty: lose in the final on purpose if for some reason 'Leodegrance' couldn't win on his own. But Haviland would not be bound by any such compunction. *Couldn't* be bound without knowing their secret.

Julian stepped forward, explaining the structure of today's lesson. She had to pay attention. 'Master Leodegrance would like to open today's lesson with a bout. Then, after you lose, he would like to show you where your error lies and how to remedy it.' She thought he might have said most of that with too much relish, especially the 'after you lose' and 'where your error lies' parts.

Haviland gave a short nod in her direction. 'I will appreciate any instruction.' She approached her end of the piste and Haviland took up his position. Julian stepped between them and dropped the white flag. 'Gentlemen, *en garde.*'

Chapter Fourteen

En garde, indeed! It took all of Haviland's concentration not to see Alyssandra everywhere.
She was in everything Antoine did, every move
he made. Leodegrance's signature wrist flick
was a damnable distraction today, calling to
mind a flirtatious fan rather than the *fleuret* of
Antoine's foil. That particular distraction nearly
saw Haviland skewered embarrassingly early in
the match. Then there was the smell—the light
scent of lavender and lemongrass that wafted
subtly whenever their blades made contact.

That was when Haviland realised how much
danger his agitated brain was really in—they
probably used the same soap or the laundress
washed with the same soap. There were all
sorts of reasons why Antoine carried the faint-
est scent of Alyssandra and none them validated

fencing like novice. It didn't help that Leodegrance seemed edgy, jittery almost. His movements were fierce and confident, but less fluid than usual. Julian was revelling in his inadequacies.

'Get your arm up! Hold your frame!' Julian barked. *'Tierce!'*

Haviland used a *balestra-lunge* combination in an attempt to launch an attack, but he had no chance to execute it. Apparently impatient with the bout, Julian inserted himself between the two, seizing Leodegrance's foil in a lightning-quick move and stood *en garde* against him. 'Come now, *monsieur*. Let's see what you can really do.' His tone was grim, his eyes narrow flints of competitive fire. But it had the desired effect. There was nothing distracting about this opponent. Haviland's mind and emotions focused singularly on one aim—defeat Julian.

Julian was not easy to beat, even on a good day. Today he was especially sharp and indefatigable while Haviland was neither. They parried and thrust endlessly. Sweat ran. Haviland's arm ached. On the sideline, Leodegrance clapped his hands and halted the match after it became apparent it would go on until exhaustion. Julian stepped forward and lowered his foil. 'Now, *monsieur*, let's talk about your dropped shoulder. Master Leodegrance has analysed your technique and has noticed this as a weakness. This is when you are most vulnerable. You will recall this was how Master Leodegrance was able to defeat you every time.'

'Twice,' Haviland ground out in correction. Haviland was sure he didn't overlook the emphasis Anjou placed on *defeated*. The bastard was enjoying this too much. In standard odd fashion, Leodegrance stood silently on the side, watching while Julian conducted the rest of the lesson. It was, however, the longest Leodegrance had ever stayed in the room. Haviland supposed that was something even if the master remained remote. The lesson ended only when Julian and Leodegrance were satisfied he'd overcome the tendency to drop his shoulder. He was sweaty and exhausted, but *this*, he thought with a surge of satisfaction, was what he'd come to Paris for—to excel, to acquire skills and knowledge he could not attain at home and to attain it from experts whom he could not access in London. Today of all days, with his mother's letter fresh in his head, the reminder was much needed.

Haviland wiped his face and hands with a towel and headed for the changing rooms, trying to ignore the old dilemma rearing its ugly head in his mind: what to choose? Family honour or personal freedom? Out of habit and practice, his mind sought to shove the dilemma away, ignore it. No. He had to stop doing that. Ignoring it solved nothing. Ignoring had only led to this point: his mother was decorating for his wedding and a girl he barely knew was designing her wedding gown. Ignoring no longer meant avoiding. It meant acceptance.

In the changing room he washed up and reached for a clean shirt. He exchanged casual words with a few others present and made his way to the club room, feeling again that stab of envy for Leodegrance's accomplishment in creating such a place. He didn't want to deprive Leodegrance of his achievement, he merely wanted such a place too. Haviland felt at home here, as if he'd found his place in the world at Sixteen Rue Saint Marc.

In the club room, he nodded at a few men he knew and settled in what was becoming his usual chair by the bookshelves. The waiter came with a glass of his preferred red wine. A new friend or two stopped by to ask his advice on parries. In between visits, he reviewed Agrippa's Italian treatise on fencing for his next lesson with Julian. They had moved on from the Spanish school to a quick study of the Italians and their love of offensive manoeuvres. But between the pages and the rich red wine, all the 'what ifs' he'd held at bay, hardly daring to believe in them, began to find their way forward in his thoughts.

The first was: what if he didn't go home? He'd certainly fantasised about that before, but always with some adolescent immaturity behind it: if he didn't go home, he couldn't marry Christina Everly. Beyond that, there'd never been any real clarity. Today, there was substance. What if he stayed in Paris? What if Leodegrance took him on as an instructor? If he performed well at the upcoming tournament, surely Leodegrance would find a place for him.

Haviland winced. Leodegrance might do that if he didn't run him through first for bedding his sister. He poured another glass of wine. What would Alyssandra think of him staying? They'd begun this mad *affaire* under the supposition that it was for escape and pleasure—two inherently short-term goals. The end had been implied since the beginning. If he stayed, that end could be put off. Would she want that? Would she want *him* if he came with reduced circumstances? He'd watched her subtly gauging the luxury of his surroundings the other night, her eyes noting the expensive carriage and the upper-class neighbourhood of his lodgings. She was used to living finely, she would not expect that to change.

That gave him pause. Haviland played with the stem of his wine glass. He'd never had to think about that before. Every woman he'd had wanted him because he had a title and was the embodiment of wealth. He supposed he'd still have a title, but it was unlikely his funds would be as extensive. If the Leodegrances wouldn't have him, he could always teach at one of the other *salles d'armes* or strike out on his own.

By his third glass of wine, the practicalities seemed less important than the vision of doing something. Practicalities would mean nothing, worries over the state of his relationship with Alyssandra would mean nothing, if he didn't take the first step and *decide*. In any situation there was always a choice. Sometimes those choices were just difficult.

What it came down to was this: could he live with that choice? Could he live with the choices his parents would make because of it? His father could not revoke the title, it was too much work. But his father would revoke the money. As much as Haviland felt the money acted as a stone around his neck, he'd never lived without it and the luxuries it brought. Could he do it? After three glasses of wine he thought he could, but it would require bravery and adjustment.

He poured the rest of the bottle and drank deeply, savouring the tannins on his tongue. He wished Archer was with him to talk, most of all to listen. Archer would understand the dilemma between family and self because he'd suffered under that burden, too. Only now, Archer was free. And Archer would be leaving them. The others didn't know. Archer would push on to Italy for the horse race in August, not stopping to play away the summer in the Alps.

It was something of an irony that the four of them had set out on this trip as one last chance to be together before they were pulled away by marriage and life, each to their own obligations, and yet, Archer was leaving and he was sitting here drinking wine, thinking of doing the same. Haviland chuckled to himself. It was a humorous and yet dangerous thought to think of Brennan and Nolan bashing about the Continent on their own, gambling and wenching their way south. Europe might never recover.

He was still laughing to himself over the image when the note arrived. There was a certain thrill at seeing the folded white sheet on the waiter's salver. Haviland unfolded it, marking its brevity with a quick scan. It contained only a single line; the address of the evening's entertainment. But it was enough to stir his blood and his imagination. Escape and pleasure seemed to be the watchwords of the day in some form or another.

Haviland smiled to himself. Alyssandra was not above a little game playing, it seemed. An address, but no given time, no specified place of meeting. He would have to hunt for her. *If you want me, come and get me.* The message implied was clear. He would have to be in pursuit. She would not make it easy for him, only possible.

The evening's venue was another musicale the French were so very fond of, this one an effort to copy the début for the king, Louis Philippe, of Auguste Mermet's new two-act *opéra comique* at Versailles a week ago. It hardly mattered what was on the venue. Haviland doubted they'd stay for the entertainment. But first he had to find her—easier said than done considering the number of people present. It had almost been impossible to greet his hostess before being jostled along.

He looked for her first out of doors along the veranda just to be certain she wasn't there. He hadn't expected her to be—it would have been far too predictable, and she *did* want him to hunt her. He checked the crowded salon where the recital would be held and where most of the guests were gathered at this point in the evening. He checked the currently deserted card rooms, the refreshment room, the outdoors once more, this time strolling through the garden. He was certain she was here already. Musicales required a more prompt attendance than a ball. At a ball, one could arrive at one's convenience, but at a *musicale* one didn't dare arrive during the performance.

Haviland sat down on a bench to think. Where would she be? He looked up at the stone facade of the house, his gaze absently scanning the windows while he thought. Most windows above the second floor were dark. His gaze moved down to the second floor where the entertainment was. He watched people spill out of the wide doors and onto the twin curved staircases leading to the garden. He couldn't stay out here much longer without calling attention to himself. A lone man in a garden was highly suspect. He might as well just brand 'I'm waiting for someone' on his forehead.

A single lamp flashed in the window of a room at the end of the south wing. It had definitely not been there a minute before. A signal. For him. Haviland smiled and counted windows. Three from the end, seven from the main salon. He stood up and the light went out. The minx was watching him. She *knew* he was in the garden. It occurred to him to exact a little revenge of his own and make her wait. Perhaps he would sit through the first part of the recital. It would serve her right, but that would only punish him, too, and by now, the hunt had him fully primed for conquest. He was ready to flush his quarry.

'*You* have led me a merry chase.' Haviland shut the door behind him. She did not look up from her book at once, but he saw the twitching beginnings of a smile play across her lips. It gave him a moment to appreciate the surroundings and perhaps to appreciate how well *she* fit those surroundings. She'd chosen a comfortable room done in rich browns and muted greens, part-library, part-sitting room with its warm fireplace and collection of sofas and chairs. She matched it perfectly in her gown of crushed gold moiré, the firelight bringing out the tawny highlights of her hair. His blood hummed as it hit him. She'd planned this right down to the dress she'd worn. Planning meant he'd been on her mind. Planning meant she was looking forward to this as much as he and that could have some very scintillating consequences indeed. His fencing match today proved he'd thought of little else.

It was hardly to his credit to be so swept away. He was made of sterner, steelier stuff when it came to *affaires*. Among a certain set of a certain type of London lady, he was known for his physical skill in bed and his mental reserve. He was famed for his ability to avoid sticky, emotional attachments. He understood the import of physical pleasure remaining strictly physical. Yet here he was, eagerly anticipating this evening like a lovestruck swain. He was only missing the roses and chocolates.

She looked up at last and he was aware of the heat of her gaze slowly drifting the length of him. This was how a mature woman flirted; boldly, directly about her intentions. No shy maidenly glances to indirectly communicate her preferences, here. Haviland swallowed, desire starting to ride him with some persistence now.

'It's about time you got here.' She wore a thick curl over one shoulder. She lifted a hand and twisted it about her finger. 'Haviland…' Her voice caressed his name with a sensual husk. 'Will you do something for me?'

Haviland gave a wolfish grin, liking this game very much. 'Anything.' He wanted to take her roughly, quickly, that gold gown hiked about her thighs. Maybe a hard, fast coupling would douse the fire that had been building throughout the day. Then they could slow down, could control the fire between them long enough to gradually warm themselves in it instead of burn with it.

Her brows lifted in acknowledgement of his boldness. 'Lock the door.'

The lock snicked quietly, ominously, in the silence of the sitting room. Privacy ensured, passion could ensue. He turned from the door, letting his gaze catch hers, let it communicate his wicked intentions; whatever happened next would be fast and it would be rough. Haviland crossed the room in three rapid strides, his hands gripping her hard by the arms, his mouth urgent against hers.

Her mouth answered his, her hands tore at his clothes, pulling out shirttails, tugging at cravats, words escaping her in little gasping fractured sentences. 'I want you, inside me, now.' Her teeth bit down on his lip. 'I've thought of nothing else all day, I've been wondering about nothing else all day.' She had the fall of his trousers free, her hand closing over him.

Haviland bore her back to the wall, lifting her. 'Wrap your legs about me.' The instruction came out hoarse, came out harsh with need. He pushed the fabric of her gown up high past her thighs, a fierce growl escaping him as his hands met bare skin. *Sans lingerie.* 'What a deliciously wicked thing you are, Alyssandra.' His voice was husky against her throat. He would not last long at this rate. Neither would she. Her curls were damp against his hand, the scent of her desire mingling with lavender and lemon-grass. Thank goodness this was not meant to be a prolonged coupling.

Haviland braced her against the wall, his muscles taut with his need, and he thrust, hard, rough, fast, and still she urged him on. 'More, Haviland, more!' Alyssandra gave a low, gut-tural moan of sheer pleasure, her neck arched, her hair falling haphazardly about her in a wild cascade. 'Don't hold back, dear God, don't hold anything back!' She looked magnificent in her pleasure, she *sounded* magnificent; a woman owning her passion, crying it in her abandon and he hammered into her like a stallion, like the wild things they'd become, pushing them to pleasure's end. She screamed, and he gave an exhalation of primal release, the tautness leaving him, satisfaction filling him. More than satisfaction, although he didn't have a word for it, for this feeling that flooded him. His body knew only that the edge which had ridden him mercilessly all day had finally been dulled, finally been conquered.

They sank down the wall onto the floor in front of the fireplace, both of them boneless heaps. He lay on his side, finding enough strength to prop himself up on an elbow; so much the better to watch her recover. He'd never watched a woman recover before, never paid attention to the little changes as she transitioned back to earth. Alyssandra lay on her back, her gaze fixed on the ceiling. He watched her breasts rise and fall beneath her gown, fast at first, and then slowing as her breathing returned to a regular pattern, *le petit mort* giving way to the peace of satisfaction.

'I don't know if I got my wish or not,' she said after a while, her eyes still on the ceiling. 'Part of me had hoped it wouldn't happen again, that last night had been a random occurrence, a once-in-a-lifetime achievement.'

Haviland studied her in the firelight. He reached a hand out absently to push her hair back behind her ear, letting the tiny diamond studs she wore dance in the flames as he contemplated her words. 'Why would you ever wish that?'

'Because it was wonderful, because it had never happened for me. Did you know that?' She turned her head to look at him briefly. The brown eyes which had belonged to a confident temptress earlier were soulful now. There was a hint of vulnerability in them—but only a hint. Alyssandra was too stubborn to admit too much. He had guessed, of course. Her response last night had been so deeply genuine, so deeply amazed for her to have expected it, to have known what waited for them.

'And if it could happen, over and over again, it meant you were the one responsible for it; you and maybe only you could make it happen.' Desperation or perhaps hopelessness hemmed the edge of her voice although she tried to hide it. He knew she would not want to appear to be either.

What ifs began to hover on the periphery of his returning reason. What if he stayed? Staying would change everything. 'Leaving is a long time off,' he argued quietly. 'I have a month yet, maybe more, before we'll even think of such things.' He didn't dare say more. He didn't know any more, only that it was possible this didn't have to end. There were weeks to go and his friends seemed content enough with Paris. Archer would leave, no matter what. His dreams of the Palio demanded it. But Nolan was winning at cards without offending anyone and

Brennan had found Paris full of willing females. Perhaps they wouldn't be in a hurry to move on. Yet. Perhaps it didn't matter what they chose to do. He might stay regardless.

She gave a half smile; half-hope, half-practicality. She'd heard the implication. 'Yet' would come no matter how he soothed. She hadn't had the epiphanies he'd had today. She was still thinking any delay was only temporary. It was the best he could offer for now. Who knew what the month would bring? Perhaps they would tire of one another by then and be glad to see the other go before the relationship could truly sour. It had been his experience that eventually all things did. Perfection didn't last, although it was hard to believe when he felt the way he did right now—sated and content.

She rolled towards him and they lay length to length, eyes meeting. 'Well, that's for later. Right now, we have a locked room. It would be a shame to let it go to waste.'

Chapter Fifteen

She'd only wanted to see him again as her lover, to see if the magic was real. Part of her almost hoped it wasn't. It would prove he was a man, as fallible, as ordinary as any other. But part of her had wanted to burn, wanted to be lit on fire once more. That part had got precisely what it desired.

And it still was not enough. Not by far.

It was as if her body was awake for the first time and, being acutely aware of that fact, it wanted to experience everything. She wanted to taste him again, feel him again. To imprint him again and again on her memory so her body would never forget what it was made for. Her eyes lit on the sideboard across the room, an idea starting to form. She rose to her feet, a little clumsy amid the tangle of clothes. Haviland's brows drew together, perplexed. She stayed him with a smile. 'Wait here.'

His body waited, his gaze did not. She could feel the heat of it with each step. Now that urgency had been satisfied, other wants, other desires, rose to take its place, the needs of a dilettante who wants to savour the experience, who is no longer in a hurry.

She turned, decanter in hand, her gaze perusing her lover with an intensity to match his. Just looking at him put a thrill through her blood. He was temptation personified in dishabille; his head propped on his hand, dark hair falling forward over one brow, one long leg bent at the knee. The fall of his trousers lay open, hinting provocatively at what lay beneath the loose billows of his shirttails. If he were to shift slightly to the right, perhaps there would be a glimpse, her mind thought naughtily. But, no, that would ruin the temptation. The secret was in the mystery, not the blatant revelation.

'I was just thinking how much I wish you were naked.' Haviland's voice was a gravelly drawl, each word a caress. Her breath caught. It was a wickedly daring suggestion; to be entirely naked in what amounted to a public room was audacious in the extreme even with the door locked. It only took one person to try the handle to confirm that something clandestine and private was occurring on the other side. And yet, they were far enough down the hall it was unlikely anyone would come looking. The odds were probably in her favour. Alyssandra set down the decanter and reached for the laces at the back of her dress.

She let the dress fall, her gaze riveted on Haviland and his response. His body went still. There was an ottoman close at hand and she raised one leg to it, untying the garter about her thigh and rolling down the silk stocking with deliberate slowness. Haviland shifted. Even at her distance, she could see the evidence of arousal assert itself against the folds of his shirt and it pleased her. She teased with her smile and rolled down the second stocking. All that remained was her chemise.

Alyssandra raised her arms, knowing full well the movement exposed her entirely below the waist as she tugged the chemise over her head. She had never been so daring. But Haviland brought out the boldness in her with his own audacity. They were alike in that regard, both of them cool and polite, aloof even among society, but behind closed doors neither balked at giving passion free rein.

His eyes devoured her, and she stood for him, letting him look his fill. Her hand closed around the neck of the decanter, and she began a seductive walk towards him, hips infused in the slightest of sways, hair tumbling down of its own accord to fall over her breasts in a riot of waves.

She set the decanter by the fire, letting the flames warm the glass, Haviland's eyes following her every move. 'Now,' she said, settling in the armchair. 'It's your turn.' A little smile played at her mouth as she borrowed his words. 'I was just thinking how much I wish you were naked.'

Haviland came to his feet and made her a bow, his tone full of mock gravity. 'Your wish is my command.'

His shirt went first. Dear lord, she should wish more often. She'd seen him naked last night, but this was different. Last night had been a means to an end, a very intimate means. Tonight, the disrobing was an end in itself. His eyes were hot as he watched her watching him.

He was stripping for her, putting himself on display for her as she had for him. There must be a name for this sort of erotic, two-way voyeurism, that raised such a specific heat in her. Her body ached, her breasts felt heavy with desire and she hadn't even touched him. He pulled off his evening shoes and made short work of his trousers so that he stood before her magnificently naked. Had a man ever looked so *beautiful*? Alyssandra felt a feminine moment of pride. Whispered speculations behind fans hardly did him justice and he was hers. *All* hers.

His blue eyes slid towards the decanter warming on the hearth. 'Did you want a drink?' His voice hinted at decadence. That suited her fine. She planned to be very decadent in the next few minutes.

She rose from the chair, her own tones husky. 'Yes, I did. Now, if you would lie down?'

'Stand up, take off my clothes, lie down. You are quite the tyrant,' Haviland scolded with feigned sternness but he complied, managing to look even more alluring horizontally in front of the fire than he had vertically. The firelight showed him to perfection. Years of fencing had honed his thighs to muscular solidity, defined the form of his arms and the lean length of his torso with its ridges and planes.

She straddled his legs and reached for the decanter, feeling the warmth of the glass beneath her hand as she pulled the stopper and wafted the decanter under her nose. She smiled at Haviland. 'Cognac. It's perfect.' Alyssandra tipped the carafe, trailing cognac along his rigid phallus.

'By Jove, have mercy!' Haviland groaned. 'That's divine.'

She gave a him wicked grin, eyes locking with his for a moment. 'Then what would you call this?' She bent to him then, her tongue flicking over the caramel rivulet.

'Paradise,' came the single hoarse word. It was probably all he could utter. Heaven knew she was nearly overcome with the pleasure of this intimacy as well. This was pleasure in its best and highest form, pleasure in the giving and in the receiving. Cognac and man combined to create salt and sweet on her tongue. Never had she found a taste to be so completely arousing, but this one was and it goaded her to extremes; she licked and sucked, bit and nipped, her hand squeezed, her tongue caressed until they were both groaning, her own breath coming in little pants as she brought him to climax, nearly as excited as he.

She held him then, with her eyes, with her hand as he spent, his own eyes holding hers intense with silent messages. Haviland raised himself up on his elbows. His gaze took on a mischievous cast, a spark dancing in his eye. 'Your turn.'

In a fluid movement he had her beneath him, their bodies pressed length to length before she could do more than register her surprise in a breathy gasp. He sat her astride, painting her in cognac, his fingertips brushing fairy-light circles around her breasts, tracing a line to her navel, leaving a thimble-sized puddle behind. 'I will smell like a drunkard,' she scolded half-heartedly. She was enjoying the feel of him too much to complain.

He leaned over her, stretching his body out above her, his mouth close at her ear. 'No one drinks cognac to get drunk. Cognac is for sipping, for savouring.' She gave a shiver at the words and their intent. *She* was for sipping, for savouring. His arms were taut brackets about her head as he slid down her, his tongue sipping and savouring as he went; breasts, sternum, navel, *ohhh!* She arched at the delicate sensation of his tongue dipping into her navel, of the pressure of his mouth covering it, creating suction as he drank the tiny sip.

Then he travelled lower, his breath warm against the damp nest of her curls. That was when she knew she was in danger of the worst sort—the danger of losing herself. It would be too easy to lose herself in this pleasure, to believe who she was, who he was inside this sensual *affaire* was the sum of them, the sum of her reality, when in fact this was a fantasy come to life for a short time. It was what she had promised herself when she'd actively begun this—if he was only here for a short while, what would it matter if she indulged? It could mean nothing and that had been the original beauty of her plan. But when he blew on her mons, when his fingers parted her folds and his tongue flicked over the nub of her clitoris, those rationales were paper dolls before flame, crackling to cinders. She raised her hips to meet his wicked mouth, to encourage it. She let herself burn. She would worry about the ash later.

She was hot and wet beneath his mouth,

wanting him with a free abandon that was positively intoxicating if the heady scent of her arousal and the cognac wasn't enough to send him over the edge. *Again.* It wasn't as if he hadn't been over that edge twice already. Haviland steadied her, his hands firm on her hips as he felt her approach fulfilment. She gave a little scream, and he lifted his head to watch release take her, a shiver that moved down her body in ripples of pleasure, leaving peace in its wake. He liked this, he realised, as he stretched out beside her. He liked watching peace settle over her features—features that weren't usually at peace. Her face was constantly on alert, constantly expressive, constantly thinking about situations, weighing, assessing. But not in these moments. In these moments, her body *and* her mind were free.

She is like you in that regard. He balked a bit at the thought. It was far too provoking. He knew he *felt* that way, but did he show it? Did he *look* like that—all peace and contentment—after she finished with him? He knew the demons he needed respite from: the pressures of family, the title, the pressure to give his life to others, saving nothing of himself *for* himself.

He knew precisely what he sought to escape. Did she seek to escape something as well?

It was hard to imagine. As a mature French-woman, she had an almost unlimited amount of freedom compared to an Englishwoman. As a woman of noble birth, that social freedom was enhanced by her financial advantages. With her beauty she could attract any lover who appealed. And yet, her experience in that venue had excluded a certain level of quality up until now. Whatever lovers there had been in her past, they had been lukewarm at best in their abilities to sate her passions. Additionally, there seemed to be no apparent pressure for her to marry. From his perspective, she had it all. What could she possibly want to escape?

'What are you doing to me, Alyssandra? I'll be nothing but a shadow by tomorrow.' He gave a low laugh, but he was only half-joking. 'More importantly, whatever are you doing with me?' He understood he was an excellent catch by English standards—Christina Everly's family certainly understood that. But for a French-woman who understood he was merely passing through? He was not quite an excellent catch for *that* woman.

Alyssandra's eyes dropped briefly to what was visible of his groin in the small space between them. 'What am I doing with you? I thought that was fairly obvious.'

Haviland gave his head a shake. If he wanted her to be brave, he had to be brave too. It was hard to be open when he'd spent so much of his life projecting a certain image even if it meant closing part of himself off. 'All teasing aside, Alyssandra, you know what I mean. Why me when there are so many better choices for a lover?'

She gave a throaty laugh. 'Better than you? That is doubtful. Every woman in every room you've ever walked into knows there would be few better.' She was serious now. He could see the change in her eyes—those brown eyes would remind him of cognac for ever after tonight. All of her would, in fact—from her eyes to the caramel of her loose hair resembling the shimmer of the liquor held to the light, and the taste of her where his tongue had slid along her skin.

He felt a moment's disappointment. 'I am a temporary lover? That is all?' He was nothing more to her than a warm body to service her needs. It was hardly different than what his family expected from him—stud service as Archer had once put it.

'Can you afford to be more than that to me? Can *I* afford it?' Her answer was sharp, those eyes of hers flashing, some of her peacefulness receding. She was on guard again, assessing again, as if every conversation was a duel.

Tell her your dreams, came the urging from his mind. But how could he? Those plans were too nascent, too fragile, as was their *affaire*, to bear the burden of his dissembling. Telling her his hopes meant also telling her about his past, about his obligations. And yet she was right. If he was to go on letting her believe all this was temporary, it was unfair to expect her to commit to the emotional aspects of a relationship if he wasn't willing to do the same.

But he didn't want to lose this. The way she responded to him, the way she physically made love to him, was far beyond anything he'd experienced with his mistresses, or anything he could imagine sharing with his bride who had made it clear to him last year during one of their two annual dances that sex would be for purely reproductive purposes.

Haviland pushed up and took to his feet. The bubble was coming off the wine of their evening. He'd rather take his leave before it had gone flat entirely, while he could still remember the warmth of her hands, the feel of her mouth and how incredible it had all been before words had got in the way. He'd asked for too much. She'd given him an honest answer. It wasn't her fault he didn't like it.

Alyssandra's hand reached up and curled around his, giving him a hard tug, her voice soft. 'I think you misunderstand me to your detriment.' She had all of his attention now. Just a few inches to the right and she would have been tugging something else. His member had the bad form to stir, apparently aware that those magic hands of hers were in close proximity. Damn it, he was trying to make a dignified exit.

Haviland looked down into her upturned face. She blushed, suddenly unsure of herself. Her dark eyelashes lowered. 'Come sit down. I'm not ready for you to go.' Her lashes flicked to the right ever so discreetly. 'And I don't think you are either, not really. You're just trying to salvage some pride that I never meant to damage.' She looked up again. 'Do I have the right of it?'

He didn't answer, *couldn't* answer. Answering would require telling her too much, telling her too many things he didn't talk about. And why? She was right, too, about expenses. There was a limit to what they could afford with each other. But he could sit and so he did, across from her on the floor, watching her draw a throw from the chair around her nakedness. The fire was starting to die and the room was cooler now. But she took his hands in hers and they were warm.

'You should know, I'm not in the habit of taking many lovers. I do not want you to think I am. To do so demeans me without justification. But it also demeans you. I would not want you to think so poorly of yourself as to define your merits strictly by your ability to perform in bed.'

Haviland wanted to say something but her eyes shone in earnest. If he interrupted her, he might miss something very important, so he remained silent and waited for her to continue.

'There has been only one other.' She looked down at her hands as if she feared he would find the confession shocking. Haviland watched her shoulders rise as she drew a deep breath. 'We were engaged. It was all very traditional. We courted for a year, our engagement was a year. We were to be wed the month after Antoine was hurt. We postponed the wedding, of course, but Antoine's recovery took longer than expected.'

'Longer than he was willing to wait?' Haviland finished the thought, grinding over the words with thinly veiled dislike. What man left a woman he was pledged to in the midst of crisis? Did the words 'for better or worse' mean so little to the man who had aspired to her hand? He hated, too, that Alyssandra was still protecting this man with her words, trying so carefully to not paint him with blame. *Longer than we expected.*

'Life flies by, Haviland. He is not to be blamed for wanting to reach out and seize that life any more than I am to blame for choosing not to. I chose to remain with Antoine.' She gave a wan smile. She leaned forward, taking his head between her hands, her fingers combing back his hair. 'You asked me what you are to me, and I shall tell you. You, Haviland North, are my escape.' She kissed him then, full on the mouth, and for the third time that night his body roused to her. He took her beneath him, bracing himself above her, sliding into her with the slow confidence of a lover who knew he had come home and was sure of his welcome, her words hovering on the periphery of his lovemaking. *You are my escape.* But he rather thought she had it backwards because he was more sure than ever she could be his.

Chapter Sixteen

What if she could be more than an escape? Did he dare indulge in all that she offered him, whether she understood she offered it or not? If he made his choice, this passion between them could be sustained beyond the confines of a purely physical *affaire*, he could give free rein to developing the emotional connection that simmered beneath the surface; the one they repressed so thoroughly because it had not been part of their original intentions.

It was the emotional indulgence Haviland debated with himself as the sun came up, throwing its spring morning rays into the courtyard of his apartments. He'd seen Alyssandra safely home after they'd unlocked the door of their impromptu lair and slipped through the ballroom, fifteen minutes apart to avoid notice that they were with each other.

She would be asleep in her bed by now and the very thought conjured images in his mind of her hair spread across a pillow; perhaps an arm thrown across the empty span of bed. These were images of peace and contentment and while they roused him, it was not in an erotic sense, but in a sense of comfort and a surge of protectiveness. He wanted to be in that bed with her; wanted to draw her against him, to feel the curve of her, wanted to match that curve to his, to feel the soft rise and fall of her breathing, wanted to watch the sun fall over her sleeping form and know she was his.

These were new feelings, *stunning* feelings in their own right when he took them out and examined them in the morning light, a cup of coffee at his elbow. These were not responses he'd had with any of his mistresses, not even the last one whom he'd kept for two years. Not once in that entire time had he contemplated anything resembling permanence with her. In converse, the permanence he contemplated with Christina was cold and empty. There were no images of sunlit mornings spent cradled together in bed, no images of nights spent behind locked doors indulging their senses until they were utterly spent to the point of exhaustion.

He'd come to France to fence, to escape for a time, and even to indulge in a physical *affaire* if it presented itself. He'd not come looking for this. But having found it, it compounded the decisions he had to make. Could his destiny include Alyssandra? Now, what had once only been a choice affecting him, now affected her. The equation of leaving his old life behind had just become more complicated and more tempting.

A door opened on the opposite side of their garden. Archer stepped out, a banyan over an untucked shirt and breeches. His feet were bare, his hair tousled, all indicators he hadn't been out to ride yet. His hands were wrapped around a steaming cup of coffee—a habit they'd all seemed to pick up in Paris.

'Good morning,' Haviland called out in hushed tones. All four bedrooms opened onto the courtyard. If Nolan and Brennan were home, they'd just have fallen asleep.

Archer took the old wooden chair next to him and settled his long form into it. 'A good morning it is. The sun is out, our rustic garden is showing to its best, the coffee is hot and, if I don't miss my guess, something or someone has kept you from your bed. Would I be wrong in assuming it was Miss Leodegrance?'

Haviland sipped his coffee and chuckled. 'No, you would not be wrong.' He blew into the steam rising off his mug. 'Paris is everything I imagined it would be and more. Leaving will be more difficult than I anticipated. I suppose I hoped that being here would satisfy my cravings, not increase them.'

Archer nodded solemnly. 'Paris is a witch of a woman to be sure. She has spells aplenty, even for a horseman like me who prefers the wide-open downs of Newmarket. And Miss Leodegrance? I would suspect she's a large part of that reluctance.'

'There's not much point in pursuing her, is there? I would just have to leave her.' Haviland side-stepped the question.

Archer was too astute and would not be distracted. 'It seems to me you've already caught her and the real question is what to do with her.' He paused, his eyes locked on Haviland's. 'Don't look so shocked. I know she was here. I saw her with you the other night when you went through the courtyard. It seems you've chosen to pursue the lovely Alyssandra Leodegrance despite your misgivings about the future.'

Archer chuckled when Haviland refused to answer. 'I don't envy you, old friend. Now she's got you spinning and you haven't a clue what to do about it.' The silence stretched out between them before Archer spoke again. 'Unless, of course, you've already decided that leaving is your only option.'

Haviland gave a wry smile over the rim of his mug. 'You're more right than you know. She does have me spinning. But you're wrong about the other.' He did have some ideas about what to do about it, rebellious ideas as nascent as the morning itself. He drew a deep breath and tried them on out loud. What would Archer think? 'I was contemplating staying in Paris for a while longer.'

'And then go home?' Archer asked tentatively. Haviland knew they were both cautiously thinking about the letter. If he honoured his parents' plans and returned home in time for the wedding there was no opportunity to go to Italy and make it back, nor was there any reason to go on to the Alps.

'I thought I might try my hand at fencing instruction, maybe see if Leodegrance or some other *salle* would take me on.' This was the riskier idea to voice out loud. He was certain even Archer's tolerance would find the idea bordering on the insane. He did and they were his ideas. They were either crazy or courageous. He'd not realised before how very thin the line between the two could be.

Archer's face broke into a broad grin. Haviland had not expected that. 'Very good. Then you haven't decided to give up yet? I'm glad to hear it. I was worried yesterday that you might have acquiesced to the pre-ordained order of your life. I see there is hope still. You aren't the sort of man who'd ever be happy walking in another's path, but it won't be easy to carve out your own.'

'I know,' Haviland said solemnly. 'But thank you for the support, all the same.'

Archer nodded. 'It will take a brave man. What does Alyssandra think about all this?'

'I haven't told her yet.' Haviland looked out over the garden, not wanting to meet Archer's eyes. The longer he was with Alyssandra, the guiltier he felt about that particular secret. It wasn't supposed to have been relevant.

'So,' Archer began slowly, 'she doesn't know about Christina?'

'Originally, it didn't matter. This was just about escape, but somehow it's become something more.' Haviland shook his head. 'Alyssandra is like me in ways I can't explain, Archer. I know it hasn't been a terribly long time, but she's like a piece of my soul. She will be with me wherever I go, whatever I do for the rest of my life.' He paused to gather his thoughts. 'Being with her isn't about an escape any more. It's about for ever.'

Archer gave a low whistle. 'Then you love her?'

Haviland nodded slowly. 'I do.'

'You're going to have to tell her.'

Haviland knew what that meant. Telling her meant telling her everything. It would be his first major obstacle in his new life. He had to tell Alyssandra about Christina, about wanting to stay in Paris, and that he loved her, that she was the reason he wanted all those things. As hurdles went, he considered it a fairly large one and it would require a leap of faith perhaps on both their parts. But he would have to leap first.

When leaping, timing is everything. It was also true that there's never a perfect time for anything. As the tournament approached, Haviland's days were filled with fencing and practice. He spent hours with Julian and the ever-silent Antoine in the private *salle*, training until his arms ached. Hours more in the club room, poring over treatises, learning and relearning the other prominent styles: the offensive of the Italian school, the defence of the Spanish, even the German school.

His nights were filled with passion, with Alyssandra in his arms. There were candlelight dinners in the tiny bistros of the Latin Quarter where students gathered to debate the politics of the city, long twilight walks in the Tuileries Garden as nannies gathered up their children for the day, a few carefully arranged appearances at social events where they arrived separately. There were nights in his rooms with the French doors open to the evening, the light breeze billowing the curtains and flirting with the candlelight.

He was a new man in these precious days, a man come to life. This was a preview of what every day could be. He had purpose, meaningful direction that drove him out of bed every morning and every evening when he came into her that purpose was reaffirmed. He didn't need estates and a title to feel alive. He needed Alyssandra. He flattered himself that she needed him, too. That the intense privacy and reserve her brother imposed on her life by extent of his own personal choices receded when they were together. He would never know if he didn't ask her. With the tournament two days away, he was running out of time.

Haviland carefully picked his moment during the peaceful interval that comes between bouts of lovemaking when she lay in his arms, her head on his shoulder, and ventured his question in the candlelit darkness. 'Do you ever think of leaving it all behind?'

Her hand stilled on his chest where she'd been drawing idle circles. Not because he'd taken her by surprise, but because the moment she'd dreaded had arrived: the moment when he'd want more than she could give. She sighed, her breath feathering against his chest. 'Always. But to what avail? Antoine needs me. I'm all the family he has left. And frankly, without Antoine, I'm nothing more than an impoverished noblewoman alone in the world.'

She feared that day would come far too quickly as it was, but that was a fear she could not voice out loud to anyone—not to Haviland who thought Antoine only bore scars on his face, or to Julian, with whom she ought to have been able to share that fear. Julian would use that fear against her to compel her into a marriage with him that made sense only on paper, a marriage that alleviated all her practical concerns about her future, but answered none of her passion. Antoine would never walk. She'd seen the truth in the doctors' faces when the first year after the accident had come and gone without significant improvement. Paralysed individuals didn't usually live long lives. Their bodies weren't strong enough. Could she really expect Antoine to live to a ripe old age? Each winter required more and more effort to keep him warm and safe from the season's catarrhs.

'Surely your brother doesn't expect you to live your entire life for him? I know his accident was grave, but it is only scars on his face. It doesn't stop him from doing what he loves.' Haviland probed gently. From the things he'd shared with her about his family, he understood how sensitive the issue was. It was an issue of honour, after all. To leave was selfish. To stay was sacrificial. Both choices were extremes.

She went back to stroking his chest and tried for distraction. She didn't want to have to explain the truth about Antoine. 'What about you, Haviland? Do you think of leaving it all behind?' Of course, she had only the vaguest idea of what 'it' represented in the question. It was times like this she was struck by how much she cared for him and how little she knew of him.

In the nearly two months he'd been in her life, she knew him as a fencer. The identity she associated with him was wrapped up in who he was at the *salle d'armes*. He'd ceased being Viscount Amersham. He was simply Haviland North. She had difficulty remembering 'it' constituted a title, a fortune, a family, and those were just the things she knew of from rumour. Beyond that day in the gardens, he'd never spoken of them directly to her.

'Sometimes. A lot since I've been here, actually.' His confession surprised her and its implications made her nervous. Was it because of her? His hand played with her hair in a slow, relaxing stroke.

'What could you possibly *want* to leave behind?' She let her voice tease a little, trying to lighten the atmosphere.

'More than you might think. No one's life is perfect no matter what it looks like on the outside,' Haviland said. It was the most he'd ever offered about his life in England and yet it was hardly enough, a subtle reminder that for all the passion he'd offered her, for all the ways in which he'd offered himself, there was still a realm of secrets he was not willing to reveal.

'Would you tell me?' she ventured. 'You once asked me what I was doing with you. Now I want to know what are you doing with me. You could have anyone.' She could feel him tense beneath her palm. She gave a soft, sad laugh. 'I thought so. For all that we have shared between us, it is still not enough to trust the keeping of our secrets. We trust each other completely with our bodies, but not with our thoughts.' She might regret such reticence, but she understood it. She could not tell him about Antoine. It made her wonder, too, just how big his secrets were.

He stirred. 'It's not that. I find I'm afraid of what knowing will do to us. I don't want to lose you over it.'

'I'd rather have you try me and let me be the judge,' Alyssandra whispered. It was hardly fair. He would be disappointed in the end. He would tell her and she could not reciprocate in kind. His arm tightened around her and she knew a thrill of victory. He was preparing. She hoped she wouldn't regret it.

'You know most of it,' he began slowly. 'I'm a viscount, but it's a courtesy title on loan from my father until I inherit the earldom.'

She huffed. 'There's more to it than that, otherwise you wouldn't be so private about it.' But it was enough of a reminder to her that he could only fantasise about walking away from that kind of responsibility. She'd always thought English heirs had it a bit rough—their lives couldn't really start until their fathers died and that in itself was a rather morbid thought to contemplate—that their successes were predicated upon another's death. And then there was the pressure of enhancing the family tree with preferably male progeny.

She raised her head, a horrible thought striking. She knew his secret. 'Dear God, you're married.' It made perfect sense. He was older than most of the young, silly, Englishmen who set out from Paris on their Grand Tours. He was an heir, there were expectations. It explained his privacy.

'No!' he protested. 'I am not married.'

Their eyes held. 'But you will be,' she said slowly. She waited for the denial, but it didn't come. 'Who is she? Do you love her?'

'Her name is Lady Christina Everly and I hardly know her.' Haviland's voice was flat in the darkness. 'She is not my choice. I don't know that I will marry her at all.'

But she was his parents' choice, that much was clear, as was the 'it' she'd so desperately wanted clarified earlier. Leaving 'it' all behind for him meant escaping an arranged marriage, escaping a family that directed his life. She also knew what such a choice would cost him—most immediately it would cost him money and access to a lifestyle that he probably wouldn't appreciate until it was gone. The wealthy were like that, she knew. She'd been in that position of taking luxuries for granted when her father was alive. His death had impacted their finances, but they had recovered decently enough until Antoine's accident had cost them once more. Again they'd recovered, but it was a near-run thing and she was acutely aware of the luxuries she enjoyed today and their cost.

'Do you really have a choice, Haviland?' She could feel the anger rising in him. She'd not wanted their last nights before the tournament to end with discord between them. After the tournament she did not know how much time they'd have left. But she wanted him to see reason. He couldn't walk away, no matter how tempted he was. He would come to hate himself given enough time.

'I do.' His tone was grim. 'I can do what I want or what they want. I want to stay here in Paris with you. I was hoping to teach fencing with your brother or perhaps somewhere else. I'm sure if I do well at the tournament, I could be an asset.'

'But the cost,' she began softly.

'The cost is this: to let them choose means my freedom can be bought.' Haviland was fierce in his rebuttal. She'd not seen him like this, so intense, outside the fencing salon.

'Haviland, it will have a price either way.' She interrupted before he could give further vent to whatever idea he'd set his mind on. She didn't want to hear any more. Her own panic was starting to rise. This was what she'd promised herself wouldn't happen. 'We weren't supposed to get attached. This was to be an escape only.' She threw back the covers and swung her legs over the bed. She had to leave.

Haviland's hand tugged at her arm. Something in his eyes broke, the fierceness receded. 'Don't go. We have time. I am sorry I mentioned it. I did not mean to frighten you off.'

She realised then what his confession had cost him. He'd been afraid to share, afraid of what it would do to them, and she'd justified that fear after minutes ago assuring him she could manage it. Ironically, it wasn't Christina that she couldn't tolerate, it was everything else, the very idea that he was willing to throw it all over for her, and she couldn't possibly accept, couldn't possibly allow that level of sacrifice.

She sat down on the bed. 'I think it would be best if I did. Haviland, these are big decisions.

You have a lot to sort through. I think after you do, you will see that I simply represent your freedom. That won't be enough for me. I can't be—I don't want to be the woman you chose simply because you didn't want to choose another.' That much was true. This was all happening too fast. But it wasn't entirely the truth, just enough of a compelling excuse.

'Alyssandra, I haven't told you the rest. I haven't told you what I've decided to do.'

She cut him off with a shake of her head. 'Now is not the time. You need to keep your mind on the tournament. Nothing else. Promise me?' She feared what else there might be to tell. She was losing on all fronts. She'd lost the emotional detachment and now he wasn't leaving, the very thing she had been counting on to save the Leodegrance secrets and perhaps her heart. It was hard to love someone who was gone. Once he left, he would wear off eventually. She would get over him. But if he stayed? She might love him for ever.

He fell back on the pillows in acquiescence, and she tiptoed out of the room and into the garden. She'd got what she'd asked for—his secret. He'd kept it because it would definitely change the balance between them and it had. But she was glad to know. It made her choices no less difficult, but far more clear. He could not give up his world for her. He only *thought* he wanted to. But she could not allow him to give up everything for a woman who would only have to refuse him.

She knew what she had to do. She had to drive him out of town for both their sakes. She had to enter the fencing competition and defeat him, remind him of his place—just one more Englishman here on a holiday, having a holiday *affaire*, before going home to embrace his realities although it would break her heart to do it. Haviland thought he had choices, but Alyssandra knew she did not, and he didn't either, not really. She loved him too much to let him lie to himself.

Chapter Seventeen

'No, I will not have it! The risk is too much. What happens if "Antoine" is beaten *before* the finals?' Antoine pushed his chair around the large estate office of their home in agitation. 'We've always arranged it so that you simply have to fight once. You face the victor in the final. You have every advantage that way. You're fresh, while they have fought for two days. You've had two days to study them, while they have had no chance to see you in action.'

'Haviland North needs to be beaten before the final,' Alyssandra said, the bluntness of her words drawing Julian's attention from the window. Julian's eyes moved slowly over her face, their eyes locking in silent battle.

'Why is that?' Julian crossed his arms over his chest.

'Because he thinks to become a fencing master in his own right. If he can win the tournament, he could begin to establish himself. People would want to study with him. We cannot afford to lose students to him or to anyone.' *Because he thinks to stay here in Paris for me.* He'd not had to lay that specific plan out in so many words for her to have divined his intentions—foolhardy intentions. What sort of man gave up the things Haviland had to become a fencing master? Well, she knew the answer to that in part—a desperate man looking to escape the confines of an arranged marriage. One should never make decisions from a position of desperation. She had to stop him from embracing what would ultimately be a calamity for him. He would eventually regret this choice if he was allowed to make it.

Julian gave a cold chuckle. 'My dear, how do you know this? I must confess, it seems implausible. He's heir to a title and to a fortune. No rational man would consider making such a choice.'

'I just do,' Alyssandra replied tersely. At least Julian couldn't say too much in front of Antoine without implicating himself for having withheld information.

'Why not simply beat him in the final if he gets that far?' Julian gave a shrug. 'Have you considered someone else may defeat him in the preliminaries and save you the trouble altogether?'

'You've seen him train. What do you think the chances of that are?' Alyssandra scoffed at the idea. She strode to Antoine's desk where he'd been working on setting up the brackets for the tournament. His desk was littered with accepted invitations from swordsmen all over Europe. She picked up a few at random and shuffled through them. 'Ralf Dietrich and his German school? Ralf was fortunate to make the semi-finals last time. Luca Ballucci? He's good, but he's over forty and hasn't the stamina if he gets too deep into the tournament. Sven Olufson? He's been training in Italy. But he needs to. He's all show and no technique when it's required. He wins early matches against novices, but he can't stay with the likes of Ballucci.'

'I will stop North,' Julian said firmly. 'He won't get past me. Set him up in a match against me early in the preliminary rounds when no one is focused on a particular fencer yet.'

At least Julian understood her strategy: eliminate Haviland early before anyone could become enamoured of his skill. It was cruel, of course, but it would be better to have this whimsical dream of his thwarted at this stage when it wasn't too late for him to claim the life he was meant for. And with luck, Haviland would never know of her part in it. Her heart sank at the thought. This was one more secret to keep from him. It also meant giving him up was imminent. Even if she was the driving force keeping him in Paris, he would have no way to stay now.

Antoine's eyes slid away from her to Julian. 'Julian, I can't afford to risk you so early in the tournament. What if you don't beat him? I need you to advance to semi-finals at the least. Who wants to study at a *salle* where the senior instructor is defeated in the early matches?'

Alyssandra bit her lip, watching Julian process Antoine's concern. It wasn't often she and Julian were on the same side of an issue. That in itself was a flag for caution. 'You don't think I can do it?' Julian was incredulous. 'I've beaten him before, quite a few times before.'

Antoine played with a figurine on a side table. Her brother was planning something. She wished she knew what. He met Julian's eyes briefly. 'You haven't beaten him since he's been training privately with us.' It was a gentle but stern reminder. Antoine seldom reprimanded Julian.

'Training with *me*!' Julian corrected in outrage. 'Who better to know him than me? I spar with him almost daily. I'm the one who has worked on his *passata sotto* and his *in quartata*, with all of it.'

'And you've trained him well,' Alyssandra intervened. 'The sign of a true master is to create a pupil who is better than his teacher.'

Antoine's brown gaze was agate hard. 'But we cannot have that on display at the tournament. If North is to beat you, Julian, it can happen no sooner than the semi-finals. Enough discussion. I cannot afford to have either of you approach North before the elimination rounds are over. We will do it as we've always done it. Alyssandra, you will face only the winner of the semi-finals.'

'Antoine, please reconsider this,' Alyssandra began to protest.

'No buts. We will take our chances with his ability to set up a *salle d'armes* if indeed that's what he intends to do. Otherwise, if he's willing to work here, I'm certainly open to offering him a position. Still, I'm with Julian. The idea of any of this coming to pass seems fairly preposterous given his background.' Antoine wheeled himself towards the doors leading outside to the garden with a stern look to them both. 'I am still the master and my decision is final.'

'So the Englishman has jilted you already?' Julian barely waited for Antoine to move out of earshot. He leaned against the desk, arms crossed, a smirk on his mouth. 'You were so willing to spread your legs for him, so willing to risk us all for your passing pleasure and now you want us to risk everything once more for your revenge.'

His crass words roused her temper, her anger bubbling. 'If that's what you think, you understand nothing.'

'I know you've been with him every night for the last two weeks. I know you send him notes at the club, arranging rendezvous.' What had he seen? *How much* had he seen? The thought made her skin crawl.

Julian advanced. She stood her ground. She would not give him the pleasure of seeing her retreat even an inch. His hand cupped her cheek, cold against her skin. 'After all you've put me through, I still want you, you needn't worry on that score. Once the Englishman is gone, you will see reason. Antoine will see reason when I explain it all to him.' He gave her a hard smile, eyes glittering dangerously. 'Really, the best thing you can do for my suit is to keep seeing him. It gives my case more substance when I go to your brother.' His thumb ran over her lip in a rough caress. 'You needn't concern yourself with that just yet, though. I will wait until North has gone so there's no risk of Antoine insisting North be the one to make an honest woman of you.'

Alyssandra's jaw tightened at the intimacy. No, he wouldn't dare risk that. Julian was too great of a strategist to make that mistake. Haviland's presence in the city was the only thing holding Julian back. 'Take your hands off me.'

Julian raised his hands in a parody of surrender and stepped back. 'For now. But mark my words, you will be mine. I've waited and wanted too long. In your heart you know it's the right thing to do, the best way to protect Antoine and the life you are so well acquainted with. It would be a shame to throw all of that away. I don't think poverty would do you justice, Alyssandra.' He backed to the door and gave her a mocking bow.

Alyssandra held her rigid posture until he was gone before she sank into a chair, a hand pressed to her mouth. Her escape had become her prison. Julian had found the ultimate way to use Haviland against her. Her first inclination was to run straight to Antoine, to expose Julian's duplicity but she couldn't do that without exposing herself, too. When she was smaller, Antoine had always been her refuge. She had run to him with broken dolls to fix, with tears to dry. But she wasn't eight any longer and she'd become far stronger than that little girl had been. Their roles had become reversed. It was Antoine who needed her now. It would crush him to know the two people he trusted most had betrayed him.

She'd been aware of Julian's attraction to her for some time now. After all, he'd already proposed once after Antoine's accident. At the time, she'd assumed he'd proposed out of a sense of honour, an attempt to make things right. But there was no honour in what he'd proposed today. Today had been blackmail pure and simple. It had been threats and coercion of the worst sort. Antoine thought he could trust Julian. How long had Julian simply gulled her brother and lain in wait for the moment to pounce? The moment to push his grander scheme?

What was that scheme? Was it solely a lust-driven obsession for her, or something larger? She knew only a little of Julian's background, that he'd risen from meagre beginnings. Did he aspire to take the *salle d'armes*? He'd never threatened to expose the great secret before.

That was without a doubt the scariest part of this morning's confrontation, the part that made her want to run to Antoine. Exposure would ruin them. But if Julian were the one to do the exposing, he would be able to separate himself from the damage. He could turn himself into the hero for bringing the deception to everyone's attention. Julian was a careful man—he would have given much thought about how to do it.

Alyssandra sighed. It was difficult indeed to fight a battle on two fronts. She had to keep Haviland from making a reckless decision that would destroy his future, while keeping Julian from destroying hers. As a woman kept behind the scenes, she had little power to thwart either of them. Not for the first time, she cursed her gender. It had kept her from proclaiming outright her excellence in a male-only sport, had kept her from finding a way to support her little family without resorting to a dangerous deception. If only she were a man—an independent man who wasn't under her brother's control like her incarnation of him was.

An idea began to form. She would have to be Antoine Leodegrance for the finals. But until then, she could be whoever she liked. Perhaps an anonymous Austrian come to try his skill. She knew very well that the tournament would take walk-in entries the first day. There was no guarantee she'd be paired with either Haviland or Julian throughout the tournament, but eventually, she would meet them and she would defeat them. She only hoped it would be soon enough to suit her purposes.

Admittedly her plan left a lot to chance. There was an easier way. She could simply tell Haviland. Perhaps there was a way to tell him without jeopardising her brother's secret. All she had to do was convince him she would not have him, that there was no reason to stay. It was testament to just how difficult that would be that she'd actually contemplated entering the fencing tournament as a more viable option. There was no 'simply' about it. He would be hurt. But in the final analysis of her options, it was the only one that left no margin for error.

Alyssandra called for her hat and gloves. It was best to get it over with before she lost her courage.

Damn her, she was going to *him*. Julian let the curtain to the front parlour fall. He paced the room, gathering his thoughts. He'd not expected this. His threat had been designed to force her into a corner, force her to realise she had no allies. The two men she might have counted on were of no use to her here. She couldn't tell Antoine without exposing herself and she couldn't tell Haviland without exposing Antoine, something her selfless little soul wouldn't conceive of doing. She would realise the only option left was to throw herself on his mercy.

He would be the man she turned to whether she wanted to or not. He would welcome her with apologies, with assurances that he'd only done this for her own good, to help her see reason and the foolishness of her headstrong notions. He would take her hands and kiss them, he would kiss her mouth, and she would give over to him, acknowledging his superior strength, his superior intellect with the acquiescence of her body. He would take her beneath him, roughly to make sure she understood who was in charge. Oh, yes, he had ways to make her understand that, pleasurable ways that had him rousing already at the prospect.

Those urges had to be subdued. He needed to think or the prize would slip away. He couldn't risk her spilling everything to Haviland North. Secrets only had power when no one knew them. If too many people knew them, or if the wrong people knew them, they weren't secrets any more, they became powerless little pieces of information. That's exactly what would happen if Haviland North turned out to be honourable. If not, it simply wouldn't be fair. If anyone was going to ruin the Leodegrances it was going to be him—he was the one who had put in the years, not some upstart English viscount who had stumbled into Alyssandra's bed on the conditions of his good looks.

Julian went to the small escritoire in the corner of the sitting room and wrote a quick note to two of his less savoury acquaintances. If his means seemed extreme, his ends would justify them. He wasn't going to give Alyssandra a chance to betray him. This next move was all his. She would be rather surprised to see that she had been outmanoeuvred.

There was movement at his open door. Haviland looked up, half-irritated over the interruption to his letter writing. 'Yes, Nolan?'

Nolan raised an eyebrow at his testy greeting. 'Don't kill the messenger. That's why I don't write letters home. It always puts me in a bad mood,' he jested. But Haviland thought there was truth to it. If he had to write to Nolan's father, he'd be in a perpetually bad mood, too.

Haviland sighed and pushed back from the desk with a penitent smile. He was learning that travel with friends meant never fully escaping them. It wasn't necessarily a bad thing. He and Archer had had several meaningful conversations. But it did take some adjustment. In London, he lived alone. 'I'm sorry, I have a lot on my mind before the tournament tomorrow.'

Nolan gave a knowing nod. 'In that case, you might be interested to know part of what is on your mind is also in the parlour. Are you receiving?'

Haviland gave a start. Alyssandra was here? He'd not expected to see her, especially after last night. They'd parted neutrally at best. He wasn't even going to the *salle* today. He would exercise in the garden instead. 'Did she say what brought her?' Something must have happened, something out of the ordinary and probably not for the good. Had her brother discovered their *affaire*? He was halfway to the door, shoving his arms through a coat before Nolan had a chance to answer.

Nolan caught his arm in caution. 'Gather yourself, man. Rushing to a woman's side makes you an easy mark. She'll think she can manipulate you. She didn't say, but I'd wager my last *sou* she's upset.' Nolan paused, his eyes going narrow in speculation. 'Dear God, Haviland, you don't suppose she's come to tell you she's with child? Make sure it's yours.' It was affirmation of Nolan's rather cynical train of thought that his mind went straight to sex.

Nolan's thought roused rapid speculation on

Haviland's part. Had she? It wasn't outside the realm of possibility, although it seemed a mite early to know. They had not always been careful in slaking their need, the heat of the moment overriding caution at the critical point. Still, he didn't think she'd know. They'd not discussed it and it hardly seemed like something she'd tell him the day before the tournament if she only suspected it. Alyssandra was the sort to wait until she was sure about something. Even so, Haviland's reaction was not one of horrific withdrawal like Nolan's. Instead, a single line ran through his mind. *It would certainly make things easier.* She would have to let him stay.

Haviland stepped into the front parlour and she rose immediately at the sight of him, her hands gripping one another tightly at her waist, her face a trifle pale. Nolan was right. She was upset. 'Alyssandra, what brings you here? Are you well?' He offered a friendly smile, trying to ease her. Whatever she had to tell him, he wanted her to know it would be safe with him.

'Haviland, I'm sorry to impose.' She flicked a glance at Nolan who was hovering at his shoulder, making it clear about who was really imposing. 'Might we walk? There is something I've come to tell you.'

Nolan gave him a 'told-you-so wink' and earned an elbow in the ribs.

'There's a quiet park not far from here where we can expect some privacy.' Haviland gave Nolan a pointed look. But his insides were reeling. Nolan was so seldom wrong about people. He offered Alyssandra his arm, overwhelmed with the sensation that the moment he stepped out the door his life was going to change.

Chapter Eighteen

Haviland noted two shabbily dressed men in his peripheral vision three streets from the house. He told himself he was being overprotective. It was the middle of the day in a big city. The streets were busy and full of all sorts, workmen and shoppers alike. Two streets later, the men were still behind them, only closer now. They'd been subtly inching towards them. Haviland wondered what they might do, *how much* they could do in public. But he'd never been a man to rely on others to dictate his response. If he waited to act, it might be too late.

He tightened his grip on Alyssandra's arm, the subtle pressure urging her to pick up her pace, his tone low and measured. 'I don't mean to panic you, my dear, but I believe we are being followed.' She started to turn her head. 'No, don't look around. They're to the left, over my shoulder. They've just started to cross the street.'

Alyssandra kept her face forward, but he felt her body stiffen with awareness. Her eyes darted to the walking stick in his hand. 'May I assume there's something inside that stick of yours?'

'Yes.' Like most London gentleman, his walking sticks were sheaths for sword-sticks.

'Good. Then we have a choice. What will it be? Shall we make a run for it, or shall we see what they want?' Alyssandra was a cool customer beside him.

'I'd rather not place you in danger,' Haviland murmured a protest under his breath. But it seemed he had no choice in the matter. The men made their move as they passed an alley. One of them gave Haviland a rough shove into the dim corridor between two buildings, the other dragged Alyssandra away from him. Haviland stumbled, cursing himself for having waited a moment too long and giving these thugs the current advantage, but he had his sword-stick out when he recovered his balance.

His first thought was for Alyssandra's safety, but it was clear from the outset the men were here for him. One of them held her, but only to keep her out of the way, which was proving to be quite the challenge since she didn't intend to be subdued. The bigger concern was the other man advancing on him, drawing a sword-stick of his own. Interesting. That was most definitely *not* the weapon of choice for street thugs. Things were not what they seemed in this alley, but there was no time to contemplate the mystery. The man thrust his sword at him, trying to catch his blade and turn it aside. Haviland deflected him, but the move made it plain the man also had some training to go with his sword.

Haviland went into battle mode, his body and mind understanding this was not a practice exercise. This was a street fight and the rules of the piste didn't apply here. Nor could he be assured this man would stop at first blood. He must assume, and quite morbidly so, this man was out to kill him or at the least wound him. Haviland struck back hard and fierce, seeking to end the encounter as soon as possible. The longer it went on, the greater the risk of injury.

Haviland thrust at the man's unprotected shoulder, the tip of his weapon striking through the cloth of the man's shirt. A bloody rose blossomed on the fabric. The man ignored the attack and the pain with a growl, a knife flashing in his good hand. That was not what Haviland was hoping for. He'd been hoping to deter the attacker, not anger him to greater lengths. He had no knife to draw, but his opponent's wounded shoulder would equalise the fight. Haviland stepped back, the two of them circling each other, reassessing.

His opponent launched a furious offensive. Haviland was ready for him. He'd gauged correctly that his opponent would recognise time was not on his side. He was bleeding, his strength ebbing with every second. If his opponent wanted victory, he'd have to act quickly. Haviland struck again, this time on the wrist and the man howled in pain, calling for his comrade as he sank to his knees. Haviland knew a primal sense of satisfaction, the fight was nearly done.

He did not see the other man let Alyssandra go and charge him from the side. Haviland went down in a pile of stinking alley debris, the man on top of him, fists ready to do damage. But Haviland's reflexes were quick. He twisted, angling his body and eventually getting his hands on the man's neck in a throttle and a leg around him to offer enough leverage to flip him over. Haviland landed two well-placed blows to the man's jaw and the man went out cold.

He rose, staggering a bit, but ready to finish off the man with the sword only to discover there was no need. Alyssandra had picked up his dropped sword-stick. It had gone flying when he'd been tackled and now she had it trained on the bleeding man. He still held his weapons, his back pressed to the brick wall, but the man had no offence left in him.

'Alyssandra, give me the sword and I'll finish this.' Haviland moved beside her, his eyes never leaving the remaining man in case he tried a last desperate lunge. Hurt or not, his sword could put a gash in Alyssandra's side if she wasn't careful.

Alyssandra wasn't listening, her gaze intent on her quarry. 'I'll finish this *enculé* myself.' She stepped in a half-circle around the man, her arm extended, her blade poised straight at the man's throat. His fencer's mind recognised the elegant footwork, the positioning. She spat another curse in French and, with a quick movement of her wrist, divested him of his sword first and then changed direction to catch his knife.

The tip of her blade returned to his throat. 'Now, tell me who sent you or I'll run you through.'

She would do it, too. There was something cool and thorough in her poise as she threatened their attacker. The man's eyes darted towards Haviland, his tone pleading. 'Don't let her hurt me.'

Haviland laughed and crossed his arms. 'Then tell her what she wants to know.' He stood at the ready—if it actually came to the skewering of this man, he'd intervene. No gentleman stood by and let a woman do his work for him, but Haviland was also a smart man. A smart man understood Alyssandra would not take well to being considered helpless. But that was something they'd sort out later. There'd been a lot of surprises revealed in this alley and not all of them lay with their attackers.

'I will give you until the count of three.' Alyssandra pushed her point against the soft part of the man's throat. 'One, two—'

'All right!' The man was nearly crying from the sword, his wound, his blood.

Alyssandra stepped back, the sword point still held at the ready. 'Tell us.'

'Julian Anjou,' the man gasped and rushed

on. 'It wasn't meant to be dangerous. We weren't to hurt you.' He was all but begging Alyssandra. 'Just the English fellow and just enough so that he couldn't fight at the tournament.' He scowled, making it clear he thought the shoulder wound was entirely too much.

Alyssandra paled and dropped her sword arm Haviland wondered if she knew how exposed she was in those seconds. He stepped up and closed his hand over hers, taking the sword-stick. 'Go, *allez*, take your friend with you. Tell Julian Anjou the next time he sends thugs after us, it will be even worse.' Haviland slammed his sword into the sheath of his hollowed-out walking stick for emphasis.

He followed the man with his eyes until he was gone, dragging his friend with him. 'Did you know about this?' Haviland turned to Alyssandra. 'Was this what you came to tell me?' His tone accused them both—she and Julian. His earlier speculations seemed foolish now. She had not come to tell him about a child. His stomach knotted. Now that his mind had time to think it through there was room for conspiracy; she'd not been frightened by their approach, she'd not been in any danger. Her struggles, even her bravado with the blade later could have been for his benefit, an attempt to absolve her of any complicity. He spat the last words at her, advancing until he gripped her shoulders, his eyes narrowed. 'Or did you come to lure me out?'

'I knew nothing about this!' Alyssandra cried indignantly, trying to shake off his hands. His words cut her cruelly. There was so much to think through it was hard to get her thoughts sorted; Julian had attacked Haviland and—*mon dieu!*—Haviland accused her of being part of it. 'How could you think such a thing? If I was part of it, why would I have pressed him for a name? I would have sent him off before he could expose Julian's plot.'

She shoved at Haviland's chest, her anger starting to replace her shock. He stank of alley garbage, his immaculate clothes ruined, and she'd been so very frightened for him. All she wanted to do was hold him, even with the stench, to reassure herself he was unhurt. How could she want a man who doubted her loyalty? She could only rail at him.

'How dare you! How dare you question me after what you put me through?' She gave her emotions full vent. 'I felt real terror when that man drew a sword against you.' She'd also known a fierce primal thrill in seeing Haviland advance on him, showing him no quarter. 'And when you fell.' Her anger broke, her voice trembled. She'd only had a few seconds to act. She'd not thought about the implications, she'd simply grabbed up the sword and done her part. 'I wasn't about to stand by and watch you die in an alley. Does that sound like I was Julian's accomplice?' Yet she understood she was asking him to believe her on very little evidence. She had her secrets. She could not truly blame him for believing the worst. He was a worldly man.

She tilted her chin up in a show of defiance, locking eyes with him. Perhaps it didn't matter if he believed her. She was sending him away regardless. She just hadn't imagined it happening this way. She'd rehearsed her speech on the way over and nowhere had she written in that script 'alleyway' or 'smell of rubbish'. Maybe, too, her pride was at stake. She didn't want him remembering her this way, with doubt and cynicism. There were other memories, better memories, to take with him when he went.

His eyes softened, his hands dropped from her shoulders and he sighed. 'You're right, of course. Forgive me?' His mouth opened and then compressed into a grim line. 'No, I won't make excuses for my conjecture. I will simply apologise.'

He bent his head to hers, foreheads touching, and they stood that way for a long while in the privacy of the alley. She'd sought him out today to let him go and now she wanted nothing so much as to keep him close. At last she spoke, saying the only thing a girl could under those circumstances. 'Haviland, will you do something for me?'

'Mmm? Yes, anything.' She could hear the laughter in his voice. 'I believe I've told you that before.'

'Good. I need you to take a bath.'

They made their way back to Haviland's apartments, heads held against the stares they acquired. Haviland looked atrocious and smelled worse. A few ladies even put handkerchiefs over their noses as they passed. But Alyssandra stared them down while Haviland laughed and called her a tigress. She didn't care. Haviland was unharmed and that was all that mattered. Other things would matter later, but for now this was enough.

* * *

'We were attacked by ruffians,' Alyssandra said curtly, meeting the eyes of his travelling companions when they entered the front parlour.

'Lovely cologne, Haviland,' the one called Nolan teased, but Archer, the one she remembered from the soirée, rose without remark and called for a bath.

'I'll have the tub set up in your room, Hav. Shall I tell Renaud to attend you?'

'No, I'll see to him.' Alyssandra was brisk and efficient, marching Haviland across the room, trying to pretend she didn't see the looks exchanged between his two friends.

'Are you sure you aren't hurt, Hav?' Nolan called to their retreating backs. 'Seems like you might have lost your balls.'

'We're ignoring you!' Haviland answered as they slipped into his room and shut the door behind them.

'Your friends care for you.' Alyssandra helped him out of his coat and bent to work on his boots. A valet would have the devil's own time getting them polished after today's events.

'We've been together a long time.' Haviland let out a sigh as the boots came off. 'Since we were boys in school, actually.' He flopped back on the bed. 'This may be the last time we all go gallivanting together, our last great adventure before...' His voice trailed off. She knew what he was thinking. Before marriage came to each of them and they took up the responsibilities of husbands and fathers and, in his case, heirs. She tugged at his hand. 'Up with you, before the water cools.'

The tub had been set up in front of his doors leading to the garden and it made a fairly romantic picture with the white-gauze curtains billowing softly in the afternoon breeze as a backdrop. Haviland stripped out of his trousers and sank into the water with a grateful sigh. 'That feels nice.'

'This will feel nice, too.' Alyssandra picked up a cloth and the bar of soap and began to scrub, heedless of the water soaking her dress. The muscles of his arms rippled under her hands where they passed over him. He lay back, giving her free access to his chest and lower. She washed the most intimate parts of him, stroking him with the warm, wet cloth, feeling him come alive in her hand.

'I dare say my own baths aren't nearly this

exciting,' Haviland drawled when it became clear they were heading for a wet conclusion.

She leaned forward, pressing a kiss to his mouth. 'I should hope not.' She rose from her knees then and held out a thick towel. 'Shall we get you dry?'

'And then we'll get you wet, unless you're wet already?' Haviland's hot eyes raked her, and heat pooled inside her as he rose from the tub, all dripping, muscled male. He could turn her to a puddle with a simple look. She would miss that when he was gone.

'You're a naughty man, Haviland North, for all your outward show to the contrary,' she teased, kneeling to dry his legs and work her way up.

'An honest one.' Haviland choked out the words as she wrapped the towel about his phallus and stroked.

'There, that should hold you long enough to get you on the bed.' She could see he was disappointed, that he'd harboured hopes of her using her mouth on him. 'Maybe later.' She gave him a wink and worked the back of her laces free until her dress gaped about her. 'I want you inside me first.'

Her dress fell, and Haviland swept her up in his arms. 'And so you shall have me.'

This was better; having him over her, having him in her, her legs wrapped about him, holding him tight. It was far better than the threat of the alley, the fear of losing him, the hatred of his doubt. She slid against him, encouraging him with her body. She didn't want to leave this room. She wanted to stay locked inside for ever, where Julian Anjou's jealousy couldn't reach them, where the outcomes of tournaments wouldn't dictate their futures, where they had no secrets between them. There were no secrets in sex, in this bed.

In these moments she could forget what she'd come here to do. She could forget that a suitable lady waited with his estates in England as part of his duty, or that she could never have him because she owed her brother her loyalty above all else.

He came into her hard, and she moaned her desire, her desperation, to hold on to this feeling for ever. 'I don't want to give this up.' Recklessly, she spoke the words out loud before she could take them back. 'I want every spring afternoon in your bed and every autumn night.'

'And the winter? The summer?' Haviland nuzzled her neck and nipped at her ear, his body still warm and joined with hers, neither of them in a hurry to part.

She stretched into him. 'I'll want those, too.'

The magic of the afternoon was taking them both, washing away the fear and doubt of the alley as assuredly as the tub had washed the grime from his body. 'I meant what I said last night about leaving it all.' He pressed kisses down the column of her throat, slowly, randomly. 'If I win the tournament, you can have them. *We* can have them.'

She put a finger to his lips. 'Shhh. Don't talk about it. Don't jinx it.' She shifted beneath him, and he rolled to his side. She felt the absence of him too keenly.

'Then perhaps we should talk about other things.' Haviland's hand caressed her hair, his touch as soft as his voice at her ear. 'Such as why Julian would go quite so far as to hire thugs to attack me in an alley and how is it that you held a man at sword point with the efficiency of an expert who had done it before?'

Alyssandra drew a deep breath. The moment of truth had come. But which truths to give him?

Chapter Nineteen

'Julian and I quarrelled over you. He sees you as a threat at the tournament.' All true, if vague. 'My brother hosts this tournament every two years. For the last two tournaments, Julian has been the one to win the coveted prize of facing Antoine in the finals. It's a great coup for our *salle*, to have our senior instructor do so well.' The first time, Julian had actually faced Antoine. It had been just a few months before the accident. The second time, it had been her behind the mask.

'He's grown complacent, then? He expects that spot will always be his?' Haviland chuckled.

'Just the opposite, I think,' Alyssandra said seriously. Julian could not be taken lightly. But if Haviland did take him lightly, it was her fault.

She could not tell him everything. 'I think he's had a taste of success and wants more. He sees possibilities, but he also sees how fragile the string is they hang by.'

Haviland's arm shifted from about her and he rolled to his side, facing her. 'Anjou grows ambitious. But for what? Or is it for whom?' Something primal and fiercely male flickered in his eyes. 'I've asked you before. You were not forthcoming, but I did not press because the nature of our relationship did not necessarily require it. But things have, ah, progressed since then. What is Julian Anjou to you?'

'He is my brother's friend. He's not forsaken Antoine since the accident. He's kept the *salle* running. I do not know how we could have managed without him.' But another phrase leapt to mind, too, without prompting: *secret keeper*. She'd understood that for a long time. But it wasn't until now, with Haviland beside her, that the phrase took on a different meaning. Before, it had been a term that connoted loyalty, if nothing else. One who kept another's secrets was loyal, trustworthy, a protector. But the reverse was also true. Secret keepers had power, leverage. They could just as easily be destroyers as

protectors. That was what Julian had become
with his threats this morning—a destroyer. One
word and he could bring down Antoine's work
of a lifetime and she'd given him the power to
do it.

'Do you feel indebted to him, then?'

'No.' That, too, was true. 'Julian had been a
junior instructor at the *salle* under my father,
even though he's older than Antoine by several
years. But he was a hard worker and very talented. My father's death was very sudden and
a bit sensational.' She paused, wincing.

'You don't have to tell me,' Haviland soothed.

She probably didn't, but she would. 'I
shouldn't mind, it's been eight years now and
all is well. The brief scandal has passed. He was
duelling over his mistress on a bridge. When
I say on a bridge, I mean on the very rim of
it, the railing, the wall's edge. My father was
famed for his balance, and that was part of the
challenge—to duel on a strip no more than ten
inches wide. He fell and drowned. It wasn't here
in the city, of course, but news like that travels
with all haste.'

She shrugged. 'Antoine and I were young,
only twenty. But Antoine was already a cham-

pion. The question was whether or not being a champion was enough to keep the *salle* open. Would instructors stay under Antoine's leadership? Would pupils stay? Would new ones come? That was where Julian stepped in. For the first three years, it was Julian's leadership that saved us. Instructors were willing to follow him and he convinced them that Antoine was worth following as well. It helped, of course, that Antoine won several tournaments and developed a reputation of his own.' She sighed. 'Does that explain what Julian is to me?' She didn't know how much more truth she could give him.

'I suspect Julian disagrees with you on the owing piece.' Haviland studied her with consideration.

'He's been made senior instructor. He is literally the face of the *salle* since Antoine can no longer perform that function,' Alyssandra protested.

'That's well and good but it's you he wants, it's you he believes he's entitled to.'

Alyssandra looked down, unable to meet his gaze. 'I know he thinks that, but he's not entitled to me. I'm not available to him.'

Haviland lifted her chin. 'Is that why you

quarrelled this morning? Did Julian send men after me because of the tournament or because of you?'

'Perhaps both.' She would never be able to sell the lie at close quarters. 'He knows our association did not end that day in the park.'

She watched anger light Haviland's eyes like a flame travelling a fuse. He understood the implication. 'The bastard had us followed,' Haviland ground out. 'I should call him out.'

Alyssandra could think of nothing worse. She pressed a hand to his chest. 'That would solve nothing except to bloody you both and call my brother's attention to things he need not worry over.' The very last thing she needed was Antoine dragged into this. He would insist on marriage if he knew. She didn't want Haviland to recognise that. At this point, Haviland would think that played into his hand perfectly. 'Promise me, whatever happens between us, I want it to be our choice, a choice made just between the two of us.'

Haviland picked up her hand from where it lay on his chest and brought it to his lips. 'I promise.' Perhaps it was unfair to have manipulated him, when she knew full well how much he valued a sense of his own freedom of choice. He would not deny her the same, at least in theory. He might feel very differently about that once he realised what her choice would be, what her choice could *only* be.

'Does this mean you've thought about what I said last night? I had hoped when Nolan told me you were here that you'd come because you had.' Hope flickered briefly in his blue eyes. She hated to disappoint him.

'No, I came to warn you, and, as I recall, we promised not to speak of those things until after the tournament,' she reprimanded lightly. She was only buying herself time, but it would be enough time for him to rethink his choices.

Haviland sighed in resignation. 'I will hold you to that promise. We will talk about it. Nothing can be decided until we do and I am not a patient man. If you won't tell me that, then tell me how is it that you are so skilled with a sword?'

His tone had turned playful, a sign that he felt the danger had passed—Julian had been explained to an acceptable extent. Haviland could understand misguided passions and male jealousy. She'd spun that tale well and it was full of truths even if it omitted others like the power of the secret Julian held and what he'd threatened to do with that power.

What he *didn't* understand was that this new question he asked was the more dangerous one by far. It represented the heart of the secret. Alyssandra moved her hand down his body, finding his phallus already beginning to stir again and closed her hand around it. She gave him a coy smile. 'Is it so hard to believe a fencing master like my father would not train his daughter, too?' She could tell him that much.

'I trained alongside Antoine when we were growing up.' She matched her words to the rhythm of her hand on him so that he wouldn't want the story to go on too long. 'My father felt a girl should know how to defend herself.' But that was as far as his enlightenment went. A girl, no matter how talented, could not compete, could not train at the *salle* with the other fencers. She would always resent him for that limitation as much as she loved him for the other. 'I still train with Antoine.' Another truth that would lead to a misconstrued conclusion. She was starting to understand one didn't have to lie to create subterfuge.

'Really?' Haviland seemed impressed. 'Perhaps you and I should train together some time.' She could tell from his voice his attentions were drifting away to other pleasures. That was probably for the best since the only response her mind could seem to make was *we already have*.

'You've failed? Two of you against one in an alley and a man taken by surprise at that?' The two men, already giving every appearance of having been beaten to pulps, stepped backwards, giving Julian space as he took a vicious swipe with his sabre, slicing through the fabric of a stuffed dummy in one of the *salle*'s training rooms.

He was to give a sabre lesson in a few minutes, the last one of the day, although he was hardly in the mood after hearing the news. He would have enjoyed handing them a beating if they weren't so battered as it was. To begin with, they were late. He'd expected them much earlier. That had been the first sign they'd fallen afoul of trouble. How long did it take to deliver injury in an alley? Fifteen minutes? They'd been gone since noon and it was nearing six. Anger pulsed through him. These idiots had failed in their very simple task! He took another swipe, enjoying the satisfaction of their fear.

'He was better with a sword than we thought,' the one with the bandaged shoulder said with a hint of accusation in his tone as if he believed he'd been led astray.

'I warned you he was good. Surprise was your best element.' Julian cursed freely. He'd given them every advantage and yet they had failed.

'You didn't warn us about *her*. You said nothing about her being a sword-wielding bitch.' The bandaged man spat. 'She put that blade to my throat and that was *after* he stabbed me and blood was running everywhere.'

'And she kicked me and bit me and scratched me,' the other man sporting a purple jaw complained.

'Bested by a woman? Tsk, tsk,' Julian scoffed. 'I'm not sure I'd be bragging about that.' He stopped his angry stabbing and stared at each of them. 'Is there anything else you'd like to tell me?'

The men looked down at their feet. 'No, we'd like our money, please, and we'll be off.'

A cold fear uncurled in Julian's belly. These

men hadn't just been beaten. They'd been thoroughly whipped. What had the one said? Alyssandra had held him at sword point? He didn't know them personally, they were arranged for him by an old friend from the streets—they owed him nothing in terms of loyalty. If circumstances were dire enough, they would not feel compelled to die to keep his secrets.

Julian whipped the sabre up, pressing the point of the blade into the stockier man's belly. They needn't know a sabre was for slicing, not piercing. All they needed to know was that blades were sharp and Haviland had already taught that lesson for him. '*What* did you tell them?'

'Nothing! We swear,' the other man avowed hastily.

Julian gave an evil grin and pushed the blade harder, watching the man gasp. 'I am not sure your friend agrees with you. Maybe you would like to try a different answer?'

'He told them your name,' the man with the sabre pressed to him confessed, ratting out his 'friend' with apparent ease. 'It wasn't me, I swear that's true.'

'No,' his companion sneered. 'You couldn't

do anything. That gentleman had laid you out cold with his fists. It was just me trying to fend for myself, trying to get us both out of there.'

Julian gave a cold chuckle. 'Don't lay it on too thick. I doubt you were a veritable hero in the alley. You gave me up quick enough. I'd say your loyalty could use a little polish.' He put up his sabre. 'Go on, get out.'

'But our money, sir?' one of them managed to stammer. Clearly he'd not frightened them enough.

Julian made a threatening gesture with the sabre that sent them scurrying towards the door. 'I don't pay men for failure and I certainly don't pay them for betrayal. Get out if you value your lives.'

Alone, Julian sat down hard on a crate of equipment, head in his hands. What did he do if he valued his own life? He couldn't simply just 'get out'. His whole livelihood was tied to the *salle*. Would Alyssandra go to Antoine and expose him? Would it be enough to turn Antoine against him? Antoine had always been his unwitting champion—dear, young, impressionable but ungodly talented Antoine. He'd recognised the vulnerability and the skill in the young *vicomte* from the start and he'd used it to win Antoine's friendship. The boy he'd been had been so desperate to give it after his father's death and the man he'd become needed him so much now. Perhaps the need would allow Antoine to forgive him.

If Alyssandra ratted him out. Perhaps she wouldn't. How could she without exposing herself and her little perfidy? There was some hope in that. What would Antoine do if confronted with his sister's *affaire* with an Englishman versus his friend's attempt to mitigate the Englishman's presence in all of their lives? Perhaps he could sell his actions as those chosen out of misguided loyalty for Antoine?

The door to the training room opened. Julian rose and took a moment to compose himself before turning. It would be his student come for the sabre lesson. '*Bon soir*, Monsieur Delacorte. I am just...'

His words died. Alyssandra slammed the door shut and strode across the room, trousers tight across her hips, shirt tucked into the waistband emphasising the fullness of her breasts. Another time he might have given those charms more appreciation, but at the moment all of his rather considerable appreciation was fixed on the sabre in her hand.

'En garde.' Her face bore no expression as she took up the position, a sure sign of the depths of her fury. Good lord, there was a reason men didn't teach women to fight. Sometimes they got angry.

Julian matched her position, his own eyes narrowing. Perhaps this was the perfect time after all to teach her a lesson about what happens to a woman who overreaches herself in a man's world. He executed a couple of feints to see what she would do. 'Come for a lesson, have you?' He parried her initial attack. 'Straight from your lover's bed? I have to inform you I do have a lesson shortly.' He barely dodged a slice at his right side.

'Then I hope you'll have enough time to get cleaned up.' She deftly sidestepped his blade. She'd become good. He'd not faced her with sabres for a while. Damn her father for training both his children in the art of all the blades. She was as gifted as Antoine and it didn't matter the sword—rapier, épée, daggers, sabres—the Leodegrances were born with a talent for them all in their blood.

She lunged, and he was too slow. Her blade sliced through the sleeve of his shirt. Fabric ripped. 'You tried to kill him today.' They circled, Julian dancing back from the edge of her sword.

'*Killed* is far too strong a word, my dear. A scratch, a nick, is all. But even that didn't succeed.' He tried to sound more nonchalant than he felt. The truth was, he didn't know exactly how far Alyssandra was willing to go. Was she intent on blood? On murder? Murder was doubtful. He didn't think she had it in her. Most women didn't. Did she intend an injury that would take him out of the tournament? That was his worst fear. He needed that tournament to boost his own importance.

Julian launched another offensive with his blade and with his words. 'What sort of man sends a woman to beg in his place? If he's spoiling for a fight, he should face me himself.' He gave a smirk. 'Or are *you* his rendition of an alley thug? Makes us even, I think.'

'He did not send me.' Alyssandra went for the other sleeve, slicing it down the centre. If he wasn't careful he was going to end up looking like a vagabond for the lesson.

Blades met in a resounding clash, steel and bodies came together, the strength of the other's arm pushing their blades into the air. He grinned. He had the superior strength here. His strength would outstrip hers. He pushed her to the wall, their arms still raised above their heads, sabres still locked. 'You were foolish today, Alyssandra, to let him see your skill. He might start to suspect there is something afoot. How do you think he'd feel if he knew what you'd been up to? Masquerading as your brother, duping people, duping *him*, into spending sums of money on lessons with "Antoine Leodegrance" when in reality they were only fencing a girl?'

'You wouldn't dare tell,' Alyssandra ground out with effort. He'd keep her pinned a little longer, make her sweat, make her think about what she risked, make her see that she needed him and his protection.

'Wouldn't I?' Julian mused. 'I could destroy you.'

'And I could destroy you. What do you think my brother would do if I told him about the alley? About the threats, that you are not so loyal as you pretend. You are loyal only to yourself and you will betray him the moment it is beneficial to you.' Alyssandra's eyes flashed, and his groin tightened. She was magnificent in her temper, all fire when cornered. That would make some rousing bedsport.

'Your brother will think what I tell him to think. He will believe me when I give him penitence for my actions and tell him it was out of concern for him that I resorted to drastic measures,' he sneered. 'He will not believe you, an ungrateful sister who would risk us all for the sake of a short-lived *affaire.'*

'I hate you,' she spat, arms showing the first signs of trembling. She would have to surrender soon and she would hate that even more.

'I know you do. But that won't matter in the end.' He relished the thought of her capitulation. He would wait for her to break, wait for her to admit defeat. He pressed against her, taking advantage of her weakening arms, knowing full well his erection would be evident.

'Me faut retourner à la pute qui m'a accouchée,' he muttered to his opponent.

Alyssandra moved, he could feel her muscles bunching for a last try. But her last try had nothing to do with their swords. Her knee came up between them, taking him sharply in the groin. She gave him a shove that put him on the floor, doubled over with pain. She strode past him.

He heard her open the door and say to someone in the hall—probably his lesson, dammit—'Give him a moment to collect himself.'

He would get her for this. He would give her one last opportunity to redeem herself. If not, the time had come to reveal the Leodegrances for the frauds they were.

Chapter Twenty

The *salle d'armes* was a crowded, bustling hive of activity when Haviland arrived the morning of the tournament. Outside, the street was bursting with energy. Vendors, sensing a profit to be made, had gathered with their wares and were doing a brisk business. He stepped inside and let the excitement of the atmosphere engulf him, let the anticipation of competition override his rage towards Julian Anjou, let the thrill of facing other excellent swordsmen from around the Continent dull the complexities of wanting Alyssandra. Now was not the time to have his mind distracted by either rage or lust.

At either shoulder were Archer and Nolan, who had come ostensibly because they were eager to see the tournament. But Haviland suspected they'd come out of concern for his safety.

He didn't truly believe Julian would attempt anything at the tournament. For one, it was too late in the game. Anything Julian wanted to do to him could be attempted on the piste should they meet. For another, it was far too public a venue to get away with anything covert.

He flexed his grip around the handle of his long sword case and approached the entrance table. Today was the day he proved to himself just how good he was. More than that, he had a chance today to prove how worthy he was of his dreams. Were they dreams only? Or was there reason to hope in them?

Haviland recognised one of the young men at the table as the student he'd helped with his *balestra*. The young man saw him and smiled. 'You'll be entering rapiers, no doubt.' He nodded at the case in Haviland's hand. The competition featured all nature of swords, but the rapier was the premiere event given that it was Antoine Leodegrance's speciality. As a result, it was also the most heavily entered event. Haviland nodded and pushed forward his entrance fee.

'We have both changing rooms available today,' the young man said. 'And we're using the day guests' salon as a warm-up centre. All the matches will take place in the main salon.' He nodded to Nolan and Archer. 'Your friends can find seats in the stands if they hurry.'

Haviland parted company from Nolan and Archer and headed to the changing rooms. Compared to the bustle in the *salle*'s lobby, the changing rooms were quiet, but only relatively so. The rooms were crowded, but the energy was friendly as men stripped out of street clothes. Most would fight in trousers and shirts covered by padded vests for protection. Haviland recognised a few of the other more advanced clients of the *salle* among the crowd who'd come to compete and went to join them.

'Is this all of us who've come to champion the *salle*'s good name?' Louis Baland, who'd been one of the first to befriend him when he'd arrived in April, clapped Haviland on the back in welcome. 'The six of us will make good showing, but isn't Anjou coming?'

'I hope not. I don't stand a chance against him,' Jean-Marc, a sandy-haired man with laughing hazel eyes, complained good-naturedly. Haviland liked him. He was a strong fencer in practice, but he lacked the competitive urge to win when the match was on the line. 'I just

want to make it further than I did last year before I have to face Anjou. It's a shame to have
to fight him all year and then have to face him
in the tournament, too. We should be exempt. I
think I'll propose that to Leodegrance for next
year,' he joked.

'North here can take him. I've seen him do it,'
another, Paul Robilliard, put in. 'I'd say North is
a great favourite in this tournament. The odds
on you in the stands are good. I can arrange a
go-between if you want to wager on yourself,'
he added quietly.

Haviland politely declined. He knew some
of the fencers wagered on themselves to lose
in order to make money. But he wasn't here to
win money. He wanted to win something far
grander.

'There's Anjou.' Jean-Marc directed their attention with a discreet nod of his head.

Julian Anjou sat alone in a corner, dressed
only in tight buckskin trousers. He was shirtless
and impressively well muscled. Louis snorted.
'Showing off his physique to intimidate us, no
doubt.' Julian's pale hair was severely pulled
back away from his face. His eyes glittered as
he acknowledged the group with the slightest of

nods, but he made no move to join them. 'He likes to be alone before he competes.'

'Do you think he can stand up?' Jean-Marc queried, his face breaking into a knowing grin and the group laughed. 'Have you heard, North? Delacorte showed up for a sabre lesson yesterday and Alyssandra Leodegrance had kicked him in the balls.'

'Everyone knows he's been sweet on her for years,' Louis put in. Haviland barely registered that last remark. He was still groping over the first one.

'What was she doing here?'

Louis laughed. 'We don't know, but whatever it was, she was wearing trousers and she was mad, mad, mad. Delacorte says there were two sabres in the room when he got there. Maybe they were duelling?' It was clear he didn't take his own suggestion seriously. The men laughed, but Haviland's mind was racing. She'd left his bed and gone straight to the *salle* to confront Julian. And not to just confront him verbally. She'd done it with a weapon.

Over him.

These men could think it was a lovers' spat between Alyssandra and Julian, but Haviland knew better and part of him was shamed by it. It was not her place to defend him. If anyone was to confront Julian, it should be him. He'd hoped to have the chance to settle things on the piste. Apparently, Alyssandra had beaten him to it. He was going to have stern words with her when he saw her next.

The announcement came that the first rounds were posted and the changing room disgorged as everyone surged into the main salon for their matches. He had to put Alyssandra out of his mind and focus on the task at hand, which apparently would be a fencer from Spain.

This would be a defensive match. His mind immediately emptied of everything except the pages of the treatise, images of the lessons flashing through his head in review—the triangles the Spanish school loved, the geometry of the steps. Haviland found a quiet space and took out his rapier, practising with a few experimental lunges and stretching his muscles. He could feel excitement building inside himself and did his best to control it. Too much adrenaline could leave one breathless, or cause one to go out too recklessly. Haviland closed his eyes and drew deep breaths, imagining the match to come, seeing himself execute flawless attacks and strong parries.

They were calling for his match when he opened them. 'On the centre piste, Mr Haviland North will face Señor Julio Navarra.' *Mr Haviland North.* He drew another breath, his heartbeat steady and controlled now. Haviland North would fight this tournament, not Viscount Amersham. He hadn't been Amersham for weeks now, not since he'd crossed the Channel. His father would say he was being selfish, but Haviland would argue he was being free. Haviland stepped to the piste, exchanged bows with the officials and his opponent and took up his stance. The officials gave the signal and everyone at the eight pistes lining the salon took up their *en garde* positions.

Fighting in a large arena with other matches going on around you took some talent and some experience not always acquired in practice, Haviland soon realised. It took far more concentration to simply block out the matches on either side of him than he'd expected. During practices in the main salon, there were any number of bouts going on haphazardly at one time, but the randomness of those bouts was hardly distracting. In the beginning, the syn-chronisation of the matches was the distraction as they went through many of the same opening strategies at the same pace. There was a beauti-ful symmetry to it that addicted the eye, but it would also see him eliminated embarrassingly early if he wasn't careful.

Haviland took deliberate stock of his op-ponent, using the early moments of the match to assess the quality and speed of Navarra's moves. Navarra was a man of middling height and years. Grey streaked the temples of his dark hair and his moustache. He was perhaps in his early forties, but his physique was well main-tained. Haviland would have the advantage on him when it came to reach and to stamina, but he was not arrogant enough to discredit Navar-ra's superior knowledge of the Spanish strategy. He needed to go on the offensive immediately and initiate the French school, force Navarra to fight outside his comfort zone.

Ten minutes into the match, Haviland caught him off guard and executed a *flèche* to his right line, earning a direct hit and five of the ten points needed to win the bout. They resumed their *en garde* positions, the Spaniard given the opportunity to initiate the first offensive movement. It would be a chance to also initiate the Spanish line of attack, but Haviland used a strong riposte to take control and land his second direct hit to the man's upper shoulder.

At the declaration of victory, Haviland felt a surge of excitement pass through him. It was only round one, but he was focused now, his thoughts centred on the tournament. He would not fight again for a few hours, but he remained on the floor of the salon instead of joining Nolan and Archer in the stands. He removed his gear and went to watch the second round of matches, to study whoever his next opponent might be. The match featuring a late entrant from Austria intrigued him. The Austrian was slim and tall, with elegant movements that were beautiful to watch as well as deadly, delivering lightning-fast defeat to his opponent. Impressive, Haviland thought. Afterwards, he came forward to compliment the Austrian, but he had disappeared into the crowd, gear and all. It was to be expected. Haviland knew from experience in some of the London tournaments that some fencers enjoyed socialising between matches and exchanging tips on technique while others preferred to slip away to a quiet spot to think and to plan. Still, he would have liked to have met the Austrian.

Alyssandra locked the door of the private practice room behind her and slipped off the mesh mask. She unbuckled the leather protective vest and breathed a sigh of relief. Her first match had gone well. She'd been fast and decisive, the first match of her round to conclude. She'd been able to slip out unnoticed and that had been her plan. The Austrian, Pieter Gruber, had done well.

Haviland had done well, too. She'd discreetly watched his match against Navarra. It was no surprise Haviland had won. Navarra was fifteen years Haviland's senior and limited in his ability to adapt to the different schools of strategy. Julian had won as well, but he had done so meanly and harshly. His match had not been pretty. He was under-matched against a young boy from Belgium. Julian had made him look ridiculous, using complicated moves and unnecessarily difficult attacks. Julian could have beaten him just as easily with straightforward efforts the boy was at least likely to recognise.

His choice was a testament to the depths of Julian's anger, however. She'd shamed him yesterday and he was determined to exercise his superiority. Perhaps she'd misstepped. It did occur to her belatedly that she ought to have left Julian alone, poking a sleeping dog and all that. But part of her could not simply ignore what he'd done and that part had begged for confrontation. In truth, she was more than a little frightened as to what Julian might do to her and to Antoine. Would he go so far as to expose them publicly? Or would he opt for a more private blackmail over public ruination? Which one would offer him more? Either would destroy Antoine.

She buried her face in her hands. What a mess she'd made. In her attempts to protect her brother, she'd become the instrument of his ruin and he didn't even know. Her conscience asserted itself. *It's not fair to keep this from him. It's his future that will be ruined, and he'll never see it coming. At least you've seen this evolve from the start.*

She'd been selfish and prideful, wanting Haviland for herself, thinking herself worthy of a little pleasure to hold the long empty years at bay. She'd even convinced herself Haviland was safe. He would move on and pose no threat to her. Yet, she'd not been able to keep him secret. She'd provoked Julian and turned him, once an ally, into a powerful enemy. Worse than that, she'd not been able to keep her heart free of entanglement. Giving up Haviland would destroy her just as assuredly as Julian's betrayal would destroy Antoine. But keeping Haviland would be the utmost in selfishness. He was a titled lord, not meant for her. Satisfying her wants would hurt both her brother and him.

There was a rattle outside the door, the click of a key in the lock. Alyssandra took a panicked step backwards. No, she would not panic. She had an alibi—she was merely practising—and she already knew who would be coming through the door. Only Antoine had a key.

She was right about the latter. She was wrong about the former. Antoine rolled himself into the room, his face thunderous. 'What the hell do you think you're doing, *Pieter Gruber of Austria*? Did you think no one would notice? No, let me rephrase that, did you think

I wouldn't? Why are you doing this? Do you know what you risk?'

'Risk? What about you, rolling around in these back corridors? What if someone sees you?' It was an entirely non-responsive answer to his barrage of questions.

'I am perfectly fine. I will ensure no one sees me. What is going on? I thought we'd decided you would only fight in the final,' Antoine reprimanded.

'*You* decided that.' This was another piece of her pride coming back to haunt her. She'd flouted her brother's authority in order to assuage her damnable pride. She could protest all she wanted that she'd entered to keep Haviland from winning so he wouldn't throw away his future on her, or that she had done it to keep Julian from hurting Haviland on the piste.

But deep inside those weren't the only reasons. She'd done it for herself, because she wanted to prove to herself just how good she was without her brother whispering her opponents' weaknesses in her ear, without having her brother study those opponents ahead of time with her through peepholes, to fight without the assurance that Julian would lose in the final to preserve the name of Leodegrance.

'Yes, I decided that. It is what makes most sense.' Antoine gave her a hard stare. 'You do understand that being unmasked is more than just public embarrassment, don't you? It can be construed as fraud and that is a crime, a punishable crime, Alyssandra. The longer our masquerade goes on, the more people we'll have duped and the more criminal it will look to the public.'

'No one is going to tell.' It was a brave lie. So much for telling her brother the truth. She would shut Julian up herself if she had to.

Antoine shrugged. 'I don't worry about telling as much as I worry about discovery.' He gave her a pointed look. 'What if Pieter Gruber is exposed to be a woman and my sister at that? And of course you'll have to forfeit if you make the final or even the semi-finals because you can't fight yourself.' They were arguing technicalities now because the larger issues were too difficult to face.

'If you're worried about discovery, help me maintain my disguise. How did you know it was me?' Alyssandra asked.

'The way you move. You move like I do...'

Antoine paused. 'I mean, the way I used to.' His tone softened and for the first time she could see the pain it must bring him to plan the tournament, to see the matches and not be able to participate. The knife of selfishness dug deeper into her gut. 'Only someone who knows you well would see it.' He grinned, trying to hide his hurt. 'Besides, I'm your twin. I'm supposed to know things like that.'

Antoine reached a hand out for her. 'Maybe we should give it all up after the tournament. We could sell the *salle*. Maybe Julian could buy it? We could retire to the country house and forget all this. I'm not going to walk again. There's little sense in continuing the masquerade. It would only take one last lie—that I have sickened in the interim—to explain the wheelchair. Then I could go about as myself at my will and so could you.'

'How long have you been thinking about this?' These didn't sound like impromptu plans born of a sentimental moment.

'A few months. I didn't want to say anything until I was sure of myself, and then lately, things have been a bit off between us. My fault, I fear. I know you're lonely. I know you gave up Etienne for me.' Rage and sadness infused his features.

'If only that accident hadn't happened, if only I'd not taken that jump without knowing what was on the other side.' His fist came down hard on the armrest of his chair. His eyes sparkled dangerously with tears. 'I've ruined both of our lives in a moment of foolishness.' Is that what he thought? How selfish of her to have let him see her moment of weakness, to have let him see any ounce of resentment that she was tied to him for life. He was her brother, and she loved him.

'No, not at all,' she was quick to answer. She could not handle Antoine's tears. They were rare things indeed and she was ill equipped to cope with them. He'd not wept when the doctors had brought him the news of his legs, he'd not cried when their father had died. She would promise him anything to forgo those tears. She didn't like the idea of selling to Julian—it would make him a fixture in their lives, but perhaps it would neutralise the threat he posed. She squeezed his hand meaningfully. 'Let us get through the tournament and we will be gone, off to a new beginning.' Even if it would be a new beginning without Haviland. Nothing had been decided between them and now it had been decided for them.

Chapter Twenty-One

By the next day the field was considerably narrowed. All events had concluded except for the foil competition, which was moving into the quarter-finals with eight fencers left. The stands were full. The unknown Austrian, Pieter Gruber, had quickly garnered a following of those awed by his footwork and wrist play. Julian Anjou had turned his matches into blood sport in his last two bouts the day before. While such behaviour was inappropriate, especially from an instructor who ought to have known better, it did bring spectators.

The athletic Englishman, Haviland North, was bound to meet one of them in the quarter-finals and the spectators held their collective breath, both loath and eager to see which of the three would fall first. The fates spared the audience until the semi-finals. All three would advance, but a pairing now was inevitable. It would be North and Anjou on the centre piste second, Pieter Gruber and the Italian master, Giovanni Basso, first.

Haviland stood at the edge of the floor, studying Basso and Gruber. He would meet one of them in the final round before facing Leodegrance. Three matches to go. The tournament was not only about skill, but about endurance. He'd fought five matches yesterday and, thinking positively, he would fight three today. Nolan and Archer were in the stands again and Brennan had come, too. Nolan was making a fortune on wagers. He was glad for it. His friends might need the money as they continued their tour without him. If all went well, that is what he meant to happen. He meant to stay in Paris, but he couldn't force them to wait.

That was putting the cart before the horse, and Haviland quickly shoved the thoughts away. There was only room for thoughts of this match and the next. The quickest way to failure was to look too far ahead. Gruber was undeniably good. If he'd wagered, he would have picked the Italian simply on reputation and years of study. He'd seen Basso duel yesterday and had been suitably impressed. The man was good and Pieter Gruber was an unknown. Gruber had apparently come alone. He had no friends here and had not travelled with a fencing group. Haviland knew, he'd asked around.

But for a man whom no one knew or ever heard of before yesterday, there was something oddly familiar about Gruber. His face was covered and, with the leather vest and protective padding, it wasn't possible to really tell what Gruber looked like. The familiarity was in the rhythm of his movements, in the fluid grace of them. Haviland gave up watching Basso and studied Gruber.

There! That arm motion. He had his answer. Gruber moved like Leodegrance and eerily so. It was more than the way someone might study another and pick up that person's gestures. Haviland had never seen such a successful mimic, but 'mimic' seemed to be inadequate to truly capture what he was witnessing. This was ingrained, innate. Gruber advanced aggressively and gave a turn of his wrist, the motion disarming Basso and bringing the match to a close.

An unreal conclusion asserted itself: Gruber

was Leodegrance. No one could so precisely match another and the odd habit of disappearing immediately after his rounds fit Leodegrance's reclusive personality. But why? Leodegrance had no reason to duel covertly at his own tournament.

Another image settled in its place—a woman with a fan, a woman with a sword-stick pressed against a thug's throat in an alley. A woman who had gone after Anjou with a sabre and kneed him in the groin if rumour was to be believed. Snippets of their last conversation came back to him, words that hadn't fully registered. *We were both twenty when my father died.* Alyssandra was a twin—a twin who had trained side by side with her brother. She would need the anonymity of the mask. Women were not permitted and it would certainly do Leodegrance no good if she were discovered.

That did not answer his question of motive, however. Why would she do such a thing and risk her brother's credibility? Whether he thought it was ridiculous or not, the tournament would be disgraced and that could hardly be what either of them wanted. Alyssandra had made no secret of the fact that the *salle d'armes* supported them financially.

You will have to face her to get to Leodegrance. He would have to face her. It seemed to be a bit of twisted irony that the woman he loved would be his last obstacle. She would quite literally be all that stood in his way. Had that been why she'd done it? Or was there someone else, something else she was protecting? Maybe he was overthinking it. It might be nothing more than wanting to prove herself. Had she finally had enough of living in her brother's shadow? If so, her reasons for wanting to compete were not much different than his own: freedom, pride in personal accomplishment, the desire to show the world for a brief moment he was more than the sum of his title and wealth—things that had come to him as an accident of birth, nothing more. He understood those reasons well enough.

He felt a presence close at his shoulder and stiffened. It wasn't a friendly presence. 'Have you figured out Pieter Gruber's little secret?' The voice carried a smirk. It was Anjou, and his proximity made Haviland want to do violence. How dare the man saunter up to him as if he hadn't ordered an attack on his person two days ago, as if he hadn't faced Alyssandra with a sabre. Haviland didn't like imagining what had transpired in that room to cause Alyssandra to go for his groin.

'Keep your distance,' Haviland growled.

'Or you'll what?' Anjou was all casual insouciance. 'Draw your foil and start our match early? Get ejected from the tournament for foul play?' He gave a laugh. 'I don't think there's anything you can do to me right here. Perhaps you'd like to save some of that vengeance for the piste? I know I will.'

It galled Haviland to think that anyone watching them would think they were acquaintances, friends even. But Anjou was right. Haviland couldn't touch him here as much as he wished otherwise without sacrificing what he'd worked so hard to achieve. Perhaps Anjou was hoping he'd lose his cool and be disqualified.

Julian changed tack, nodding towards Pieter Gruber, who was exiting the floor yet again, to hide in seclusion until he was called. 'She's a fool, of course. After I beat you, I'll beat her and perhaps teach her a rather public lesson about interfering in the games of men.' Julian smiled coldly, his intentions thinly veiled. He meant to expose Alyssandra. Had he thought that through or was anger talking? Surely he'd harm himself in the process.

'You won't beat me,' Haviland answered, keeping his gaze forward. He would not give Anjou the satisfaction of looking him in the eye. 'You haven't beaten me for some time.' And now, knowing that Alyssandra was at risk, he certainly couldn't allow it. Julian facing Alyssandra would be disastrous. He was hunting revenge for last night and possibly more. There was far more bad blood between Alyssandra and Julian than she'd alluded to.

Julian shrugged, unconcerned. 'I'll take my chances all the same.' He paused for effect. 'It's not me you should be worried about, you know. I am a straightforward fellow. You know exactly where you stand with me. I don't like you. I want you gone. Defeating you is the fastest way I can get rid of you. But Alyssandra is a different matter. She's not been plain with you from the start. I know this because I know the real truths. I know what she hides from you.'

A cold finger ran down Haviland's back. Julian was merely trying to get a rise out of him. Julian would like nothing better than to pierce his calm and distract him. Unfortunately, it was working. He could not discard this latest probe as the jealous lashing out of a thwarted suitor. Julian was not spinning lies in the *hope* of hitting a target. He was spinning truths knowing full well they would hit a target.

He'd known there were secrets, things to hide. Privacy meant secrets and one did not get much more private than the Leodegrances— Antoine with his odd habits in the lessons and Alyssandra and her penchant for withholding information. She had done so since the beginning when she had not disclosed her name until it was too late. She'd kept him hidden, too, not wanting him to call at the house and conduct a proper courtship, not wanting him to address her brother. She'd not told him she was a twin or that she fenced.

What else hadn't she told him? What had there truly been between them besides great sex? Sex so good that he'd believed there was something more, something worth fighting for, breaking free for. It was horrid to think, after all his years of practising detached physical affairs, that he'd fallen into the trap he'd tried so hard to avoid. And he'd fallen unaware.

The announcer called for their match. 'Are you ready?' Julian sneered. 'I'll take you apart a piece at a time.'

'And risk being thrown out of the tournament yourself? You were warned yesterday one more infraction would see you expelled. Leodegrance won't tolerate it,' Haviland said coolly.

Julian scoffed. 'Leodegrance will do nothing, he *is* nothing, that's how little you know. Are you familiar with the concept of smoke and mirrors, North? Do you think this is the first time Alyssandra has masqueraded as a man? She's rather good at it—too good at it, don't you think?' He strode off to take his position at the end of the piste, waving to the crowd who cheered as he passed on his way to be helped into the padded vest and mask waiting on his side of the arena. Then it was Haviland's turn to step forward, to take the adoration of the crowd. He raised his arm in acknowledgement, smiling, wiping away any trace of unease. He would not give Julian the satisfaction of knowing what his insinuations did to him. Julian would not win any game with him, mental or physical. But, by Jove, did he really mean what Haviland thought? That Alyssandra was *the* Leodegrance? But how could that be? She couldn't be both Pieter Gruber and Antoine Leodegrance in the prize round, assuming she won the match between them. And she might win. If Julian was right and she was the face behind the mask during his lessons, he had never beaten her. Would she lose on purpose to preserve her identity or would she win to prevent him from achieving his goal? Did she care for him so little that she would thwart him in such a manner?

Haviland let the piste assistants help him into the equipment. Where was his foil? It should have been back from cleaning by now. He never let his foil out of his sight and it made him nervous not to have it now. At the last minute, a boy acting as squire ran up with his foil.

Haviland's hand closed around the grip of his foil, letting the feel of his weapon centre him. He had to empty his mind. A full mind was what Julian wanted. Julian would like to turn him against Alyssandra. What was he going to put his trust in? Julian's viperous tongue or Alyssandra's passion? He took an experimental swipe with his foil, exhaling a breath, purifying his thoughts with the exhalation. He closed his eyes. Words could lie, but the body couldn't. For now, he would simply believe in her.

'I don't believe Julian's presence in the prize round is a foregone conclusion this year.' Antoine pressed his eyes to the peepholes. He could only see the match from one end since the stands erected for the occasion obscured viewing the matches from the sidelines. 'What do you think, Alyssandra? North or Anjou? This might be the highlight of the tournament. The crowd is excited. Listen to them.'

Alyssandra joined him in the locked room, glad to see he was in better spirits. 'Haviland will beat him,' she said tersely. He had to. The alternative was too disastrous to think of. She had gone too far with Julian the night before. She thought of the note she'd received after her match, tucked into Pieter's gear. Julian had made his intentions clear. She was frightened of what he might do to Pieter Gruber on the piste if she gave him the chance. He would not care if he was ejected from the tournament. No one would even pay attention to his infraction if it revealed Pieter Gruber was a woman and Antoine's sister besides.

'Haviland? Is that how it is these days?' Antoine looked away from the match to study her. 'That's a long way from Viscount Amersham or Mr North. When he first came, he was merely the Englishman to you.'

She met her brother's eyes, unwilling to hide any longer. Too much had been hidden for too long. 'Don't worry. It's a temporary *affaire*, nothing more. It will end shortly.' When she beat him and prevented him from winning the tournament and he realised his dreams weren't worth his future.

'Why would it end? Does he not care for you?' Antoine asked carefully.

'He's not in a position to offer for me, if that's what you're thinking.' Alyssandra busied herself with looking through the eyeholes, but that only put Haviland firmly in her view, most particularly his backside in her view.

Antoine was silent for a moment. 'What position would that be?'

'He's on a Grand Tour with his friends. He plans to go on to Italy and study there.' It was the safe answer. She couldn't bring herself to say the rest—that there was a woman expecting to marry him back home in England. Never mind that he didn't love her, or that she didn't love him. And certainly never mind that Haviland had declared his plans to be otherwise. He wanted to stay in Paris, wanted to stay with her. Haviland would do his duty because his honour demanded it and in a fight between his honour and his freedom, honour would win. Alyssandra would see to it even though it hurt. The woman she would be sending him back to would never know him, never know how he looked when passion took him, or how he danced on bridges in the moonlight. He would never do those things with that woman. Those memories belonged to her alone.

'Perhaps he needs a reason to stay,' Antoine mused. 'If you gave him a reason, he might be persuaded. I know I told you to be careful with him, but since you weren't…?'

Alyssandra scolded softly, 'He already questions why a man with scars would need his sister so much. I think Haviland staying is the last thing we need.'

'But the first thing you need,' Antoine countered. 'You care for him.'

'I care for you more.' She looked away in order to end the argument, her attention going back to the match. It was as close as she'd ever come to admitting out loud just how deep her feelings for Haviland went. 'Watch, Antoine. They're about to begin.' She sent up a prayer that Haviland be safe. Julian would stop at nothing, but surely Haviland knew that and would be on his guard.

Antoine wasn't ready to let it go. His voice was quiet beside her. 'But if you could have him, would you want him?'

Yes and always, her heart answered silently. But it was an impossibility. If he knew what she'd done, Haviland would never forgive her deception. He would never accept a relationship that had been begun with the intent to conceal secrets.

Chapter Twenty-Two

'I think I'll start with your heart. Oh, I forgot, I already have,' Julian sneered and parried. But Haviland knew the words were an attempt to regain ground. He was giving Julian no quarter and it showed. He meant to end this bout as quickly as possible. The sooner this was over, the sooner he could get to Alyssandra. Until he saw her, Julian's words could have no power.

Haviland made a hard thrust, catching Julian's blade. It should have turned Julian's foil aside, but instead he felt a tremor run up the length of his own blade. It caught him off guard, giving Julian an opening to advance. Julian brought his foil across Haviland's in a strong sweep. Haviland was ready for him, but his weapon wasn't. His blade quivered, undeniable proof something was wrong. Haviland parried, blocking the move, but Julian could see the blade was in distress. He struck again and again with the same sweeping thrust, hammering on the weakening foil. Each blow taxed the strength of Haviland's arm in his attempts to keep the foil steady and recover fast enough to meet the next onslaught.

Reality sank in. At this rate, the blade would break and soon. Julian had seen it weakening and was shamelessly exploiting that fact. He was going to lose. Haviland moved to launch one last offensive, but his blade hadn't the strength. On the next thrust, it met Julian's foil and snapped five inches from the hilt in the place Julian had been relentlessly catching. He could hear the crowd give a collective moan of disappointment, a few gasps of disbelief. For the fraction of a second he, too, was caught up in the disbelief staring at the broken foil. But Julian wasn't done yet.

Julian didn't stop for the broken blade. Even though the officials had immediately stepped forward to call the match, Julian carried on his attack, driving for Haviland's shoulder. Out of instinct, Haviland blocked with his foil, but a broken weapon was no match for Julian's speed and wrath. The buttoned tip of Julian's foil pierced the padding at his shoulder in a legal touch. 'Now I've won on points. No one can claim otherwise,' Julian hissed under his breath as the officials had them separate and return to their own ends of the piste. The officials conferred together briefly. One official stepped forward and proclaimed the outcome of the match to the crowd.

'Victory in the second semi-final round goes to Julian Anjou on the grounds that his opponent is unable to continue. The final touch to the shoulder will not be counted.'

Down the length of the piste, Haviland watched Julian's face mottle. That was not the decision he was looking for. He'd wanted a decisive victory, one that nobody could question. He didn't want anyone to think that, but for the broken blade, the outcome might have been different.

The crowd applauded, but the applause lacked some of its earlier excitement. For them, the outcome of the much-anticipated match up had been anticlimactic and in some ways inconclusive. There was a small commotion at the officials' table where the matches were set and another announcement was made. Pieter Gruber had forfeited his place in the final. The tournament would move straight to the prize round—the chance to directly face the tournament's renowned host, Antoine Leodegrance. The match would be held in an hour, giving the victor time to recover and it would be fought with rapiers, Antoine Leodegrance's famed weapon of choice. Julian tossed Haviland an 'I told you so' look while the crowd murmured its surprise and disappointment in rising volumes.

Haviland felt his gut clench. The forfeit seemed to confirm all that Julian had hatefully intimated. Alyssandra was playing a dangerous masquerade. And now Julian had what he wanted: a chance to prove himself in public once again as the great instructor, a man who might dare call himself Leodegrance's equal. But if that was no longer enough, he had a chance to expose Alyssandra. Of course, he'd have to choose. Julian couldn't have them both. Perhaps Julian's own ego would keep Alyssandra safe in the end.

Haviland stepped from the arena. He looked down at the snapped blade still in his hand, his fingers running over the rough break. His fingers suddenly stalled and he brought the blade up for closer inspection. Blades *did* snap due to rust and misuse, but he took impeccable care of his. He examined the exposed cross-section and swore under his breath. This blade had been tampered with. There was a notch where Julian had hammered away until the blade had given. There had been only one time when the blade had been out of his sight and that was when it had been taken for inspection before the semi-final. Since the semi-final was fought with personal blades, they were always examined. If Julian was willing to go to such lengths to ensure victory and reach the final it was further proof Julian meant to do the Leodegrances harm. What Julian had done was tantamount to a declaration of war.

Julian had made his choices. He had his own choices to make as well. To go and bow to duty or to stay and pursue his freedom here? That would depend on Alyssandra. Had she used him for pleasure alone? Was there truly nothing between them to build a future on? Maybe in the end, this hadn't been any different than his other affairs. He'd just wanted to be so much more than a temporary bedfellow with a title, a phallus with a fortune.

It was hard to think of their time together that way. Perhaps that's why he'd been so eager to set aside seeking those answers from Alyssandra. He'd had excuses aplenty to wait. The affair was short term, the affair was physical only, there was the tournament to concentrate on. But now, those items did not apply. There was no longer a reason to wait. The tournament was over. He had lost.

Dear God, Haviland had lost! Alyssandra set back from the viewing holes with a sigh of disbelief that mirrored the crowd's. She'd had not been prepared for that. The depths of her disappointment, her incredulity, revealed to her just how much she'd counted on Haviland's victory, how much she'd come to rely on him.

'It's hardly his fault,' Antoine said, sounding as disheartened by the result as she. 'Foils snap. It happens. It is rather unfortunate. If it's any consolation, Julian looks displeased too. The officials are announcing the decision.'

Julian wouldn't like winning on a technicality, but he would take it gladly. He'd been losing up until the point Haviland's blade had weakened. Under the circumstances, he couldn't have wished for better if he'd arranged it. That thought made her sit up a little straighter. Had he? Could he have had Haviland's weapon tampered with? A man who hired thugs in alleyways would not shy away from notching a blade. 'Antoine, you don't think Julian had anything to do with the blade breaking, do you?' She said the words carefully. It was a bold accusation to make.

Antoine looked aggrieved by the suggestion that one of the men in his *salle d'armes* would be capable of such treachery. 'Blades break,' he said firmly. It was easier for him to believe that statement than she. He didn't know what she knew. Julian had done violence to Haviland on two occasions.

She was about to delicately push the subject matter when a loud call in the corridor pierced the shelter of their little room. Someone was calling her. Not someone, Haviland was calling her. And he was calling her *by name*.

Alyssandra shot a worried glance at her brother. Haviland was in the hall, *shouting*. She could only hope there was no one nearby to hear. What was he thinking? If he had known how much she needed to preserve her identity, he wouldn't be outside shouting her name. *Or maybe he didn't care*, came the niggling thought. Maybe he knew and was beyond discretion. 'He's come for his reckoning.' Alyssandra stood and swallowed hard. Haviland had every right to be angry. Her secrets were a betrayal of all they'd shared. It would be better this way, to let him leave her in anger. But it wouldn't be easier.

Antoine furrowed his brow, cocking his head to listen. 'That doesn't sound like an angry man.'

Alyssandra disagreed. It sounded like a man who'd come for answers, and she couldn't quarrel with that. In her heart, she knew she'd treated him abominably, sharing with him only the intimacy of her body when he had shared his mind with her, opened himself up to her. *You didn't have a choice. You had a brother to protect*, came the old argument. But it did little to soothe her.

Haviland was pounding on the doors now. They could hear the heavy thump of his fist on the panels as he came closer. 'I will go out and meet him. I will try to protect you,' Alyssandra promised. There was no way out of this viewing room except through the door. 'If Haviland gets through the door, there's nothing left to hide.' She drew a deep breath. She was so tired of secrets, but it was almost over. She had to face Julian on the piste and then it would be done. She and Antoine could go to the country and put this chapter of their lives behind them. One more match, one more victory. She had to stay strong now when they were so near the end.

She stepped into the corridor, Haviland spying her immediately. He stopped. His features collected themselves into aristocratic coolness. He looked as he did when she'd first met him: calm, unflappable, untouchable, as if the world did not dare to bother him with its petty troubles. Almost. He'd not stopped to change after his match. He was dishevelled, dressed only in breeches and shirt showing signs of sweat. His dark hair fell forward over his brow. He'd come straight to her. It was either a sign of how deep his anger went or something else she dared not name. Naming it would make it all that much harder to let him go.

'Are you Pieter Gruber?' he asked in even

tones, his eyes locked on hers, waiting, watching for the truth unflinchingly. Perhaps it was good he wasn't yelling wild accusations and calling her every slanderous name known to womankind. If he was, it would make it easier to sell a lie because she wouldn't care about his reaction.

'Is that what Julian told you?' She could be cool, too, even though she was hot with worry, hot with desire, beneath the surface. Just looking at him here in the dim corridor made her want him, made her want to die from the knowledge she might never have him again, never lie beside him again. Once he figured it all out, and she was sure he would now that he was so close, he wouldn't want any part of her. He might even for a while hate himself for being duped. She'd never wanted that, never meant for that to happen. 'I saw the two of you talking before the match. Is that the sort of poison he was pouring in your ear like the snake he is?'

'*He* was talking.' Blue eyes flashed at the insinuation he and Julian had somehow made up.

'You were listening. Apparently.' Maybe if they could fight over something, she wouldn't have to answer the question.

'I'm sorry that you think I'm a man who

would be served his opinions by a man who has little credibility to recommend him,' Haviland parried, arms crossed, eyes darkening dangerously. Her attack had been thwarted and now it was time for him to go on the offensive. 'I had already made up my mind. Once I saw Pieter Gruber use his wrist I knew it was you. I know how your body moves, all grace and glide. I know what your body looks like, what it *feels* like. Did you think I could be in bed with you, or run my hands over your naked body, and not know you?'

His words were a rough caress. She did not miss the scold in them for underestimating him. But they were not meant only to punish. He was teasing her with pleasure, too, using words to conjure hot images, to kindle the heat in her belly. To what end? To lure out her last secrets? Could she trust him not just for herself, but for her brother? It wasn't always for herself that she held back. She would find a way to live with the repercussions, but she could not assume that Antoine would. And what would trust result in? Would it be worth it? Or would he leave anyway, disgusted with her for one reason or another?

'Yes, I was Pieter Gruber and, yes, it was selfish and risky. But I deserve a chance to prove myself and I did. There was no man my equal,' she said defiantly. Perhaps this truth would distract him from the larger one.

He raised a brow as if he doubted her confession. 'Is that truly why you did it?' He started circling her, and she started to move clockwise, refusing to let him stalk her.

'You think it isn't?' she challenged. She was more comfortable quarrelling than disclosing. This was more familiar territory. She'd been quarrelling with Julian for years. She knew how to protect herself here.

'No, I don't.' Haviland was cool. 'If it was, you wouldn't have forfeited the final. You would have *enjoyed* besting Julian, you would have been *thrilled* to be taking the stage in the finale against your brother. What better way to make your point than to face the great Leodegrance and perhaps even best him? And yet, when the moment came to prove yourself against truly great talent, you bowed out. That makes little sense. Only a coward would falter at the last, afraid to seize greatness for themselves.' He paused. 'I did not take you for a coward, Alyssandra.'

Those clipped, crisp English tones, so superior, so all knowing, provoked the tiger in her. She had to tread carefully here and not give that rash tiger free rein or she'd be saying too much. There was nothing to say so she fell back on her strategy of questioning to distract. 'What exactly do you think explains it, then?' They'd started circling one another again, crossing foot over foot as they stalked.

'I think Pieter Gruber and Antoine Leodegrance are the same person, making it impossible for them to face each other in the finale.'

'A woman masquerading as her brother? Do you hear how absurd that sounds?' She wanted him to reject the proposition for himself before she had to affirm it. 'Now, consider this: the brother is regarded as the finest swordsman on the Continent.'

Haviland was not daunted. 'Consider *this*: his sister is his twin and was trained beside him by their father.' He paused and cocked his head. 'It seems less far-fetched now, coupled with the fact that the brother suffered from an accident three years ago.' His features softened. He broke his circling and stepped across to her, his hand going to her cheek. 'Did he die?'

She could see that storyline spinning across his face, pity and sorrow mixed together. It was an explanation that made sense to him, an explanation his code of honour could forgive: her father dead, her brother killed in an accident, a young woman suddenly left alone to fend for herself so she turned to her inheritance—a *salle d'armes*, her own formidable talent and her family name. And Julian had supported it for his own gains, waiting for a time when he could strike out for himself or marry into it.

'No, he didn't die.' The words were in her mind, but she'd not been the one to speak them. She watched Haviland's eyes move past her to the door she blocked. The voice spoke again. 'I'm Antoine Leodegrance and I'm very much alive.'

They both turned and stared at the man in the wheeled chair. For once she had the luxury of seeing Haviland caught entirely off guard. This was too much for even his noble hauteur. She knew with a certainty that whatever pity he'd felt for her was gone, replaced with something indecipherable.

Haviland stared. Two simultaneous thoughts flashed. Antoine Leodegrance did *not* have a scarred face. Instead, he had a face that very strongly resembled Alyssandra's, high cheekbones and all, right down to the chocolate-brown eyes. Secondly, he was in a wheeled chair. It was not scars that prompted his privacy, but that fact that he couldn't walk. Antoine smiled in the wake of the stunned silence. 'Perhaps this isn't best discussed in the hallway. Alyssandra, if you would please help me inside.' He gave his attention to Haviland. 'This chair can do some amazing things, but backing up is not one of them.'

'Of course,' Haviland said automatically, still trying to take it in as he followed the Leodegrances inside. Alyssandra was pale and, for the first time since he'd known her, she was visibly unsure of herself and unsure of what to do next. She shot him a glance he wasn't meant to see and realised where the uncertainty came from. She didn't know what *he* would do next. Perhaps she was right to carry that uncertainty. What would he do next? He had the feeling that this revelation should change everything, but he didn't know how. Was he supposed to stop loving her because her secrets were revealed?

Antoine pulled out a pocket watch. 'There is

still forty-five minutes before the match. I think there is time for our tale.' He looked at Haviland. 'But I'm sure, at this point, you've figured out an accurate sketch of it.'

He had. His original thought was not far off except for Antoine's role in it. He wasn't dead, but he was incapacitated and it had fallen to Alyssandra to literally become the legs of the *salle*. The masquerade was ingenious in many ways, making the most of their shared likeness and their shared talent. Haviland had understood that aspect well enough the moment Antoine had opened the door. It was the details he was lacking.

Antoine gave Alyssandra a small smile full of affection, his attention riveted on her as he began. 'I love my sister, Mr North, and she loves me. So much so that she has dedicated her life in recent years to my care and well being to the detriment of her own.'

His dark-brown gaze swivelled to Haviland. 'You are aware that slightly over three years ago I was hurt in an accident. You might even have heard that it was a riding accident? I'm not sure how much news of that nature would be of interest in London. I took a jump stupidly, not knowing what was on the other side. It was muddy and slippery and my horse landed badly. I was thrown and this is the result.' He gestured to his useless legs. 'The doctors were hopeful the damage wouldn't be permanent and, under that assumption, we took up the masquerade. Alyssandra could be me for a few months. We could keep the *salle* open and it would be business as usual.'

He shook his head, a shadow crossing his face for the first time. 'But the months became a year, the doctors became less optimistic. A year became two years. Alyssandra's fiancé lost hope that she would ever leave me, ever feel free enough to marry and have a home of her own. He broke with her.'

He paused and looked down at his hands. 'I think that was when I started to realise I had to end the masquerade for Alyssandra's sake. I was going to be tied to this chair for the rest of my life, but it was not fair for her to be as well. But these things take time and timing. I couldn't just close the *salle* and disappear. There are practicalities to be met. What would we live on without the membership fees?' Antoine said apologetically as if the delay in acting on his thoughts had needed explanation.

'It is not a sacrifice to be with you,' Alyssandra inserted swiftly, fiercely when he paused. 'You do us both little credit to talk about yourself that way.'

Haviland smiled. That was the woman he knew, selfless and giving. Some of the worry inside of him began to ease. Despite his comment to the contrary, he had allowed himself to be influenced by Julian's words more than he'd cared to admit; perhaps not in the way Julian had intended—that she was a master plotter, a woman of covert, insincere attentions—but in a more personal way. He'd doubted Alyssandra's feelings for him, doubted the quality of their intimacy.

Julian had failed on both accounts. The masquerade had not been wrought out of duplicity but out of love, out of a need to protect themselves and each other. Haviland saw the underlying message in Antoine's apologetic remark. He was Alyssandra's brother, he had to provide for her. And Alyssandra recognised his pride demanded it. He saw now why the masquerade had been maintained. Alyssandra was protecting her brother's pride while he protected their livelihood.

'But now it has to end,' Antoine continued. 'She cannot do this indefinitely. After the tournament, I will look for a buyer and sell the *salle*. We will remove to our country house in Fontainebleau and start again somehow. Perhaps it is what should have been done from the start. Now, Monsieur North, you know our little secret.'

It was a request for judgement. Haviland knew what Antoine was asking. Antoine wanted to know what would he do with their secret? Would he expose them here at the last with them so close to escaping detection? More importantly, what were his intentions towards Alyssandra? Haviland understood, too, that Antoine had taken an enormous risk in what he shared. Men did not take such risks unless they felt that risk was somehow justified. Antoine must be very sure of him.

Was he that sure of himself? He let his gaze rest on Alyssandra, lingering on the fall of caramel hair, the sharp jut of her chin, the depths of her dark eyes. There was sadness in them and he wished he could take it away. There was little doubt in his mind that he'd been the one to put it there in the first place. He was starting to understand Alyssandra's choices.

It occurred to him in the silence of the room that he'd been wrong. All along, he'd viewed the tournament as the watershed, the event that would define his future. But it wasn't. Winning the tournament or taking third as he had done, didn't change anything *for* him and it certainly hadn't changed *him*. It had merely been an exercise, a chance to show off an accomplishment, but nothing more. *She* was his watershed. What he did *with* her, what he did *for* her, would define his future. She had given up her secrets for him. Would he give up his family for her? Not for a fencing salon, not for personal freedom, but for her because she was his freedom, his dream. But the time for such an announcement was not yet.

'I think Alyssandra needs to prepare for her match,' Haviland said at last. 'Monsieur Anjou must not be underestimated.' She needed her mind on Julian, not on him, not on any emotional turmoil. He tore his gaze from Alyssandra to give attention to Antoine. He bowed. 'You have done me a great honour with your revelations. Your secret is safe with me. When the tournament is over, we will speak again.'

Walking out of that room past Alyssandra without touching her was the hardest thing he'd ever done. He supposed he could have stayed. Antoine would have allowed the company, but he sensed Alyssandra and Antoine needed time alone, perhaps not solely as brother and sister, but as coach and athlete.

Knowing didn't make passing her easier. He wanted to stop and kiss her, wanted to tell her a million things to watch for, how to fence against Julian, how Julian preferred to go for the right line on his opponent. But he recognised those things served no purpose. A kiss would distract her, and she already knew how to fence Julian. She'd been fencing him for years. Anything he might tell her she already knew.

At the door, Antoine called out to him, 'Do not worry, Monsieur North. Julian is no danger to her. He knows his part. There is just as much glory for him in losing the finale, if not more. A defeated Leodegrance is bad for business and Julian depends on that business as much as we.' He smiled confidently.

Haviland wished he were that sure. Julian

might know his part, but Haviland wasn't at all certain Julian would play it. He shot a glance at Alyssandra, counselling caution. Antoine would have to be told about Julian's perfidy, but now was not the time. By Jove, he did not want Alyssandra to go out there. Every instinct protested against it. What sort of man let his woman go out to face danger?

Alyssandra held his eyes, firm and unwavering. *I will be fine. I've done this a hundred times.* He had his answer. A brave man. A man who trusted in her abilities. She was not outmatched. She'd beaten *him*, hadn't she? It had been her behind the mask conducting the lessons, meting out the defeats until she'd helped him correct his dropped shoulder. Perhaps, too, he could do her more good out there, where he could keep an eye on Julian. He gave a short nod as he opened the door. 'I'll see you both afterwards.' This was a different kind of bravery, a different kind of honour. But Alyssandra would tolerate nothing less. It would take some getting used to.

'He's coming back.' Antoine smiled triumphantly.

Alyssandra returned his smile. She hadn't the

heart to ruin his happiness. Antoine thought everything was solved. And it was, in a way that had nothing to do with his disclosures to Haviland. 'You should have told me you meant to tell him everything,' she said, reaching for her gear. She would have to go soon.

'I didn't know myself that was what I intended,' Antoine confessed. 'When I heard him out there, I knew I had to tell him. He loves you, Alyssandra. It's in his voice, in the way he looks at you. You love him, too, I think.' His voice softened, and he looked young again, the way he looked before pain marked his days. 'Maybe he's the reason Etienne wasn't meant to be the one?'

That brought tears to her eyes. 'You're a hopeless romantic, Antoine.' She brushed at her cheeks and shook her head. She had to tell him. 'Maybe he does love me, but nothing can come of it.'

Antoine cut her off. 'You're the daughter of a French *vicomte*, you're a lady in your own right. There's nothing wrong with your birth. You're perfectly acceptable—'

'Antoine, listen,' she interrupted. 'It wouldn't matter if I was the Queen of England. He's promised to someone else. It's been arranged since they were children. Two families are counting on him to fulfil the contract when he goes home. He's an honourable man, Antoine.' She couldn't tell him the rest, that Haviland wanted to stay in Paris, wanted to teach fencing, wanted to be with her. Antoine would hope too much.

The news crushed him. She could see the life go out of his face. Oh, she hated doing it to him. 'Then he should not have dallied with you.' Antoine's voice was grim, bitter.

'Don't blame him. We started it, you and I, with our subterfuges. And I proved less resistant to his charm than I would have thought.' Perhaps she should feel regret over having waved her fan that very first night. But she didn't. She would lose Haviland, but she wouldn't lose the memories.

Antoine relented, but remained unconvinced. 'I guess it was all for naught. I thought if he knew, if he understood…' *He would forgive her and the path would be clear for him to propose and everyone could live happy ever after.* Antoine didn't need to finish the sentence. She knew his thoughts, knew how his mind worked.

'It's not all in vain.' Alyssandra picked up her rapier. 'I will finish this tournament and we will have a new life.' She bent down and dropped a kiss on her brother's forehead. 'All will be well, you'll see.' Eventually it probably would. She'd got over Etienne. She would get over Haviland, she promised herself. But it would take a long time and it would hurt. It already did.

Antoine's hand closed over her wrist. 'Wait, why is North worried about Julian?'

She smiled brightly, too brightly, and pulled away. 'I do not know. I will beat him.'

The bitch would not beat him. Julian stood on the sidelines of the piste, waiting for the final to be called. He couldn't notch her rapier, as well. He caught sight of Haviland shouldering his way through the crowd and moved to intercept him. He had something for the Englishman too.

He made sure to stand next to North on the sidelines. 'What a day this will be. First I beat you and now I'll beat your woman.'

To his credit, North refused to be drawn. 'You didn't beat me. You notched my blade.' His tone was low and calm, his eyes straightforward, never straying from the curtained cubicle where Alyssandra must be right now getting ready. 'Did you notch hers? If not, she'll beat you.'

Julian smiled. He was going to mess with North's mind until the Englishman was paralysed with fear. 'Two broken blades in two consecutive rounds against me would be far too suspicious. No, I have something better for her. Shall I tell you what it is?' Just then, his page ran up to him, delivering his rapier. 'Ah, and here it is. Thank you, my boy. You didn't touch it, did you?'

'No, sir.' The boy nodded and ran off.

'Good lad, because if he had…' Julian leaned towards Haviland with an air of confidentiality '…he might be dead. I poisoned the tip, you see.' He watched Haviland's jaw tighten. 'I think it adds a little excitement to an otherwise dull sport, don't you? Really, what's the point of fighting with only wooden fleurets to pierce one's chest? It's like knife fighting with dull blades, firing guns without bullets. It's much more exciting this way.' He held up his blade to the light. 'It's cobra venom, it's invisible. All I have to do is knick her arm or leg. It won't matter if it's a legal touch or not. The result will be the same. I just have to give the poison a chance to work. The surface of the skin isn't enough, it has to enter the bloodstream.'

Then it would just be he and Antoine. He might not have the security of marriage any longer to bind him to the family without Alyssandra, but Antoine would need him for ever, would need the quality of his name to keep the *salle* drawing high-paying customers because to all the world, Antoine Leodegrance would be dead. Best of all, Antoine would never know what he'd done. It would be a shame to lose such a beauty, but she had made her position plain and refused to budge when she'd come after him with that sabre.

'You can tell her if you want to. There's time.' Julian smirked at Haviland's silent outrage, his fists clenched at his sides as he realised there was nothing he could do in a crowd. 'Or do you think it would distract her too much to know? What you have to ask yourself is will she fight better knowing her life is on the line or better if she was ignorant of the fact? It's your very own roulette game. Or maybe you don't care either way. You know, she has played us both, North. She's led me on for years. Maybe you've finally figured out she came to you only to protect her brother. She flirted with you so you'd stop asking questions about the two of them. She's done nothing but deceive you. If you didn't want to tell her, I wouldn't blame you.' He gave Haviland a little nod. 'If you'll excuse me, I need to get ready for the final.' Julian was through waiting. Fortune favoured those who took action and it was going to smile on him in about twenty minutes.

Chapter Twenty-Three

Murder! Haviland let the horrifying knowledge galvanise him into action. There were mere minutes in which to act. His mind raced ahead of his body as he pushed his way through the crowd gathering on the floor for an up-close look at the bout which would take place on a raised stage. There was no time to go to Antoine. Even if there was, there was no guarantee Antoine could do anything to stop the match without revealing himself. Neither could he go to Archer or Nolan in the stands. He'd never make it through the press of people to reach them and still warn Alyssandra.

His mind had already resolved that issue, too. He impatiently elbowed aside a few bystanders that refused to move. The crowd was nearly impossible. He wouldn't risk playing with her mind because she wasn't going to fight. He needed to take her place. The crowd would be expecting a man anyway. With a mask on, he doubted they would see anything but what they expected to see—Leodegrance on stage, at a distance from them.

Haviland turned sideways and edged through the people congregated at the foot of the stage. There were curtained cubicles set on either side for garbing up. She'd be there, but she'd already be garbed. As the champion, she'd be stage left. She was there, practising with her rapier—one of the *salle*'s premier blades. Haviland had seen them under lock and key in the glass case of the private instruction rooms.

'Leodegrance…' he began, careful not to use her name in case they were overheard.

She stopped mid-lunge, startled by the intrusion. He strode towards her, a hand to his lips, warning her to be silent, to do nothing to give her away, although he suspected she was far better at that game than he. Close enough to whisper, he delivered his news. 'Julian has poisoned his blade. Likely it's the tip, perhaps part of the blade itself. Definitely the fleuret.'

He wanted to rip the damn mask from her

face, wanted to see her reaction, but it was far too risky with a crowd just feet away beyond the curtain. What was her reaction? Did the news frighten her? 'He means to do murder.' Motives didn't matter at this point. All that mattered was that Julian not have a chance to do it.

'Give me your helmet and your rapier.' Haviland's tones were stern, leaving no opportunity for argument. He didn't want her to feel there was a chance to contest his decision.

She backed up, shaking her head. She risked low, fast words. 'You will not die for me.'

'I don't mean to die. I am safer out there. Julian means to murder you. He'll recognise me, but no one else will. Perhaps he'll swap out his rapier or perhaps he won't even try if it's not his intended target,' Haviland reasoned. 'Who will protect Antoine if you fall? Who will protect the *salle d'armes*? Julian will have everything he wants with you gone.' He did not give voice to the rest of that argument. If Julian did succeed in harming him, it would accomplish nothing, move none of Julian's avaricious goals closer to achievement.

'Haviland, you have a family, people counting on you,' she argued. 'You simply can't throw yourself away.'

'Neither can you. I will beat him,' Haviland answered swiftly. They were running out of time. He could hear officials taking their places, the rustle of papers and the murmur of conferring voices. He ran his hand down the side of her mask as if it were her cheek. 'And when I get back, I mean to marry you if you'll have me.' He hadn't meant to do it quite that way. He'd meant for there to be champagne, roses and candles. But the words tumbled out, a promise that he had not been daunted by her brother's disclosures, nor his family's expectations, nor would he be daunted by Julian's poison. After all, Julian's rapier would never pierce his padding. Julian would have to go for a very specific mark on his arms or legs.

Haviland smiled, his world shrunk, the crowd noise faded. Thoughts of Julian and poison receded. There was only the two of them in their tiny curtained alcove. 'Do you want to marry *me*? There's no reason you can't any more. You don't have to protect Antoine from me. It's just up to you. Can I be enough for you?' It might have been the bravest question he'd ever asked.

'What about Lady Christina? Your family? Wanting and being able to are different things.'

Haviland pressed a finger to her lips. 'Your decision is not about them. What about you? What about us? *You* are my priority. It doesn't have to be us or them, but that will be their choice to make. I've already made mine.'

'My brother...' she began.

'I have a plan for him, too,' he breathed, his mouth close to hers, close enough to silence her with a kiss, long and full. Barely a day had passed since they were together, but it felt an eternity. His body was hungry. He wanted to touch her, taste her, hear her little sighs as they took pleasure in each other. 'Don't worry so much.' He pushed back her hair, his hand cradling her head. 'I love you, Alyssandra. That's the best reason I can think of for getting married. That and the fact that it makes it official: you are not alone any more.' He pressed his forehead to hers. 'I am learning that sometimes being brave is about trusting others to do right by me. Perhaps you need to learn that lesson, too.'

Outside the curtain, the announcer began his speech. He went through the standard rules; the bout would be fought with weapons from the *salle* itself, making the rapiers identical so there would be no technological advantage for either side. Haviland didn't listen further. He was too intent on the woman before him. One more victory and he could focus on what was truly important.

He took her face in both hands and kissed her one last time. She reached up and put the mask over his head. She bit her lip and then it all came in a rush. 'Watch out for Julian's—'

'Right-side attacks,' he finished speaking for her and they laughed together. 'I know.' She needed something to do, something to take her mind off the bout. 'I need you to change your clothes and go up into the stands. Find my friend, Archer Crawford, have him go for the inspector. Then tell your brother. I want you with him. I need to know you are safe.'

It was time to go. The announcer was making introductions. The crowd's momentum was starting to build. He heard Alyssandra behind him. 'Keep your shoulder up.' He smiled to himself and climbed the steps to the stage, hearing the words that went unspoken in that four-word phrase. Alyssandra loved him. A man waited with a poisoned blade, but all was right in the world.

* * *

The world slowed. Alyssandra pressed her eyes to the peepholes in the viewing room. She'd done all Haviland had asked of her. There was nothing left to do but watch. She'd rather watch from the stands, but she'd been conspicuous enough when she'd gone up to find Archer. This was not a venue open to female attendance and she'd promised Haviland she'd stay with Antoine in case…in case the unthinkable happened.

Beside her, Antoine was still as stone, shocked to his core at Julian's betrayal. Even now, she thought he didn't quite believe it. But he believed *her*. Julian had been wrong about that. She sucked in her breath as Haviland avoided a graze of Julian's blade on his sleeve. Julian had recognised immediately his opponent wasn't her, but it had not deterred him as Haviland had hoped.

Haviland retaliated with an aggressive move that brought their blades close together, crossed and tangled. But Julian was strong and he pushed back. Both blades spun out of their competitors' hands, landing on the floor. 'No!' she cried out, grasping for Antoine's hand. She felt anew the panic of having a front seat to a man's murder. The man she loved. He was going to marry her. *If he survived this.* Had she sent him to his doom?

On the floor, there was a scramble for the blades. Then it hit her. The blades were identical! How would they know? It would be a relief if Haviland came up with it, but a horror, too. Would Haviland kill Julian? Would he have a choice? She'd not sent him to be a murderer any more than she wanted him murdered. The scene on the floor had turned violent. Ignoring the officials' call for a break while rapiers were reclaimed, Julian tackled Haviland. The two went down and the piste became a brawl; punching, kicking, rolling as they grappled with each other awkwardly through the thick padding of their vests and masks. Julian was trying to rip the mask off Haviland's face.

'No!' Alyssandra exhaled as they rolled dangerously close to one of the blades. Exposure wasn't the only risk Haviland ran out there. It would be too easy to be accidentally pricked. But the brawl couldn't last long—already she could see the officials moving in to separate them, but not fast enough. The two had scrambled to their feet, coming up with rapiers, although it was impossible to tell who had which. One look at Julian's ashen face suggested, however, that *he* knew.

'Haviland has the blade,' Alyssandra whispered. It should have relieved her to know the blade was out of Julian's hand, but it had just the opposite effect. Haviland had to fight carefully, had to consider every strike.

'He should use the *passata sotto*.' Antoine scowled when an opportunity to score passed. 'He could come up under Julian's blade and strike at Julian's flank.'

'And risk killing Julian?' Alyssandra responded. 'All it will take is a nick of the blade.' Haviland was in an impossible situation. Then Julian made a sudden move, a startling turn in an attempt to disarm Haviland. She saw it all in slow motion. Haviland threw up his arm to ward off the unorthodox move, his blade catching Julian's sword arm, slicing into the sleeve of his shirt. Julian went to his knees, rapier clattering away, his other hand gripping the sliced arm, red showing on the fabric of his shirt.

Alyssandra fought back a scream and raced from the room. She did not care who saw her.

She knew only that she had to get to Haviland. He would need her. Haviland's mask was off when she reached them and he was kneeling beside Julian, gripping the man's shoulders. She fell to her knees beside Haviland on the floor. But there was little she could do.

Julian was dying, writhing and cursing on the floor, and it was a horrible sight. Julian was the enemy, he'd threatened her, but it was not in her nature to enjoy death. 'We have to do something!'

'I need a knife!' Haviland shouted. 'I need someone to hold him.' A knife materialised and Haviland ripped apart Julian's sleeve, careful to avoid contact with the blood.

Julian screamed at the sight of the knife against his flesh. 'You don't need to kill me any quicker, the poison will do it soon enough.'

Alyssandra fought to hold his shoulders, watching in fascination as Haviland scored an 'x' over the tiny scratch with the knife and pressed his mouth against the wound. He sucked and spat, sucked and spat again. Over and over until the crowd had gone silent, the mass panic ebbing. Nolan and Archer made their way to

Haviland's side with the inspector while officials began to usher spectators out.

'I need a bandage,' Haviland said, hoarse from his labours. Alyssandra grabbed up a piece of ruined shirt and handed it to him. He tied it around the wound site. 'I think you'll live, Anjou.'

He'd saved Julian, his enemy. Alyssandra stared at him with admiration, her heart filling with love all over again as if she didn't have reason enough to love him. Not many men would make the effort on behalf of a man who would have willingly killed them. She went to him, letting him wrap a warm, strong arm about her. Archer and Nolan helped Julian to his feet. But they weren't out of the woods yet. There would be explanations—why hadn't Antoine Leodegrance been under the mask? Why had the blade been poisoned? The whole situation was starting to unravel. It would only take a few words from Julian to expose everything in a very public fashion.

'You should have let me die.' Julian shook off their hands and snarled at Haviland with such vitriol that Alyssandra nearly recoiled.

Haviland met his hatred coolly. 'You owe me a life and I want Antoine Leodegrance's. That is a fair trade for what I've given you today.' He was asking for a confession and for protection of Antoine's identity.

Alyssandra watched the last bit of honour stir in Julian's eyes. 'You shall have it.'

The inspector stepped forward, and Nolan made introductions. 'Inspector Bouchard, this is Alyssandra Leodegrance, the *vicomte*'s sister.' Nolan gave her a cheeky grin. 'Miss Leodegrance, this is Inspector Bouchard. He and I play cards on occasion.'

Alyssandra smiled back. Everything was going to be all right.

And it was. Especially later that night as she lay in Haviland's arms, candlelight dancing about the room, her body and mind sated from desire fulfilled. As soon as they were able, they'd come here and retreated from the world, making love in a celebration of life both past and future. She'd almost lost him today to the slightest prick of a rapier, proving how dear and precious each moment was and how small the obstacles one raised to their own happiness could be when weighed against what one had to gain.

She stirred in his arms, turning to face him. 'I love you.' She'd missed the opportunity to say it today and it had almost been her last chance.

'I know,' he murmured drowsily.

'You don't know,' she argued playfully. 'I didn't say it until now.'

He nuzzled her neck. 'Yes, you did, when you told me not to drop my shoulder. That's how the great fencer, Alyssandra Leodegrance, says "I love you".'

She laughed. He had understood after all. 'Out of curiosity how does Haviland North say "I love you"?'

He rolled her beneath him, and she gasped. 'Don't you know? With his mouth, with his eyes, with his hands. Perhaps it would be better if I showed you.' And he did, beginning with a trail of hot kisses that ran all the way to the damp curls between her thighs and ending with their bodies joined in a star-splitting climax that left them exhausted…until the next time.

Epilogue

When Haviland North, fourth Viscount Amersham, imagined his wedding it had always been in a big church filled with hothouse roses and hothouse people, a useless white runner on the aisle for the bride to walk upon once before it was thrown out, and an icy, beautiful but remote woman he hardly knew floating towards him in another useless piece of expensive frippery while he stood straight and immaculate at the front, showing not a single emotion. But now, when he pictured his wedding, what lay before him was not that. It was better. Much better.

The little church in Fontainebleau was turned out with simple vases full of late spring flowers, looking its best even though the wedding was attended by only seven people counting the reverend and his wife, Nolan, Brennan, the bride and groom and the bride's brother. The wooden floor was bare of any decorative runner and the woman walking towards him drew every emotion he possessed to the fore of his mind. He was certain they were written on his face for all to see. The only item this wedding shared with his original vision was that the bride was beautiful. But that was where all similarities ended. Alyssandra was radiant in a gown of buttercup yellow that made her skin glow and her caramel hair shine. She vibrated with life as she looked at him, love in her eyes. She was his—his partner in all things.

And there were a lot of things to partner. In the time before the wedding, he'd encouraged Antoine not to sell the *salle d'armes*, but to keep it in the family by turning it over to him. Antoine would be able to live in the country while he and Alyssandra divided their time between Fontainebleau and Paris. Alyssandra would pioneer fencing classes for women in the private instruction rooms of the *salle*. But all that would be after their honeymoon in Italy.

The only sad note for Haviland today was that Archer had left the previous week, going ahead to Italy to prepare for the annual horse race in

Siena, the Palio. But they had said their fare-
wells with promises to catch up with him there
as part of the honeymoon. Antoine met Alyssandra at the end of the aisle and placed her hand
in Haviland's, the aisle not being wide enough
to accommodate both of them and his chair.
Country life agreed with him, Haviland was
pleased to note. Or perhaps it was the house-
keeper they'd hired to open the house. Haviland thought she'd rather taken a fancy to the
vicomte. Either way, Alyssandra need not worry
about leaving Antoine for their wedding trip.

In the month since the tournament much had
been settled. Julian had been sentenced to house
parole in Lyons so that he would not be a con-
stant reminder in their lives. But Haviland's parents had not been one of the things settled. His
father had written a vituperative letter derid-
ing his decision to marry elsewhere and to stay
there. He had expected that. However, there had
been a surprise. His mother had enclosed a private note wishing him happiness. There was
hope in that direction, then. And he was optimistic that, given time and eventually grand-
children, his parents would relent. He didn't hate

them, he just loved his freedom more, loved Alyssandra more than even that.

The reverend began the service—where Nolan had found a Church of England man in France he didn't know. He didn't bother to question it. The reverend intoned the words, 'with my body I thee worship', and Alyssandra beamed up at him, mischief sparkling in those dark eyes. 'I'm already thinking about tonight,' she whispered naughtily.

Haviland raised an eyebrow. 'Really? To-night? Is that the best you can do because I'm already thinking how I will worship you this afternoon.'

She blushed, and the reverend coughed. Haviland didn't mind. He was *alive*, he could feel it in his bones. He'd set out on this journey with all his hopes pinned on Paris, and Paris, the city of love, had not disappointed.

* * * * *

MILLS & BOON®

The Thirty List

At thirty, Rachel has slid down every ladder she has ever climbed. Jobless, broke and ditched by her husband, she has to move in with grumpy Patrick and his four-year-old son.

Patrick is also getting divorced, so to cheer themselves up the two decide to draw up bucket lists. Soon they are learning to tango, abseiling, trying stand-up comedy and more. But, as she gets closer to Patrick, Rachel wonders if their relationship is too good to be true…

Order yours today at
www.millsandboon.co.uk/Thethirtylist

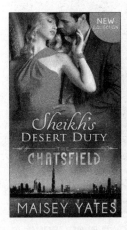

MILLS & BOON®

HISTORICAL

AWAKEN THE ROMANCE OF THE PAST

A sneak peek at next month's titles...

In stores from 3rd July 2015:

- **A Rose for Major Flint** – Louise Allen
- **The Duke's Daring Debutante** – Ann Lethbridge
- **Lord Laughraine's Summer Promise** – Elizabeth Beacon
- **Warrior of Ice** – Michelle Willingham
- **A Wager for the Widow** – Elisabeth Hobbes
- **Running Wolf** – Jenna Kernan

0615/04